THE STORYTELLER

AARON STARMER

SQUARE
FISH

FARRAR STRAUS GIROUX

NEW YORK

SQUARE
FISH

An imprint of Macmillan Publishing Group, LLC
175 Fifth Avenue
New York, NY 10010
mackids.com

Our books may be purchased in bulk for promotional, educational, or
business use. Please contact your local bookseller or the Macmillan
Corporate and Premium Sales Department at (800) 221-7945 ext. 5442
or by e-mail at MacmillanSpecialMarkets@macmillan.com.

Library of Congress Cataloging-in-Publication Data
Starmer, Aaron, 1976–
    The storyteller / Aaron Starmer
      pages   cm. — (The Riverman trilogy ; 3)
    Summary: Along with stories, Keri Cleary records in her diary the strange
and terrifying events surrounding the disappearance of Fiona Loomis and
Alistair Cleary's efforts to find her in Aquavania, a world where wishes can
nearly come true, as well as the repercussions of the shooting of Kyle Dwyer.
    ISBN 978-1-250-10418-2 (paperback)   ISBN 978-0-374-36314-7 (ebook)
    [1. Missing children—Fiction. 2. Storytelling—Fiction. 3. Brothers and
sisters—Fiction. 4. Family life—Fiction. 5. Diaries—Fiction. 6. Friendship—
Fiction. 7. Fantasy.] I. Title.

PZ7.S7972Sto 2016
[Fic]—dc23

                                                                  2015004696

Originally published in the United States by Farrar Straus Giroux
First Square Fish Edition: 2017
Book designed by Elizabeth H. Clark
Square Fish logo designed by Filomena Tuosto

1   3   5   7   9   10   8   6   4   2

LEXILE: 700L

To Michael and Joy

THE
STORYTELLER

THE CHRONICLES OF KERRIGAN CLEARY

SOMETIMES I'M A SISTER WHO GIVES ADVICE AND TEASES AND all of that, and sometimes I'm just a girl who wonders how the kid who sleeps in the next room could ever be related to her. Only natural, right? We all love our brothers, in spite of the fact that none of us has a clue what's really in their hearts.

Even before Fiona Loomis took off, or got killed, or who knows . . . before this neighborhood was all sirens, search parties, and ladies standing by their windows at all hours . . . weeks before someone shot Kyle Dwyer in the stomach, my brother, Alistair, had changed. Puberty: it got him and it got him good. At least that's what I thought at first. That's not what I think now. Because when they found him in our front yard, looking up at the stars, that wasn't the boy I knew, and that wasn't even the one I didn't know yet. That was someone from outer space.

Here's what we can say so far: Kyle Dwyer will live. For

now. He's in a coma, so he isn't talking. Can't tell us who shot him. My money is on Charlie because, well, he's Charlie, and Charlie has always been a bit off. But Charlie is nowhere to be found, and the police bagged up Alistair's wet and bloody clothes. They say Alistair is the one who made the 911 call.

"It's not how it looks," Alistair told me two nights ago as he stood in our hallway, dripping wet and terrified. "Just make sure they know it's not how it looks."

I didn't make sure "they" knew anything. I love the kid, but he has to speak for himself. He has to start talking. He put a padlock on his mouth, though. Swallowed the key. Mom and Dad think he's still in shock. It's only been a couple of days, so they may be right. A psychologist tried to get him to open up and will try again. The police gave it a try too. Nothing doing. Not enough evidence to arrest him, I guess, but they can't help but think this has something to do with Fiona Loomis.

Everyone thinks that.

The town prays for Kyle Dwyer. A sentence I thought I'd never write.

The town misses Charlie Dwyer. Another sentence that tests the laws of logic.

The town is sure my brother shot someone in the gut. Ding, ding, ding! That's three in a row.

Oh, the town. Forgot to tell you about that. The town is Thessaly, up here in the forehead of New York State, where no one notices us until a couple of kids go *poof*.

Oh, and me. I'm Kerrigan Cleary. Keri to friends. I'll admit,

Keri Cleary is a bit of a tongue twister. *Keri Cleary carried cherries for cheery chipmunks.* Say that ten times fast. What can I do, though? It's the name I got and I can't get another.

Oh, and one more thing. I haven't even told you the date yet, which I guess is pretty much necessary for this sort of . . . endeavor. I hesitate to call this a diary, even though that's what it is. Hopefully it becomes more than that. A place to confess. A place to tell stories. Truth and fiction.

Anyway, I'm writing this on:

TUESDAY, 11/21/1989
EVENING

Which is two days after Kyle was shot and Charlie disappeared. A day after they found my brother sitting in our yard, looking up at the stars. Hours after I started thinking up a story about a wombat.

Yes, a wombat.

That's yet another thing. There are no wombats here in Thessaly, at least that I know of. Most of my neighbors probably don't even have a clue what a wombat is. For the record, it's a marsupial, which means it has a pouch like a kangaroo or koala, and lives in Australia. It looks a bit like a woodchuck, but it isn't related. Not even close.

How much wom could a wombat bat if a wombat could bat wom?

Dumb joke. Forget it.

The story is the important thing. In it, this brother and

sister find a wombat on the side of the road, and the wombat has a sign around her neck that reads: PERFECTLY FINE WOMBAT. This is the type of story where kids believe signs like that, so they take her home and make her their pet.

I don't think I'm ready to write any of it down yet, but I do have a pretty good idea how it'll end. In a waterfall. Images and ideas have been crashing into me like a meteor shower for the last day, and the image of a waterfall is the clearest. The story starts with a brother and a sister on a road. It ends with a wombat and a waterfall. That's what I've got so far.

I've never thought of myself as a writer. Don't get me wrong, I've written stories before. For school. A few times for fun. But this is the first time I've really felt like I needed to do it. I'm finding out that if you have the ending from the get-go, then you're in good shape. Problem is, I rarely have the ending from the get-go.

Here, for instance, is a different story, a shorter story, one about endings that doesn't really have an ending. I don't care. That won't stop me from writing it.

THE ENDING

———————◆———————

JUSTINE BARLOW WAS A RUNNER. SHE WORE SWEAT SUITS. She drank Gatorade. Every morning, when her cuckoo clock cheeped six times, she got up, got out of the house, clipped a Walkman to her waistband, stretched against a tree, hopped in place a few times, and then set off into her neighborhood.

It cleared her head. It kept her heart healthy, which was important because hers was a good heart. She gave money to the homeless, even when they weren't begging. She said "Good morning" to people and meant it.

Why not? Mornings *were* good. Cold mornings, rainy ones. It didn't matter. They were new beginnings. Justine had recently graduated from college, was living on her own for the first time, and had her entire life ahead of her. "Each day is a blank page," she told people. "A fresh thing to write on. Have fun with it."

Running was hard work, but it was fun too. The

sounds—the barks, beeps, and buzzes—always entertained and they were never the same, even if her route was, a four-mile loop that passed by the school and the reservoir, through the center of town and back home past the rickety old houses on Palmer Street. The images were always different too. The trees that went from green to brown to white to pink to green, depending on the season. The babies who went from slings to strollers to feet to bikes. Change. Beauty. Life. All that crap.

And death. That came later.

It started with one baby bird, clear-feathered and dead on the sidewalk beneath an oak tree. *Poor little thing must have fallen from her nest,* Justine thought. She even considered burying it, giving it a proper funeral, but she knew that wasn't how nature was supposed to work. A stray cat or raccoon would eat it and poop it out, and then the poop would become dirt and plants would grow from the poop and other birds would eat the plants. This was called the circle of life.

So the next morning, when she saw two dead birds on the sidewalk, she thought, *Poor little things,* and she ran on.

The next morning she saw four. *Poor little things.* The cats and raccoons were going to be plump as can be.

It kept doubling, though. Eight the next day. Then sixteen. Thirty-two. Sixty-four dead birds by the end of the week, all along the same running route.

Justine was disturbed. "Have you noticed a lot of dead birds lately?" she asked her friend Laura.

"Always see some in the spring," Laura said. "It's a shame. The world is a tough place."

"How many have you seen this spring?" Justine asked.

"I don't know. Normal amount, I guess. I haven't counted."

Justine had been counting. She had started by keeping tabs in her head, but now she put little check marks in a pocket notebook as she ran.

One hundred and twenty-eight baby birds the next day. Two hundred and fifty-six the next.

Was this an omen of something worse to come? How could other people not be noticing? She asked around. "What's with the birds?"

People would reply by looking into the cloudless sky and shrugging.

The birds weren't imaginary. They were flesh and blood. Cold flesh and cold blood, that is. Justine knew because she poked them with her finger. There weren't enough cats and raccoons to possibly eat them all, so she started scooping the bodies up in plastic grocery bags like little logs of dog poop. Or at least that's what it looked like to her neighbors.

"You probably have yourself one of those Great Danes," a postman joked as Justine jogged past with two sagging plastic bags.

Strange thing to say, Justine thought. *If that's the case, then where's the dog? I don't just run around scooping poop. No sir. This is death. Something serious is afoot.*

"Aren't you worried?" Justine asked him. It wasn't the type of question she normally posed. For her entire life up until that point, she believed in a world without worry.

"Worried about what?" the postman asked.

"All the death."

He too looked up at the sky, but he kissed his fingers. "Our time comes when our time comes," he said, and returned to his route.

Justine returned to her route, but she couldn't run anymore. Too many birds to pick up. When she made it home, she buried them all in a hole in her backyard as a suspicious neighbor boy watched from a perch in a tree house.

"It'll be okay," she assured him, but he didn't respond. Maybe it was the wobble in her voice, the tone that said it would, in fact, not *be okay*, that it was actually going to be pretty damn horrible.

Because Justine could do the math: 512; 1,024; 2,048; 4,096; 8,192. That was just one more week's worth if it kept doubling, and she was sure it would. It meant in two more weeks there would be a billion dead birds. A month after that? She couldn't fathom such a number. Enough to cover the entire earth, she suspected. It seemed biblical. Beyond biblical.

She locked herself in the house. She started making phone calls. The police, senators' offices, her parents.

"What will we do to stop it?" she asked.

They all laughed her off. "You're too sensitive," her father said. "Heck, your mother's cat alone probably kills one hundred birds a year. These things have a way of balancing themselves out."

Two weeks before, she would have agreed. Two weeks

before, she wouldn't have boarded up her windows. But that's what she did now.

The next day, the birds started showing up in her house. In the toilet, down the chimney, in the air-conditioning ducts. The numbers held true. She ticked them off in her notebook and filled the bathtub with the bodies.

There would be no more running. Mornings weren't *good* anymore. There was only the inevitable sunrise and the inevitable double dose of dead baby birds. Within a few days the bathroom was full. Justine didn't dare look out her windows. Not because she feared seeing more dead birds outside, but because she feared seeing none.

She was the problem. *She* was the cause of all this. They followed *her*. Was this punishment for her positivity? Or was she simply going crazy? Whatever the case, she couldn't face the world anymore. Each day was definitely not a blank page. It was a black page. And it didn't matter what you wrote on it; it would always be black.

Within five more days, the birds filled the house. There was nowhere to stand, to eat, to sleep. Justine huddled in the corner, surrounded by the stinking mess.

I can't do it, she thought. *I can't go on like this.*

But before she could act on her dark thoughts, something came out of the pile of death. A bird, a real live hummingbird. It hovered in front of her face.

"What does it all mean?" she asked the hummingbird.

The hummingbird didn't say anything because hummingbirds can't talk, obviously. Though she swore it had compassion in its eyes. The hummingbird hovered there for what seemed like hours. Then it fell dead on top of the pile, as Justine's cuckoo clock, buried by birds, tried in vain to announce a new day.

The End?

Wednesday, 11/22/1989

AFTERNOON

PEOPLE WANT CLOSURE. IT'S BEEN TWO AND A HALF WEEKS since Fiona Loomis disappeared, and people want her home safe and sound, but if they have the choice between never knowing what happened to her and knowing that she's dead, then I hate to say it, but they're going to pick dead. No one will 'fess up, obviously, but it's the truth. A story with a clear ending, happy or sad, is an acceptable story.

They still don't know anything about Charlie. No ending to his story either, and no ending to Kyle's, who's still hooked up to the machines and full-on comatose. The superintendent canceled school yesterday and today, so we essentially have the week off. With one missing kid, he told us to go about our routines. Two kids changes things. This isn't a fluke. Something's happening. Someone's doing something.

I stood outside of Alistair's door last night. I was going to try to reason with him, but what can I say anymore? *Please speak to us? It's okay, we won't judge? We love you no matter what?* A lot of people say *no matter what*, but how many people actually experience *no matter what? No matter what* will fill up your head with a real mess.

So, yeah, I stood there, saying nothing, and I listened. I could hear some faint beeps. I could hear him whispering, like he was talking to himself. Eventually, Mom saw me and glared at me like only she can glare. I tiptoed over to her and she whispered, "He's not ready yet. One more day."

Mandy isn't as patient as Mom. I tell people she's my best friend, but she really tests me sometimes. Like when she calls me up and says things like she said this morning.

"You gotta get your brother to talk. The longer he's silent, the guiltier it means he is. He's probably working on his alibi, making sure it's super airtight."

"How the hell do you know that?" I snapped.

"TV. Books. Every place," she said. "It's a well-known fact that most missing person cases are solved in, like, forty-eight hours, and what's it been now since Charlie disappeared? How many hours are there in two and a half days?"

"He's already met with the police twice."

"Does he have a lawyer?"

See what I mean about Mandy? Pushy. Nosy. Whatever you want to call it. Alistair does have a lawyer, of course. Or at least my parents have one. Dad works at the hospital in Sutton, and they have a few lawyers on staff. One of them is a family friend named Ms. Kern, and she gives Mom and Dad advice on documents and things like that. So she's been going to the police station with Alistair. I'm not sure what she does, because Alistair isn't under arrest and has been totally silent, but she's there just in case.

"He's got people looking out for him," was what I decided to say to Mandy, because that's all she needs to know.

"Heavy Metal Fifi made sense," Mandy replied. Heavy Metal Fifi—or HMF—was our nickname for Fiona, because we saw her a few times listening to heavy metal music while she was riding her bike.

"Made sense?" I asked.

"She's a lonely girl and they're easy prey for sickos," Mandy said. "But who's going after Charlie Dwyer?"

"I don't know," I said with a sigh.

"Honestly, I don't think it's your brother, but I got this theory. What if it's Fiona's uncle? He's a war vet, like Rambo, which means he torched villages in Asia and stuff. Maybe he, like, did something with Fiona because she found out about that. Then Kyle and Charlie found out about it, and so he tried to cover up some more. And now Alistair knows all this and he's scared. Weren't you saying Alistair blamed the uncle for Fiona disappearing in the first place?"

"Alistair was confused," I said, which was an understatement. Mom and Dad haven't told me everything, but I know that after Fiona disappeared, Alistair was making all sorts of strange accusations. Like I said, he hasn't been himself.

"One thing is for sure," Mandy said. "Creepy uncle drives by and honks at you, offers you Fruit Roll-Ups or something? Run, run, run."

"Goodbye, jerkface," I said.

"Sayonara, onion butt," she said in her super high *I'm going to annoy the crap out of you* voice.

I hung up.

EVENING

This thing was supposed to be about me. You get a diary and you're supposed to write about yourself in it. You're supposed to confess your deepest and darkest secrets. That was the thought, anyway. Dad bought this for me as an "early birthday present" two years ago. Which was a bunch of bull. The reason it came early, or came at all, is because things got a little *Are-You-There-God-It's-Me-Keri*-ish around here one embarrassing morning when Mom looked in the bathroom trash and found some of my stained pants and . . . undergarments. She probably talked to Dad about it, and he had the brilliant idea of getting me something to *express myself* with. He's a social worker, you know, and is all about sharing feelings. Well, I didn't start writing in this stupid thing until yesterday, nearly two days after Kyle was shot, Charlie disappeared, and the police came upon Alistair sitting in our yard, staring up at the stars. And wouldn't you know it, this is my diary, but all I'm writing about is my brother.

I'm not ready quite yet, but I need to write the wombat story down soon. Not sure why, but the wombat might help.

Thursday, 11/23/1989
(Thanksgiving)

AFTERNOON

THE BIRD WENT IN AT EIGHT A.M., AS IT ALWAYS DOES. FOOD will hit the table sometime around four p.m., like every year before. I don't know what the Loomis family has planned. Maybe they'll escape back to their lake house or wherever it is they go. The Dwyer family will be in the hospital. Bedside, with a phone nearby, hoping for any sliver of good news. While we, the Clearys, will eat our taters and stuffin' and pretend like nothing ever happened.

Rub a dub dub, thanks for the grub. Amen!

Okay, it might be a bit different than that. We'll sit there silent through most of it, as we have been through all of our meals lately. Mom will pick. Dad will scarf. I will try to make jokes, and Alistair might even smile at a few of them. But he won't speak. Because that would be helpful, wouldn't it?

I'm so glad Grammy and Pops and Nana and Grampa aren't here. And Uncle Dale and Aunt Mia. They all said they'd come, but I heard Dad on the phone saying that he "didn't want things to be overwhelming." Too late, old man.

Old man. That's what Alistair calls him. A buddy name, I guess. I call him Dad. But he's starting to seem like an old man. Sighing a lot. Slumping into chairs as if they're meant to break a fall from hundreds of feet up. I don't blame him. I feel it too, the falling. Mom, on the other hand, is staying strong, which looks like staying stiff to me. Hands in the sink washing dishes, stiff. At the computer, playing Solitaire, stiff. Standing by the car, about to leave for another shift at the post office—because the mail only takes holidays and Sundays off—looking out at the neighborhood before opening the door. Stiff.

When your family isn't talking much, you watch a bit more TV. At least I've been watching more. Mostly stuff I normally wouldn't watch. Like the news. You know what the big story this morning was? Besides all the tales of pardoned turkeys and all the people going wild back in the USSR?

The Littlest Knight.

He's a boy they found in a lake somewhere in the Middle East. Jordan? Syria? I forget. One of those. He was dead, and his body floated up on shore a few days ago. No one knows who he was, but he was wearing a miniature suit of armor called scale mail. Apparently it's a type of armor from hundreds of years ago. It's one of those weird random stories that people love talking and wondering about, but I couldn't bear to watch much more than a few minutes of the coverage.

I switched over to the parade instead. The New York City

one, obviously. It's funny; our parades in Thessaly are nothing but Little League twerps and beer-gutty bagpipers. In the big city they get the big floats, the humongous balloons. I started to zone out as I watched it and I imagined that there were balloons of Fiona and Charlie in the mix. Monstrous cartoon versions of them, floating between the skyscrapers.

Mom sat down next to me and broke me out of the daze. She put her hand on my knee and said, "Maybe next year we can drive down there, get a hotel, and see this thing in person."

"That'd be fun," I said.

It would be fun. To be a year in the future. To ditch this place and time for a bit. To eat Thanksgiving dinner in a restaurant where no one knows who the hell we are, to eat lobster instead of turkey, to gaze out a window and see people you'll never see again in your whole stupid life.

THE FINE ART OF FORGETTING

MANY YEARS AGO THERE WAS A PRINCESS NAMED SIGRID, AND she lived in a tower made of onyx, which is a type of stone that's as black as black can be. Sigrid was an only child, destined to inherit a kingdom that stretched from one sea to the next. Every day, she sat on a swing that hung over her balcony at the top of the tower and she watched her subjects work in the market and the fields. Her heart was always bursting with empathy, and whenever she saw someone in turmoil, she called to her trusted advisor, Po, and made a request.

Make sure that man gets his broken leg fixed.

Make sure that mother has enough food for herself as well as her children.

Make sure that family has a warm home in which to live.

Po would always nod and respond, "Yes, my lady," but he knew that all requests had to filter through her parents, and her parents, the king and the queen, kept the purse strings mighty tight.

"She is given to whimsy," the king said at first. "Indulge her for now, but we cannot afford to do this all the time."

All the time is what Sigrid wanted, however. She was a humanitarian, and a humanitarian's work never ends. She kept passing her requests through Po, and her parents kept growing more and more annoyed.

"I fear we must turn to the Dorgon," the queen finally said, a shocking but inevitable decision.

The Dorgon was neither man nor woman. It was a vile beast made of mud that lived in a bog not far from the tower. It possessed one talent, the construction of potions, and while the potions always worked, they came at a steep price. Payment was always in blood.

"I agree with the queen," the king told Po. "Give the Dorgon our kingdom's lowliest citizen in exchange for a potion that will cure young Sigrid of her constant do-goodery."

"And what sort of potion might that be?" Po asked.

"We do not want to silence her kind heart," the queen said. "We simply want to make the kindness temporary. A potion of forgetting should do the trick."

Po was a loyal subject and did not ask any other questions. That night, he went to a tavern, where he sat down next to a man named Tom Rondrigal. Rondrigal was a known liar and cheat, a thief and a scoundrel who would cut the throats of his own children if there were a gold coin in it for him. Po challenged Rondrigal to a drinking contest, something Rondrigal would never pass up, and the two proceeded to throw back flagon after flagon of mead.

Rondrigal was a legendary drinker who had never been bested, but Po had a trick up his sleeve—or, to be more specific, under his shirt. He had the ability to untie his belly button and tap into his stomach. Using the tentacle of an octopus, he created a spout that led from his stomach to a hole in the floor. The mead went in and the mead went out and Po didn't get the least bit drunk.

Rondrigal certainly did. So drunk, in fact, that he passed out in his chair and Po was able to drag him out of the tavern and put him under a blanket on Rondrigal's horse-drawn cart. Po had the king's blessing, of course, but even if he didn't, he feared no punishment for kidnapping this horrid man whom everyone in the kingdom despised.

"You'd be wise to toss him off a cliff," the tavern keeper called out as Po pulled away. The tavern erupted with laughter.

The Dorgon was brisk with his business. As soon as the cart pulled up to the bog, the creature emerged and croaked, "You'll be wanting a potion?"

"I will," Po said. "A potion of forgetting. A girl is too careless with her kindness. She does not need such a burden."

"It is understood," the Dorgon said as it pulled Rondrigal from the cart and down into the bog. It was only a few moments later that the Dorgon surfaced with a flask of colorless liquid, tossing it at Po. "She will not forget what she already knows, but this will steal her ability to make new memories," the Dorgon said. "She'll need to drink a drop every day."

"I will make sure that she does," Po said.

The Dorgon burped and replied, "Next time, bring me one who doesn't taste so sour."

Back in the onyx tower, Po put a drop of the potion into Princess Sigrid's evening stew. It must have been flavorless, because she didn't notice it. She simply bid Po a good night and went to bed.

The next day, when Po arrived, Sigrid was out on her swing, looking over the land. In the center of the market below, a woman sat on a stump crying.

"Please see what ails that poor soul," Sigrid said, her voice as full of empathy as ever. "And make sure her life is set right."

Surprised, because the Dorgon's potions were legendary for their effectiveness, Po asked, "What was that, my lady?"

Sigrid turned from her swing, shook her head for a moment, as if it were full of dust, and replied, "I seem to have forgotten."

Po smiled. "Come inside then and rest a bit. No need to look out onto the world all morning."

"I suppose you're right," Sigrid said in a resigned tone. She came inside for the remainder of the day.

Every day went like this. Po would arrive in the morning and Sigrid would be on her swing, asking about the unfortunate people below. Po would reply, "What was that, my lady?" She would turn, instantly forget her worries, and go back to her room. In the evening, she'd have a bowl of her stew, which always contained a drop of the potion, because Po gave it to the cook with explicit orders.

"This is medicine for Princess Sigrid. If it does not flavor her stew, then she will become very ill and you will be to blame. Understood?"

"Understood," the cook said, and the cook was always true to his word.

The king and queen were thrilled that the plan had worked, but Po found himself disturbed. Because every morning, before Sigrid's forgetfulness set in, she fixed her eyes on the same place: the stump at the center of the market. And every morning, that same old woman was there, crying. Sigrid would always forget about the woman moments after taking her eyes off of her, but every morning she'd witness that pain anew.

Guilt started to pile up on Po. In the past, Sigrid would have used her power to ease this woman's suffering, but now her forgetfulness made that impossible. The woman suffered on, and Sigrid was compelled to watch every morning. It wouldn't have bothered Po if Sigrid watched a different person every morning. It was the infinite nature of this one woman's suffering that bothered him.

Po had a bit of gold saved and figured he could fix the problem on his own. So one morning, he lingered in the market until the old woman arrived and sat on the stump. She was a fragile person, with rosy cheeks and thin lips. Her eyes were so tiny that a single teardrop could cover one of them, and when she cried it was almost like a stream of eyeballs pelting the ground.

"What ails you?" Po asked her as he approached. "And how may I help?"

Wiping her face, the woman looked up at him and said, "Find my son. He's been missing quite a while."

"Who is your son?" Po asked.

"Tom Rondrigal," the woman said.

Po paused. He considered his options. "I think I can help you," he finally said.

"You can?" she asked. "Because I love him so much. I know he can be boorish, but I am—"

"Not to worry," Po said. "I will help you. I know where he is. I'd like to take you there." Then he led her to Rondrigal's horse-drawn cart that he had kept for himself since Rondrigal's death. He asked that she climb aboard.

She recognized the cart as her son's, and was duly suspicious, but she had little to lose. She was quite old and didn't have much time left in the world. Po guided the horse through the forest and directly to the bog where the Dorgon lived. The Dorgon emerged, but it did not frighten the woman. She had lived in the kingdom her entire life. She knew of its dark corners.

"So," the woman said with a sigh, "the Dorgon took my son?"

"He did," Po admitted.

"And now you intend to feed me to the Dorgon as well?"

Po didn't answer. He simply climbed down from the cart and looked the Dorgon in the eye. "You made me a fine potion," Po said. "I'd like you to make more of the same."

"The one you brought me isn't too sour?" the Dorgon asked.

"I don't think so," Po said. "But see for yourself."

Po threw himself upon the Dorgon, and the Dorgon pulled Po into the bog.

When the Dorgon emerged minutes later with the potion, the old woman was still there. "What is it?" she asked as she took it from the creature.

"You are to drink it every day, when sadness visits you," the Dorgon said with a burp. "But it's best that you not know exactly what it does."

The old woman nodded, climbed onto the cart and, as she guided the horse through the forest, she sipped the potion. She kept her eyes fixed on the shiny onyx tower poking up through the trees.

Friday, 11/24/1989

MORNING

There's an early memory I have of Alistair. He was a tiny kid, nothing but a rib cage and a noggin. Probably four years old. We were in the backyard, playing TV tag or freeze tag or some other version of tag. The sun was getting low and Mom and Dad were inside making dinner when I heard yelping out in the swamp.

"What was that?" Alistair asked.

I'd heard it before with Dad and he told me what it was, but I wasn't sure if I should tell Alistair. He was a real fraidycat. Even the most harmless things could inspire his nightmares back then. I'm only a year and a half older than him, but when you're little that's a huge difference. Huge.

"Nothing," I said to him.

"Sounds like sad kittens," Alistair replied. Not that we ever had sad kittens. Not that we ever had kittens at all.

"It's nothing," I said.

"They sound hurt," Alistair said, moving toward the swamp.

I grabbed him by the shirt. "They're fine. It's dinnertime. Let's go inside."

"We should bring the kitties inside. They probably need milk."

"They're fine." I pulled him to the door, but he broke away and started running toward the swamp.

"Kitties, kitties, kitties," he cooed as he went.

I was forced to tackle him.

"What are you doing?" he cried as he squirmed in my arms.

"Coyotes," I whispered.

He froze. "What?"

"They're coyotes. Pups. But they have parents. Or a momma at least. Something that feeds them."

"What do they eat?"

"Deer. Squirrels. Whatever their momma can catch."

Without taking a breath, Alistair whispered a question through his teeth. "Kids?"

My arms wrapped around my brother, I looked into the dark swamp. At the edge was a big rock shaped like a frog. "Frog Rock," I said. "It protects us from them. But don't go past it. You promise?"

Teeth still clenched, Alistair nodded.

For at least a few years, Alistair kept that promise. He climbed that rock, played around it, but never went past it. Fiona used to come over when she was little and she'd go past it, but she was always braver than my brother.

Years later—come to think of it, only a few months ago,

actually—I saw her bury something out by that rock. Which was weird. Alistair dug it up. At least I assume he did, because a few weeks ago, after I told him about what I saw, I noticed a mound of dirt out there, like a fresh grave. With all the rain and snow we've been having, it's flattened out now. When Fiona learned that I told Alistair, she said that it was a love letter to him that she buried. Could be, but I suspect it was more than that.

EVENING

Love letters. I don't get those.

Okay, that's a lie. I got one. Once. Last year. Seventh grade. Valentine's Day. A secret admirer. No joke. It was signed *Your Secret Admirer.*

Someone slipped it into my locker. I don't remember the exact words, but I think it said my eyes were "an azure sky" and my hair was "amber waves of grain." *Azure* is blue, I think. My eyes are brown, for the record. And amber waves of grain? That's in . . . well, not "The Star-Spangled Banner," but one of those patriotic songs. So it appeared that Uncle Sam had a crush on me. Don't get me wrong, I love a top hat, but . . .

Anyway, the letter ended with a plea to meet the guy behind the maintenance shed after school, which is more than a little creepy. I suppose he didn't think it was creepy. Probably thought it was a private place where we could talk and no one would bother us. I didn't go, of course, but I'm actually pretty sure I know who sent it. The Looney Tunes stationery gave it away.

Glen Maple. He's harmless, I guess. No top hat either, as far as I know. And not really the sort of guy who murders you behind maintenance sheds. At least I don't think he is. But then, it's always the ones you least suspect, right?

Actually, no. Not Glen. He's fine.

But he's annoying. Like, *man, I hope he loses his voice* annoying, because he's always doing these terrible impressions of cartoon characters and he answers every question every teacher asks and is wrong more often than he's right and there's a point when he's wrong so much that he doesn't seem to care about being wrong. I know that's mean to say, but it's the truth.

Anyway, I saw Glen today, when Mom and I went to the grocery store. He was with his dad at the bakery counter, and they were ordering a cake. I overheard him saying, "Mom likes angel food," and I snorted a chuckle because that's funny when heard out of context, and he looked at me, but it wasn't with that *oh my god, I want to kiss you all over the face* look that I'm used to from him.

It was an *I feel sorry for you* look.

I didn't say anything to him. I walked over to Mom, grabbed her elbow, led her to the cereal aisle, and told her, "I'm buying Lucky Charms and you're not gonna say a darn thing about it."

It made her laugh.

Saturday, 11/25/1989

MORNING

YOU'RE AT BREAKFAST, OKAY? YOUR MOM IS CUTTING THE grapefruit with one of those weird bent and jagged knives, right? It's squirting all over the place, including your dad's shirt, and he's saying, "Hey now, watch the fine poly blend." And you're looking at the paper, and of course there are stories with the names Loomis and Dwyer all over the thing, and you push it away before you give in to the temptation to see if any of them have the name Cleary in them, and you take a sip of pineapple juice and a bite of your Lucky Charms, which you're almost never allowed to have, and you announce, "I've been writing a few stories in my diary and I'm going to write one today about a girl made out of candy canes, but someday I'm going to write one about a wombat with glowing fur," and your brother, who hasn't said a thing in close to a week, looks up from his bowl of Life—what can I say, the kid loves Life— and he says, "You're writing about what?"

THE CANDY CANE GIRL

---◆---

SOME PEOPLE CAN'T HAVE BABIES. IT'S SAD BUT IT'S TRUE. Their bodies aren't built for it. Some of those people also can't adopt babies. Just as sad, maybe sadder, and just as true. Their lifestyles aren't built for it. But most people want families. Most people need families.

Everyone can have candy canes. If they want them, at least. Even diabetics, because there's insulin for that, right? Around Christmastime, there are candy canes everywhere, available for free. In glass jars at banks, hanging from pine branches, tossed by Santa from fire trucks. If you took every single candy cane you saw, you'd have about a hundred pounds of them in a few days.

You wouldn't take every single one you saw though, would you? That's because you aren't Hazel and Howard Clumpet. The Clumpets liked candy canes. A lot. Every December they filled their bathtub with them. And while they did eat a fair amount of their loot, they always had more than they needed.

Maybe that was the problem. They weren't healthy people, the Clumpets, and it's a good bet that a diet consisting mainly of peppermint and sugar isn't the best for making babies. In any case, they couldn't have babies, and the adoption agencies rejected the Clumpets as soon as they visited their home and found the furniture buried in candy wrappers.

"We'll always have each other," Hazel told Howard after they were rejected by every adoption agency they could find.

"Each other isn't good enough, is it?" Howard exclaimed. "This family won't be complete without a daughter! Don't you understand that?"

Hazel did understand that. The man told her that every stinking day. "Well, why don't you build us a daughter out of candy canes, then?" she hollered at him.

"Maybe I will!" he hollered back.

Howard rarely made threats—mostly because he was too lazy to make good on them—but when he did make threats, they were rarely idle ones. As ludicrous as it seemed, he became determined to build a girl out of candy canes.

Do we need to mention again that Howard was lazy? Because that's important. Lazy guys aren't the best builders. When they sit next to a bathtub full of candy canes, licking them until they're sticky and then sticking them together until they form arms, legs, hair, spleens, and all that other body stuff, they do it lazily. And they end up with dripping, deformed things, staining the white bathroom tiles candy cane–red.

"She's hideous," Hazel cried when she saw what Howard had made.

"Her name is . . . Candy," Howard said. "I love her. And you will too. Because she is our daughter."

"I won't love anything that can't say it loves me back."

"Fine," Howard said. "Then I'll teach Candy to talk."

Rather than instruct the misshapen sugar girl himself, he propped Candy up on the sofa and made her watch sitcoms with him. He'd laugh at all the bad jokes and slap her on the back, saying, "Well, that was a humdinger, wasn't it? Learning to talk yet, my love?"

Candy wouldn't respond. She wouldn't even move. She sat. And dripped.

"Eat her already," Hazel said after a few weeks.

"You're a monster," Howard said. "How could you say that?"

"Oh, come on," Hazel said. "Like you haven't thought of it."

Actually, he had. Every night, sitting there, smelling the peppermint, Howard was tempted. When Hazel wasn't looking, he even nibbled.

A wee bit off the toe, that's all I need.

How about a little hair? We'll consider it a haircut.

She won't miss an earlobe. Who misses an earlobe?

Soon it became obvious what he was doing. Chunks were missing all over Candy's body. He tried to hide them by covering her in a quilt, but Hazel became wise to his tricks.

"The jig is up!" she howled. "Let's eat her and be done with it. She's a pile of candy canes, for crying out loud!"

With a sigh, Howard agreed. And they both strapped on some bibs, because they were slobs, but not *total* slobs.

For a few hours, they chomped away on Candy. Her hands, her feet, her striped kneecaps. "Scrumptious," Hazel moaned when they had eaten as far as her head. But just as they were about to eat her face, a sound snuck out from the thin striped lips.

"Gur Ferm Griggid."

"Amazing," Howard gasped. "She said *I love you*."

"She didn't say nothing," Hazel said as she licked sugar from her fingers.

"Gur Ferm Griggid," Candy said again.

"That does it!" Howard stood up. "We're getting more candy canes and making her whole again."

"Gur Ferm Griggid, Gur Ferm Griggid," Candy said.

"Sounds more like *I am delicious*!" Hazel said, puckering her lips. "Let's finish her off."

"No!" Howard shouted. "I am her father and I want her to grow old and wise, just as I have."

"Ha!" Hazel shouted. "Wise? That's rich."

The two shouted at each other for hours, while Candy kept saying "Gur Ferm Griggid" over and over again until the saliva from her lips melted her face and the liquid soaked into the sofa.

Saturday, 11/25/1989 ...
Continued

ANOTHER STORY WITHOUT MUCH OF AN ENDING. SORRY.

Double sorry, actually, because I guess I didn't tell you how this morning ended either, did I? How the rest of the day went? I'm a total jerk like that. Well, let's just say when your brother has been mute for what seems like forever (five days) and then finally speaks, it's monumental, right?

Yes and no.

So I brought up the candy cane story and, more importantly, the glowing wombat story and Alistair started talking and Mom immediately hugged him like he'd graduated high school or something and Dad put up a hand, a sort of *slow down, give him a moment.*

"I need to talk to Keri," Alistair told them. "Alone."

It's strange. Twelve-year-old boys don't usually get everything they ask for, at least not in this house, at least not until today. But even though Mom started to say, "Wait, but we—"

Dad cut her off with a hand on her shoulder and a whisper in her ear and before I knew it, they were in the dining room and I was sitting alone with my brother in the kitchen.

"How do you know about the wombat?" he asked me.

"You wanna know about . . . wombats?"

"Yes. I do."

"Umm . . . They're marsupials and they live in Australia and—"

"Your wombat. You said his fur glows. Is that right?"

"*Her* fur. And yeah. It's kind of her thing."

"Who told you about the fur?"

"Who told me?" I said as I noticed Mom's head peeking around the door frame and Dad coaxing her back into the dining room. "No one told me."

Alistair scooted his chair closer and leaned in so he could whisper, "If someone didn't tell you, then you came up with it yourself, and if you came up with it yourself then that really means something, doesn't it?"

I almost said *Well, it means that girls can be creative too, you male chauvinist pig,* but I wasn't sure the time was right for being a wiseass, so I said, "I don't know what it means. I don't know what any of this means."

Alistair nodded sympathetically. Then he pulled a small padded envelope out of his pocket. It was addressed to someone named Jenny Colvin. I didn't recognize the name of the street or town, but it was someplace in Australia. As in the country. Of Australia!

"It's stamped and ready to go," Alistair said as he handed

me the envelope. "I need you to slip it into the mail. Too many people are watching me. I'd rather you handle it."

"Your handwriting is out of practice," I said, because it looked like it had been addressed by a six-year-old.

"I wrote it with my left hand," he said. "Didn't want Mom to spot it if she was at work sorting mail."

"Smart," I said, but I didn't know if it was smart at all. Like this entire conversation, it was mainly weird. "So who's Jenny Colvin? Your girlfriend? Who conveniently lives half-way around the world?"

I regretted the girlfriend crack instantly. I was pretty sure Fiona was Alistair's girlfriend. With her gone, and with his best friend gone, it was beyond cruel to joke like that.

If it bothered him, he didn't show it. "I don't know who Jenny is," he said. "Not really. Only that she's very smart and very capable. A few other bits and pieces too. Her address and a phone number. Oh yeah, that's the other thing. I've been making some long-distance calls. Talking to operators in Australia to find out that information. I don't like lying, so when Mom and Dad get the bill, do you mind saying it was you who made the calls? They've got so many other things on their minds that they probably won't bug you too much about it."

This was probably true, though these days I could use a little bugging. Still, who am I to complain? It was a fib, at best. A white lie, which are the good ones. And while I don't really like lying either, I agreed. Because that's what you do when your brother needs you.

"Okay," I said. "So who was I supposed to be calling?"

"Same person. Jenny Colvin. You can say she's your new pen pal. Or whatever seems to make the most sense. You're creative. You'll think on your feet."

Loyalty combined with flattery will rope me into just about anything, and he must have known that. "What's in the envelope?" I asked.

"A tape," he said. "A message for her. If I call her, she can hang up. But if she has this tape, she'll be tempted to listen."

"Will she try to get back in touch?" I asked.

"I hope so," he said. "If she calls, I might want you to talk to her for me."

"Why?"

"Because she'll be afraid of me."

"Why?"

"Because I'm someone she should maybe be afraid of."

I shook my head. The weirdness was too much. I had to ask. "What in the hell happened to you, li'l bro?"

"I've grown," he said.

Tilting my gaze, I looked him over from head to toe. "What are you, five foot five, five foot six now?"

He tapped a finger on his head. "Up here. Up here it goes on forever."

NIGHT

The dam released and he's been speaking all day. He hasn't said anything about Fiona, Charlie, or Kyle, or anything else about the wombat or Jenny Colvin. He's acted relatively normal. "Pass the ketchup" and that sort of thing. I don't know what it was about our strange chat, but it set him at ease. Or at least made him more approachable. Dad can sense this, obviously. It's his job to sense. A few minutes ago, we were all watching some stupid show and Alistair was laughing at something and Dad picked up the clicker and turned off the TV and said, "Now it's our turn."

That was his way of saying, *Good night, Keri. Skedaddle.*

Sunday, 11/26/1989

MORNING

THEY LEFT EARLY, BEFORE THE SUN WAS EVEN UP. MOM, DAD, and Alistair—back to the police station. Presumably because Alistair is ready to talk. About wombats?

I'm home alone, which isn't unheard of (I'm fourteen, you know), but considering that there's still a crazy person out there stealing kids and shooting people in the stomach, I'm surprised they think this is a good idea.

Unless they think Alistair is that crazy person. Which from what he was telling me, maybe . . .

God. This is so messed up.

I'm not *really* alone, for the record. Mandy is here. If that counts. She came over as soon as the others left, and I guess that was enough for my parents. She's in the bathroom, which means she'll be a while. She treats bathrooms like crime scenes. She doesn't come out until there is absolutely no evidence that she's been in there.

When she got here, she hugged me right off the bat and said, "I love you."

Girls say stuff like that to each other all the time, but Mandy rarely says it to me. So it means something. That she loves me, I guess. I hope.

I love Mandy too. I do. How could I not? We've been friends forever, and do you know what love is? It's when you try to picture your life without someone and you can't.

I love Mom. Dad. Alistair. Mandy. They all frustrate me, but life without any of them would be impossible. I have to remember that when I think about the Dwyers and the Loomises. Their families are facing lives without the ones they love. Apparently, Kyle is stable and the coma he's in is actually caused by doctors, who did it to keep him alive. They'll probably be able to wake him up when they're ready.

But Charlie? Fiona? Still not a word about them.

Or maybe a lot of words, pouring from Alistair's mouth into the tape recorders at the police station.

Worst-case scenario:

"Where are they, son?" says the cop.

"Buried by Frog Rock," says Alistair.

"Why'd you do it?" says the cop.

"Because a wombat named Jenny Colvin told me to," says Alistair.

Best-case scenario:

"Where are they, son?" says the cop.

"Wombats," says Alistair.

"What in the Sam Hill are you talking about, son?" says the cop.

"Wombats," says Alistair. "It's a resort in Australia run by Jenny Colvin. They've got phosphorescent stuff in the water there. Very romantic. Those two fell in love and ran off. First Fiona left, and then Charlie. So people didn't suspect it. Don't worry. They're fine."

Yes, yes, yes, I know. I'm making jokes when I shouldn't, but what the hell am I supposed to do?

Actually, here's what I'm going to do: when Mandy comes out of the bathroom, I'm going to tell her that I love her, because I do, and I don't tell her enough. Things have changed. They're changing by the second. I have to hold on to everything I have.

Monday, 11/27/1989

AFTERNOON

Mandy's mom came over last night and cooked tacos for us and waited for my family to get home. It was about nine o'clock when they finally did, and Alistair went straight to his room and Mom and Dad stood in the hall with Mandy's mom whispering. Mandy's mom gasped and put a hand over her mouth. Then she hugged my mom, but it was an awkward hug because they aren't really friends.

My parents told me they had to sleep on some things and would explain stuff in the morning. *Fantabulous, Ma and Pa!* Like that's the sort of thing that will help me calm down and get a solid eight hours.

Seriously, though. I guess I understand. They were gone the whole day. A lot to absorb.

I probably slept two hours of the eight I was in bed and then dragged myself downstairs for breakfast. Everyone else was up all night too. Floorboards were creaking at all hours and every eye was glassed over as Mom poured the OJ.

"Dad will be driving Alistair back to the police station this morning, and I'm going to walk you to school."

"What?" I said. "Why?"

"Because we need to talk through what is going to happen and we don't need everyone chiming in."

I turned to Alistair. He didn't look sad or happy or scared or relaxed. He was eating an orange, and his eyes were glued to the sink where Dad was washing last night's dishes.

"But I want Alistair to chime in," I said.

Alistair turned to me and said, "Mom will get you up to date. It's better that way."

They were simple words, but he said them in a way that made it seem like I was his little sister instead of his big one. They were comforting and yet made me feel small at the same time. Whatever they were, they managed to shut me up.

Minutes later, Dad and Alistair were out the door, side by side, wearing matching knit caps that Nana got them last Christmas.

A few minutes after that, it was Mom and me walking outside. She didn't really say anything until we were crossing the driveway. It was as if she was scared the house was bugged and we could only talk in the open air.

She took a breath and said, "Your brother shot Kyle."

I kept walking because I expected her to say more. But she didn't. I could hear her breaths, like a phone's busy signal but in her chest.

"So what's going to happen to Alistair?" I asked.

"Ms. Kern is his lawyer for now, but we might have to hire someone who's more experienced in these situations."

"What type of situation is it?" On the inside, I was cursing myself for joking about this in my diary yesterday. On the outside, I was shaking. I put my hands in my pockets.

"It was an accident," Mom said. "He and Charlie had been playing with the gun in that old clubhouse of Kyle's. Kyle tried to wrestle it away from them and it went off. Alistair ran home to call 911, and Charlie must have run off somewhere."

"Whose gun was it?" I asked.

"Ummm . . ." Mom put a hand on my shoulder. "It was Alistair's. With the whole Fiona thing, he was worried. He wanted to protect himself."

"How the hell did Alistair get a gun?" Mom hardly blinked when I said *hell*. What does a swear matter when your twelve-year-old son packs a pistol?

"That's the next step," she said. "Figuring out who's really responsible here. The person who gave Alistair this gun. He won't say. He's made up some story that's too strange to be-lieve. He's probably scared to tell the truth, but it's important that we find out. It might be the key to finding Charlie. So that's what he and Dad are doing right now. Talking to the police about it."

I figured it had to be Kyle's gun. Kyle was the type of guy to have a gun, the type to spin it around on a finger and wink at you and say, "Let's get dangerous, toots."

Okay. That's a weird thing to write. Do guys really call girls *toots*? Probably not, but the fact remains that if any guy around here would have a gun, then that guy would be Kyle Dwyer. But why would Alistair be afraid of admitting that? Kyle isn't in the position to be doing much of anything to anyone.

"Will they arrest Alistair?" I asked.

"Right now, it's still a conversation," Mom said. "Speaking of which. What did you two talk about the other day?"

I put my hand in my coat pocket, where Alistair's envelope to the mysterious Jenny Colvin was buried. I wasn't going to tell Mom about that. I decided to tell her the odder bit, the bit that got Alistair excited in the first place. I didn't have to lie in that case. "Wombats," I said.

"What?"

"Seriously. Wombats. When I said I was gonna write a story about a glowing wombat, he was interested. I don't get it either."

We had reached the entrance of the school at that point, and a school bus drove by going about fifteen miles per hour. Even though we were walking in the grass about five feet from the curb, Mom put her arm over my chest to protect me until it was long gone.

"Alistair didn't say anything about a boy named Luke Drake, did he?" she asked.

The name sounded familiar, but I had no idea why. "No. Who's he?"

"It's about something Alistair told us he saw once," she said as she kissed my cheek, which meant she was leaving me here. "It's not important."

Not important? Yet she asked about him.

TONY THE GUN

THERE ONCE WAS A GUN NAMED TONY. HE WAS A SWEET LITTLE gun, a please-and-thank-you sort of gun. He lived with his parents in a gun shop on a highway leading away from a big city. His parents were an Uzi and a sniper rifle, but you would never have guessed that. Tony was tiny. A popgun is what customers called him. As in, *Look at that darling little popgun! Perfect for a beginner! Or for a lady's purse!*

Five bullets fit in Tony, and he liked bullets because they were smooth and made him feel less hollow, but since Tony lived in a gun shop, he had only been loaded a few times, and only in the back, by the owner, who sighed as he did it, saying, "Your time will come. Just you wait. Someone will find a use for you."

Tony sure hoped so. Someone found a use for his parents. They were sold to a man in a camouflage jacket who came into the shop looking for some "pinpoint accuracy and elephant-stopping power." Which left Tony alone, hanging in a display case next to pink holsters and pellet guns. Pellets guns were the worst. They all had names like Petey and Zeke and they thought that fart jokes were the funniest things, and Tony didn't like fart jokes at all. Not because they were rude, but because they were rarely funny.

One day, a little old lady came into the shop looking for something dainty, and the owner said, "I have just the thing!"

He pulled Tony from the display case and handed him to her. With a trembling hand, the woman raised Tony and pointed him at a mirror that hung on the other side of the shop. The sight of this hunched, frail little person clutching his handle made Tony afraid. What if she dropped him?

She didn't. Instead, she said, "I'll take it!" and slapped a wad of cash on the counter.

From that day on, Tony lived in the old lady's nightstand, next to a ball of rubber bands, a pill bottle, and her dentures (when she wasn't wearing them). It wasn't an exciting life, but it did have one advantage to life in the gun shop: he was loaded.

"I'm very important," Tony told the ball of rubber bands as often as he could.

"Then why are you in this drawer with us?" the ball responded.

"She's waiting. She'll use me. She has to."

It was a long wait. Or what felt like a long wait. In the drawer, it was hard to tell day from night. Especially when the old lady stopped opening it to take out her dentures. Months passed. Possibly years.

If you lose track of time, you lose track of your mind. You don't go crazy necessarily, but your thoughts wander. They go on permanent vacations. So when the drawer finally opened one day, and light finally poured in, Tony had forgotten what light was or even what *he* was.

A hand reached into the drawer and pulled him out. The hand had nineteen fingers, and each finger had six knuckles. It raised Tony and pointed him across the room at a dusty and cracked mirror.

In the reflection, there was a creature the type of which Tony had no words for. Maybe it was an animal he'd never seen before. Maybe it was an alien. Maybe it was something he once knew of, but had forgotten.

Whatever it was, it was weird and gross, with a bulbous head and knobby knees. It turned Tony away from the mirror and pointed him at another weird and gross creature that stood on the opposite side of the room. The two creatures babbled gibberish at each other as Tony felt his trigger being pressed down.

A click.

A spark.

Then a bullet rocketed through Tony and the second creature fell to the floor.

I remember, Tony thought. *I'm a gun. A glorious gun! And this is what I've been meant to do all along!*

The first creature shrieked and turned Tony around to

look down his barrel. The creature's five eyes were wide with curiosity. They say curiosity killed the cat. Whether that's true or not doesn't matter because, at the very least, it killed this thing. With the barrel pointed in the center of its five eyes, the creature pulled the trigger again and another bullet came rocketing from inside Tony.

I'm a gun! A spectacular gun!

As the creature crashed to the ground, Tony flew from its hand and landed on a rotting dresser next to a window. The two creatures lay dead on the floor. In the bed, there was a skeleton, presumably the remains of the old lady who had bought Tony so long ago. In the yard, which was a sea of giant weeds, sat some sort of spacecraft.

For eons, Tony remained in that room. He never saw a man, woman, or creature again. But soon the dresser collapsed from the rot, and the weeds in the yard became trees, and the house fell down around him. The spacecraft crumbled too, and then oceans rose and covered Tony and the rubble. And when the ocean dried up, lava melted Tony and he became part of whatever was left of the Earth.

His last thought was a happy thought. Sure, he was dying alone, but he had served a purpose. He had shot a bullet from his barrel. Two bullets, actually, and both had hit their targets.

He had done his part.

Tuesday, 11/28/1989

AFTERNOON

THEY DIDN'T TAKE ALISTAIR INTO CUSTODY. THAT WAS AN option, since he's making a crazy claim about the gun. He says he found it in a box, buried near the Oriskanny. He actually took them to the spot, a bend in the river somewhere. They asked him why he was digging there, and he said he was looking for something.

Somewhere. Something. Mom and Dad refuse to tell me the exact details.

"We're going to let the police investigate," Dad said. "But we can't have information getting out at this point."

"Who am I going to tell?" I asked.

Dad raised his eyebrows.

"I'm not telling Mandy," I said.

Somehow, Dad managed to raise his eyebrows higher.

"Oh come on," I said.

"Facts," he replied. "Mom and I have agreed to tell you the facts of the case."

"What if I ask Alistair?"

"Alistair has agreed to not discuss the case with anyone besides us and Ms. Kern."

"So I'm the least important member of the family, then? Less important than Ms. Kern." I think I said it to bug him, but when the words came out, I started to actually feel them. Like, *Yeah, why does Ms. Kern get more information than me? Because it's her job?*

Dad gulped back his words for a second and started to shake his head, but then stopped. "We love you. So, so much. And don't think for a second that we don't, even if we sometimes get consumed with Alistair's problems."

"How can I have anything bigger in my life than Alistair's problems? How can anyone?" I was shouting the words by this point.

Dad's job is to set people at ease, to give them a place to point their confusion and rage. But he didn't do his job. All he did was shrug.

EVENING

I finally tore open the padded envelope addressed to Jenny Colvin. How could I not? I haven't mailed the thing, after all. I still intend to. A promise is a promise, but the promise had nothing to do with not listening to it.

There was a tape inside, but nothing else. The label on the tape read: *PLAY ME*. I slipped it into my Walkman and lay down on the bed. The sound was fuzzy at first, and then Alistair's voice filled my ears.

"Greetings and salutations, Jenny," Alistair said. "I hope this recording finds you and finds you well. You've gotta be wondering what it's all about, so I'll get right to it. You have been chosen, Jenny, out of . . . well . . . You're the only qualified candidate for this job. Do you know where the Steerpike Fountain is? Of course you do, it's a few blocks from your house. Every day at two p.m., I will open a portal there. When you're ready, step through and you will enter the Captured Worlds of Aquavania. It's where the rivers lead, where daydreamers like you have been trying to get for ages, where the swimmers go.

"An atlas and spacesuit will be waiting for you there, which will help you get to Quadrant 43. I'll get you as close as I can, but even I don't have control of everything. I'm still learning how to use my power. In Quadrant 43, you'll board a space station where you'll meet some kids named Chip and Dot. They're doing vital work. I was told that in your world you created something that extracts and projects thoughts. Well, these two are in the extraction business. Only they're extracting souls. Now they need to project them. They could use your intuitiveness.

"I suspect they'll be a bit prickly at first, but ask Chip about the pendant he wears. Tell both of them that you want to help them resurrect the Astronomer. They'll know what you mean, and they'll come around. Once you've gained their trust, I'd like you to tell them that I want to help too. They've gone to great lengths to protect themselves from me, which you undoubtedly understand. But I'm not a danger. I want to help. At the very least, they know that I've gotten rid of all the ciphers, and the Captured Worlds are a more peaceful place than they've been in ages. Now I'm trying to do what I can to get everyone home again. Werner, Chua, Rodrigo, Boaz . . . Fiona. Everyone.

"As for me, I go by many names. Alistair is one of them. And yes, you guessed it, another one is the Riverman. But I'm not after your soul. I would have gotten it already if I wanted it. Because I know what you need, Jenny. You need to be courageous. You need to be a hero. You need to be a swimmer. Now is your chance. I hope you take it."

That was it. That was the entire tape.

What. In. The. Half. Baked. Hell!

I listened to it seven or eight times, trying to figure out what it was about. Each time I listened, I was more confused. Finally, I put the tape back into the envelope, sealed it up with Scotch tape, and stuffed it in my backpack.

NIGHT

I'd rather be in school. School!

What a pathetic thing to write. Kids everywhere should be calling for my head. "Nerd!" they should scream into the air like a bunch of Barbarians.

Or "Geek!"

"Dweeb!"

"Renob!"

Yep. You heard it right. Renob. It's *boner* spelled backward. Don't ask me. It's something kids say.

Now, of course, I'm not going to jump up on one of the tables in the cafeteria and declare, "I love school!" What kind of maniac do you think I am, Stella?

Stella? Where the hell did that come from?

Ha. I think I just named you! Stella.

Stella! Stella! Stella!

I heard someone yelling that in a movie once, and now, diary, you are officially known as Stella. People name their diaries all the time, so I'm doing it too. Just so you know, I don't plan on being polite. I won't be starting each entry with a *Dearest Stella* or *My Good Friend Stella* or whatever. I'm going to be emotional sometimes. I'm going to be honest. On occasion, I'll be overwhelmed and I might even say awful things that I don't mean.

Screw you, Stella.

Up yours, Stella.

Kill yourself, Stella.

Actually, that last one is not a bad idea, Stella. If you ever decided to throw yourself off a bridge, no one would ever read you. And that'd be a good thing. Because the danger of writing something like this is the possibility of someone reading it. Someone like Phaedra Moreau, who would find it and start telling people, "Not only does Keri Cleary love school, but she

56

loves Mandy Druger! Odds are that every school has a lesbo, and now we're lucky to have two. Oh, and how about Keri's brother, Alistair? What a pathetic dope. It'll be a shame when they strap a straitjacket on him and ship him off to the loony bin."

Not that I can't handle Phaedra Moreau. Everyone knows Phaedra talks crap because she is crap. For instance, this morning she was hanging out on the front steps, sucking on a candy cane and whispering numbers to girls as they walked into school. Six. Eight. Three. Nine. And so on.

Weird? Not for Phaedra. Simply more of her crap. I heard later from Mandy that she was rating girls' outfits on a one to ten scale.

I got a five. Simply spectacular.

Okay, I've gotten off topic. I blame you, Stella.

The point I was trying to make is that I could live in school and be happy, even with weasels like Phaedra there. Or happier. Sitting at a desk or in the cafeteria. Standing at my locker and watching people walk up and down the hall. Listening to Mr. Geary blab on and on about the formula for the volume of a cone and how that's going to be important to know if I ever want to go to college and not be a homeless person. It's all better than thinking about the fact that your brother is delusional, that he speaks of strange things with strange people in strange places, all in an attempt to distract you from the only truth, which is the worst truth.

Your brother shoots people with a gun he dug up next to the river.

Wednesday, 11/29/1989

AFTERNOON

On the walk to school, I still had the tape for Jenny Colvin. I guess I should have given it to Mom, Ms. Kern, or the police. But it's too late for that now. I didn't want the thing around anymore, and since I strive to keep promises, I kept this one. I dropped it in the mailbox outside school. Messages, even cuckoo crazy ones, deserve to reach their destinations.

Besides, the very existence of Alistair's tape inspired me to send my own message. I wrote a letter last night when I couldn't sleep, when all I seemed to hear were Alistair's footsteps in the hall like every night for the last few days. It was a short letter, and I addressed it to Glen Maple.

Remember him? My secret admirer from last year?

The letter read: *Meet me behind the maintenance shed. Today after last bell. Sincerely, Your Secret Admirer.*

I delivered it between classes. I pretended to bump into Glen's locker and I slipped it through the air vents.

It felt awesome. It felt awful. It felt completely like something I would never do, but I needed to do it, Stella, because you deserve to hear about something other than my brother. You deserve stories of kids being kids, of romance and regular stuff.

The afternoon was drizzly and cold—no surprise, this is Thessaly—but the shed has an overhanging roof that kept me dry while I waited. It was at least fifteen minutes before he showed up.

"Thank heavens to murgatroid," he said when he poked his head around and saw me.

Yep. *Murgatroid.* It's a word, I guess. From a cartoon, if I'm not mistaken.

"Don't say things like that," I told him.

"Sorry," he said. "I'm just relieved you're not Wart Woman."

An awful nickname some kids called Kendra Tolliver, a nice enough girl in the seventh grade. "Don't say things like that either," I replied.

"Sorry." He hung his head low, so low that I knew he wasn't really sorry. He was frowning, but it was a smiling variety of frown. The edges of his lips still curled upward.

"You didn't know who wrote the letter?" I asked. "But you came anyway?"

"I was hoping it was you," he said as he looked at me in every place except my eyes.

"It's me," I said with a shrug. "So what's next?"

"Ummm," was all he could say.

"You're not kissing me," I told him.

"Ummm."

"And I'm not telling you anything about my brother."

"Sure. He's so, like, not . . ." He pretended his mouth had a zipper and he zipped it shut.

Then we stood there silently for a few seconds until I said, "So you're my boyfriend now. If that's okay with you."

"Super okay," he replied.

"You don't tell anyone yet, though. Let me do that."

"Sure."

"Sit with me at lunch tomorrow," I told him. "People will know by then."

"Bitchin'," he said, and I realized at that moment that he said stupid things like that not because he thought they were funny, but because he actually thought it made him sound cool.

"Until then," I said, and I ducked out from the overhang, opened my umbrella, and hurried home.

EVENING

The family is in a holding pattern. Waiting for the next thing to happen. In the movies, everything happens so fast. Someone is shot. Someone is arrested. Someone goes to court. Someone goes home or someone goes to jail.

In real life, there are negotiations. There are late-evening phone calls, there are early-morning meetings. Then there is nothing. Delays. There is sitting around having dinner and watching TV.

I skipped TV tonight. Because of you, Stella.

Damn you, Stella, always begging me to write stories in you. Moronic stories. Stories without endings. If you don't share your stories with other people, do they even count? If you don't share your stories, do they even need an ending? I know, it's that stupid *if a tree falls in the forest* sort of question, but I mean it.

So I'm back to the wombat. That's a story with an ending. A beginning too, but I still have to write the thing. I can't get the images out of my head. I think about them when my mind wanders in class. I dream about them, for crying out loud. Now's as good a time as ever to finally get the story down on paper.

Right, Stella? Are you ready for it? Will you protect it?

THE PHOSPHORESCENT WOMBAT

IN A PLACE WHERE THE PINES WERE THICK, ALONG A COUNTRY road with dandelions sprouting from the cracks, a wombat wobbled under the weight of a sign that hung around her neck.

PERFECTLY FINE WOMBAT, the sign read.

It was raining, the drops coming down hard, massaging the wombat's head and back. It was a warm day, so the rain wasn't a bad thing. It was quite pleasant, actually. A lovely sort of rain.

Sprinting through the forest and down the road, with plastic tubs of wild black raspberries they'd picked, a girl named Rosie and her younger brother named Hamish came upon the wombat. "Well, look at that," Rosie said.

"Ugliest puppy I've ever seen," Hamish said.

"It isn't a puppy," Rosie said. "That there is a wombat."

"A womwhat?"

"Wombat. From Australia. Like a koala that can't climb. Or a kangaroo that can't jump."

Hamish got down on all fours for a closer look. Water dripped from his floppy bangs. "Then what does he do?" he asked.

Rosie didn't need to get on all fours to answer. "First off, he's a she. Notice the lack of dangly bits. And why does she have to do anything?"

Hamish leaned in closer, until the wombat showed her teeth. He pulled back, pushed his bangs up, and said, "Everything needs a purpose. Guess hers is to be mean and ugly."

"You're mean and ugly," Rosie said, a comment that made the wombat smile. At least it looked like a smile. Maybe it was gas.

Whatever the case, Rosie whistled a welcoming whistle and the wombat waddled over to her, stood up on her hind legs, and swayed because of the weight of the sign around her neck. Rosie bent down and picked the wombat up.

"Show-off," Hamish said.

"Perfectly fine wombat," Rosie said, bobbing her chin at the sign because she needed both hands to hold the slippery beast. "Means she's fine and perfect and I'm taking her home."

"Means she's perfectly *fine*," Hamish said. "That's entirely different. Might as well be *spectacularly regular*."

Rosie stuck out her tongue and set off down the road with the wombat under her arm. When Rosie was only twenty feet or so away, Hamish could barely see her, on account of all the rain. But he could see a faint glow.

Yes, that perfectly fine wombat was glowing.

* * *

They took the wombat home. Well, to their summer home, a small cabin on the rocky coast of an island in the Atlantic. Their parents asked the standard questions:

What are you going to feed it?

Where will it sleep?

Who's going to clean up after it?

Rosie gave three answers:

Table scraps.

In my bed.

Hamish.

Hamish didn't object. He knew Rosie could convince their parents of just about anything, and if he was forced to live with this wombat, then he'd rather clean up her poop than have her sleep in his bed, especially since she glowed.

"It'll be like having a night-light pressed against your face while you sleep," he told Rosie. "No thank you."

"Oh, come on, she doesn't glow that much," she replied. And she was right. At first. But, like a dimmer on a lamp slowly turned up, the wombat was getting brighter day by day. They didn't notice the brightening during those first few weeks, but they did decide to name her Luna, on account of the fact that in the nighttime, she resembled the moon.

Rosie gave Luna showers every day, hoping to wash off whatever it was that made her fur glow. Luna adored the showers, but no matter what or how much soap Rosie used, the glow remained.

64

"Do you think she's sick?" Hamish asked one afternoon. Though he'd been resistant to Luna initially, the boy had come to truly care for her.

"Dr. Hoover will know," Rosie replied.

Dr. Hoover was a veterinarian who lived on the island with a menagerie of animals—dogs, cats, goats, parrots, ferrets, snakes, and other things. She had years of experience with all sorts of beasts, even a wombat or two. However, Dr. Hoover had no idea what was wrong with Luna.

Standing back from the examining table where Luna sat and munched on a radish, Dr. Hoover cocked her head and shrugged. "Seems perfectly healthy. She's small. A juvenile. Maybe she'll grow out of it. Or maybe it's some sort of genetic mutation."

"Cooool," Hamish said, because all the genetic mutations he knew about were from comic books and resulted in super-powers.

It was hard to say whether Luna's glow counted as a su-perpower, but it certainly got her plenty of attention. Rosie and Hamish would walk her on a leash along the roads of the island, where cars and bikes would stop and people would gawk.

"She's a wonder, isn't she?" Rosie said to a man who slowed down his convertible to have a look one afternoon.

"She most certainly is," the man replied, and he handed Rosie a business card.

Rosie read the writing aloud. "Hal Hawson, Hollywood Producer."

"I'm heading back to LA tomorrow, but call the number on the back. That . . . whatever that thing is . . . needs to be on TV. And I've got the perfect project in mind. It might mean your parents can quit their jobs."

Before Rosie could flip the card over to read the phone number, the convertible was speeding away.

A week later, their family was in California. Luna was fitted for a tuxedo and scheduled to appear on *Pocketful of Hullabaloo*, a daytime variety show popular with folks who thought women in leotards juggling chain saws was the height of human achievement. Luna's job there was a simple one: sit at the back of the stage, tuxedoed and atop a Grecian pillar. And glow. That was it.

It became a regular gig. There was a promise of paychecks that Hal Hawson honored with a wink and a smile. And for one hour a day, Luna wasn't Luna. She was a wombat lamp known as Mr. Nickelsworth.

Sometimes, one of the performers would turn to Luna and say, "What do you think about that, Mr. Nickelsworth?"

Luna, being a wombat and all, couldn't reply, so she simply sat there on the pillar glowing, and the performer would invariably make some joke like, "Well, you're very bright, Nickelsworth, but you aren't very bright."

The studio audience found these jokes hilarious every time.

The family bought a house near the TV studio, and Rosie ferried Luna to work in the basket of her bike. Every other

Tuesday, they'd stop to deposit Luna's sizable paycheck in the family account at the Sunfirst Bank, where Rosie always told the teller, "Soon as this wombat can talk, we'll cut her in on the dough."

Without fail, the teller would chuckle and shake his head and stamp the receipt.

But back at home, Rosie's father was noticing something. "Is it just me, or is Luna not growing?"

Her mother was noticing something too. "Is it just me, or is Luna's fur getting even brighter?"

It wasn't just them. Luna was the same size she was the afternoon they'd found her, which was tiny for a wombat, but her fur, once mocha-brown, had more of a shine to it every day, a neon green tinge.

It hardly mattered, though. Luna was famous, or as famous as a wombat could be. The studio audience at *Pocketful of Hullabaloo* would hold up signs that said things like A NICKELSWORTH IS WORTH A DOLLAR, AT LEAST! And after each taping of the show, they'd ask for autographs. Hamish would take the scraps of paper, the photos of Luna, and anything else the fans wanted signed and he'd bring them backstage, where he'd sign them himself.

Shine on! Love, Mr. Nickelsworth, he'd always write. And people were more than grateful. All things considered, there were worse fates than being a shiny runt of a wombat.

No one ever asked Luna how she felt about her life, though. If they had asked, she might have wiggled her feet and showed her teeth, which was the only way she knew how to communicate. She would have tried her best but failed to explain that she enjoyed wearing the tuxedo and bicycling in the wind and falling asleep when rain was pattering on the roof, that she liked the feeling of Rosie's sharp—but not too sharp—nails on the soft spot behind her ear, that she adored it when Rosie would give her a shower because the water on her head felt like liquid sunshine and always reminded her of that day along the road when Rosie first found her, that she didn't care much for the taste of radishes but loved how they crunched, and that she didn't remember where she lived, or who with, or what she did in those days before Rosie and Hamish spotted her along the side of the road.

As for not growing, and as for the glow in her fur, she would have said that this worried her. She would have confessed that deep down, she knew something was wrong. But she also would have said that she didn't think about it too much. Mostly, she thought about food.

That's right. Luna had ideas and emotions, but there was no way that anyone could tell. To the world, she was simply a dim-witted, dimly lit marsupial. Little did they know, she was so much more than that.

TO BE CONTINUED . . .

Thursday, 11/30/1989

AFTERNOON

To be continued is a terrible thing, I know. But life is *to be continued*. You want *to be continued* as long as possible. Which makes me sad about my walk to school this morning. As I rounded the corner toward the parking lot, I saw a dead baby bird on the sidewalk. It's almost December. I didn't know birds had babies so late in the year. But there it was, nearly see-through and dead. Tiny. A baby hummingbird.

Sure, it reminds me of the story I wrote about the jogger named Justine Barlow, and I want to say it's only a coincidence. And it probably is. But maybe it's also an omen. Telling me that good news might not be good news after all. Because there was good news this morning. Plenty of it.

Before leaving for school, before the baby bird, I called Mandy and told her I was dating Glen Maple. Instead of telling me I'm crazy or pretending to throw up, she said, "That is so awesome. I am so happy for you."

Which was . . . good.

A minute after I hung up, just as I was about to step out the door, the phone rang. I figured it would be Mandy calling back to say, "Ha, ha! It's Opposite Day! Glen Maple is gross. Why would you ever want to date him?"

But it wasn't. It was Mr. Dwyer. Charlie and Kyle's dad. He had some even better news. Or so it seemed.

Kyle Dwyer is awake.

THE STATEMENT OF
KYLE DWYER

———— ·——·—— ————

IT WASN'T TOO LATE, BUT IT WAS DARK OUT. SUNDAY, NOVEMBER nineteenth, right? Yeah, had to be. Because Saturday was the eighteenth. I know because Saturday was Jared's birthday, and he couldn't celebrate on Saturday because his parents had a whole fancy dinner for him with his grandma and grandpa and everyone. So that's why we went out on Sunday. Had a few beers by the silos at the Finnerman farm. Didn't get plastered or anything. Played the radio, sat in the back of the van as the rain came down. Four of us. Kim and Heather were there too.

We talked about stuff, Fiona Loomis mostly. She'd been gone for at least two weeks, I think, which is, like, forever for a kid to be missing. Seemed even longer because we actually kinda knew her. We polished off the twelver around, I don't know, seven thirty or eight, and I was feeling really bummed out. Been a rough month around here, ever since Charlie blew his fingers off.

I dropped everyone back at their places and I felt like driving to clear my head, but the rain was coming down harder and it was a bitch to see out the windshield, so I headed home.

A couple of weeks before, on Halloween actually, Alistair Cleary told me that he was afraid that Fiona's uncle was some sort of psycho, the type looking to hurt kids. It's funny, I thought the guy's name was Damien for the longest time, which is totally a psycho name. But it's Dorian. Close enough.

I couldn't be sure that Alistair's suspicions were true, but after Charlie lost his fingers, I wasn't taking any chances on any other kids getting hurt. So I drove to Syracuse a few days later, to this street I heard about, a place where people score. Salina? Yeah, Salina. Like salt. I started asking around about getting a piece, and a guy shows up in a red Trans-Am. Skin was a little dark. Maybe Mexican, I don't know. Didn't ask. Didn't care. Didn't even get a name. In the parking lot of a hot dog place, he sold me that pistol. Two hundred bucks. Money I'd saved for a rainy day.

How 'bout that? A rainy day.

(Laugh)

Anyway, reason I bought it was because we have Neighborhood Watch here, but has that ever amounted to anything? Think of all the stuff I've gotten away with over the years.

(Laugh)

Actually, don't.

Point is, if there's some psycho roaming our streets and the cops aren't doing anything about it, then it's on people like me to keep the peace. I told Dorian as much. Out in that

72

field where he flies his toy planes. But then you know all that, right? We went over this before when you were looking for Fiona.

Best place I could think to hide the gun was in my old clubhouse. No one uses that shack but stray cats. So I put it in a crawl space underneath some old signs. Anyway, on that night, Sunday the nineteenth, I got home and I went to check on the gun, make sure it wasn't getting soaked by the rain. Not sure if that would ruin it, but what do I know?

I pulled it out and I was sitting in the clubhouse with it in my hand and I was pointing it at the cats and going *blam, blam, blam,* pretending to pick them off one by one. Kinda sick, I know, but I was trying to get my mind off what I really was thinking about. Which was . . . shameful. We all have our problems. Some of us, me at least, aren't always the best at dealing with them.

I don't know what Alistair and Charlie were doing, but they showed up in the yard. To feed the cats, I guess. Or maybe collect rainwater. They had a glass pitcher with them. Or maybe a vase. I don't know, something glass. They're goofy kids like that. Always have been.

They must have heard me in the clubhouse, because Alistair slipped in right as I was turning the gun to my head. Not my proudest moment. But, you know, I was bummed, it was raining, and I had a few beers in me.

Alistair, being, like, the best kid there is, tried to stop me. Instinct told him to grab the gun, and so he went for it. He pulled it down, and I pulled it back. It went off.

Now Alistair is going to tell you that he pulled the trigger, maybe even that the gun was his, but it's only because he's covering for me. Because he knows I've got a record, what with the knife thing and all that other business.

Or maybe he's confused. Craziness like this happens and a kid like him won't know what's what. His brain will start making things up. Trauma will do that to people.

Truth is the truth, though. It was me. It was always me.

The shot didn't take me out, obviously, so I stumbled into the yard to lie down. Alistair ran off to call 911, and Charlie was crouched by my side, trying to help. He's a good kid, Charlie. He cares a lot. Really does.

That's all I remember. I blacked out after that. I have no idea what happened to Charlie. I wish I did. Man, do I wish.

Friday, 12/8/1989

EVENING

SOMETIMES I DON'T FEEL LIKE WRITING AT ALL. I CLOSE MY diary and stuff it under my mattress and I ask myself why I even bother. It seems so selfish, writing.

Look at me, look at me. I'm interesting! Stop what you're doing and look at me, for I have tales to regale you with! Hark, hark! Look at me!

I avoid writing until I can't avoid it anymore. Until writing comes knocking at my door like a friend I've neglected.

Oh, Stella, you again? You're so damn needy.

Alas, I have returned because I had to share Kyle Dwyer's "statement." I found it in Dad's briefcase yesterday. I know I wasn't supposed to see it, but the briefcase was next to the couch and Mom and Dad and Alistair were in the kitchen and . . .

Okay. I'm lying again. Why do I lie to you, Stella? Because you're judgy, Stella. You judge.

The truth: Late last night, I was curious about what was going on with Alistair, so I got up, went into Dad's desk, found the statement, and copied it down. It's a transcription of what Kyle told the police a few days after he woke up. Ms. Kern must have made a copy for my parents. It's called a statement, but I guess it's also sort of a confession, though I don't know what crime Kyle is confessing to. Being a suicidal dope?

Okay, that's not cool. I shouldn't joke about that. I'm sorry. Just because I write something doesn't mean that I mean it.

Seriously, though, owning an illegal gun is probably the crime. There might be some other technical stuff that Kyle is guilty of. Endangering the welfare of a . . . little brother? I don't know. The point is, Alistair is off the hook and Kyle is on it. And Kyle is the one with the hole in his belly, the one who may never walk again.

Man oh man.

So things have calmed down. A little. Alistair has been relatively quiet. Or he hasn't been saying outlandish things, for what that's worth. Of course, I haven't told him that I've listened to his tape. I'm not sure what good that would do. If things are going better for him, then I should make sure they keep going better. No reason to derail any progress. Maybe the tape was some sort of inside joke. Maybe it was . . .

It was weird, and I prefer not to think about it.

There's still no Fiona. Still no Charlie. I see the missing posters for Fiona at the post office and on utility poles outside the Skylark, and they're already faded and brown from the weather. You know how you can make a piece of paper look old by dipping it in coffee and leaving it out in the sun? That's how the posters look, and they're not even a month old. The snow has been especially heavy, and we're hardly into December.

Glen and I have been "dating" for over a week now, and it's actually pretty cool. We've had lunch together every day. We know each other's locker combinations, so we can slip each other secret notes and gifts between classes. Glen has already given me chocolates in a heart-shaped box. I know that's a bit of a cliché—but come on, chocolate.

We interrupt this program to acknowledge the glory that is chocolate.

Another sweet thing: Glen has been walking me home after school because Alistair isn't back in classes yet and it's not necessarily safe for me to walk alone. Glen lives in one of those nice houses on Clutter Hill, so he takes the bus, but he'll walk with me anyway, turn around and jog back to school, and hop on the late bus that comes at four thirty. It's very thoughtful, and my parents appreciate it.

"She's in good hands," Glen said to my dad the first time he walked me home last week. There are all sorts of ways Dad could have responded. For instance:

1. *Just see that you keep those good hands to yourself.*

2. *And whose hands would those be?* (with exaggerated glances over both shoulders)

3. *She will be soon enough. Now hand her over, hotshot.*

He didn't say any of those things, though. He grabbed Glen's shoulder, gave him a little shake, and said, "Good man."

Good man? He's fourteen. So am I. If he's a man, then I guess that makes me a woman. Do I feel like a woman? Ummm . . .

I am woman, hear me roar!

That's supposedly something strong women say, and though I'm inclined to roar a lot lately, I'm not sure mine is a womanly roar. I guess if these were the good ol' days, Glen and I might be considered adults. We might even be married already. At the very least, we'd be working in a factory with all the other kids. If these were olden tymes—the *y* makes the times especially olden, much more olden than the *good ol' days*, at least—we'd be Romeo and Juliet, all cleavage and pantaloons, poisoning ourselves in a graveyard because that's what kids were into back then. But alas, these are modern times, and we're in eighth grade, and that means sitting next to each other at lunch and walking home together and holding hands.

Maybe it's because he's not as nervous now, but Glen has calmed down with saying a lot of the stupid stuff he used to say. I appreciate that, but I also don't mind the stupid stuff that much anymore. When the stupid stuff is said for my sake, then I guess it's not so stupid.

"You're like the jelly to my peanut butter," he told me today at lunch as he bit into a PB&J.

"Why am I the jelly?" I asked.

"Jelly is sweet."

"Jelly is sticky."

"Jelly comes in lots of flavors. Like you. You're a compli-cated girl. Peanut butter is just peanut butter."

"Not true. It can be chunky or smooth," I said.

"Which am I?" he asked as he peeled back the bread and peered at his sandwich.

I paused. Was I supposed to be the doting girlfriend, who always says the nicest things to her beau? Or was I supposed to be Keri Cleary, world-renowned wiseass? I decided to stay true to myself, because I don't know if I have it in me to be someone I'm not. "Chunky," I told him. "You're as chunky as they come."

He scowled for a second, like he was really hurt, and I was worried that maybe he was. We haven't been together long. I know him, but I don't *know* him. I almost apologized, but slowly the scowl transformed into a smirk and he pushed me playfully on the shoulder.

"Exactamundo," he said as he stood from the table. "Call me your big chunk of hunk." Hands up and balled up, he flexed his tiny muscles. Not that I could see his muscles through his sweatshirt, but it doesn't take a genius to realize they had to be tiny.

"Heads up, Hulkamania," Trevor Weeks said as he slipped into a seat next to us. He was tossing a Granny Smith to himself like it was a baseball.

"Young Mr. Weeks," I replied, "to what do we owe this honor?"

Trevor caught and then bit the apple in a fluid motion, and

with a full mouth, he said, "My woodshop class is crashing the early lunch with all you eighth graders because we're field trippin' it to the mill this afternoon. Thought I'd stop by and ask how he's doing."

Trevor didn't have to elaborate on the *he*.

"He's fine," I said.

Glen was still standing there, muscles flexed. Crouching down, he whispered into Trevor's ear, though loud enough that I could hear. "She doesn't want to talk about him."

True. But Trevor was Alistair's friend, and friends deserve occasional updates. "It's okay," I said to Glen, and, "He's fine," I said to Trevor again.

"Good, good," Trevor answered. "I never thought he did it, by the way. Even though we fought that one time, I know he's always been, like, a pacifist."

"Thanks," I said. I didn't know what fight he was talking about, but it was a relief to finally have someone say something nice about Alistair. Not that people were saying mean things, but most questions were of the *so what the hell happened?* variety.

"Tell him *hey* for me, and that I hope to see him back here soon," Trevor said.

"I will," I said. "He'll probably be back after Christmas break. Which is pretty soon."

Glen finally sat back down, though his glare was still fixed on Trevor. "Bye-bye now," Glen said.

After another bite of apple, Trevor stood and said, "Later

taters." Before leaving, though, he paused, squinted at Glen, and asked, "Wait, are you two, like, boyfriend and girlfriend?"

Glen is rarely stunned into silence, but his response was to scrunch up his face in anger and not say a thing, so I put my arm around him and pulled him close and said, "We sure are."

Trevor nodded. "Cool."

Cool. It's basically what Mandy has been saying too. And basically what my parents are like.

You've got a boyfriend? Cool.

It's Glen Maple? Double cool.

I wasn't sure what I was expecting. Not anger, really. Maybe . . . something more. Talk. Debate. Something other than a nod and a "cool."

Forget it. Cool is good. Cool is cool.

Alistair hasn't said anything about it yet. Ever since Kyle woke up, my brother has kept to himself, at least when I'm around. Not mute like in those first few days. But lost in thought, like he's considering all the angles. Even more than everyone else, he seems to be trying to figure things out.

Saturday, 12/9/1989

MORNING

SOMETIMES A KNOCK CHANGES EVERYTHING. EARLIER THIS morning, I knocked on Alistair's door, he invited me in, and I found him lying on his back in bed.

"Trevor Weeks says *hey*," I said. "He's looking forward to seeing you again."

"That's nice," Alistair said, but he didn't look at me. There was a fishbowl resting on his chest, and even though it was empty, he was staring at it like there was something living inside it. He hasn't had a fish since he was probably five or six, so I don't know why he has a fishbowl, but people keep things for sentimental reasons, I suppose.

"I think a lot of kids are excited that you'll be back," I said.

"It'll definitely be different," he said.

"No kidding."

This is pretty much how our conversations have been

going. Small talk, nothing more. I get most of my information about how he's doing from Mom and Dad, and half the time that's from overhearing them chatting in the kitchen while Mom is cooking dinner and Dad is making the salad. So when Alistair moved from the small talk to the big talk, I was more than a bit surprised.

"No word yet from Jenny Colvin," he told me.

The mention of that name drenched me with guilt. Why had I betrayed my brother's trust? "Oh," I replied. "I forgot about . . . her."

"Really?" Alistair asked. "You listened to the tape, though, didn't you?"

"What? I . . . No, I'd never . . . No."

Alistair placed the fishbowl on his nightstand, rolled over onto his side, and smiled at me. "It's okay," he said. "I wanted you to listen. It was weird, wasn't it?"

My heart was buzzing, definitely not up for deceit. He was giving me a pass, so I took it. "It was beyond weird, Alistair," I said. "It was certifiably insane."

This made him chuckle. Then he sat up and ran his hands across his comforter, sending little waves to the edges. "Do you believe in other worlds?" he asked me.

"Like other planets?" I asked.

"Like other dimensions," he said.

"I don't know," I replied. "I like the *idea* of other dimensions."

Liking ideas is a good way to be noncommittal about things. For instance, if you ask a girl out and she says she *likes the idea* of going out with you, then it means that she's not going out with you.

Alistair nodded and said, "How about this idea, then? If there were another dimension, would you like it to be very different from this one, or very similar?"

There are tons of books out there about kids who hop through space and time and visit magical worlds, so I guess I've always assumed that other dimensions are very different from ours. But maybe they don't have to be.

"I've never really thought of it until now," I told him.

"Yeah," he said. "Most people don't think about it until they have to. Can I be honest with you about something?"

"Sure," I said.

"I go to another dimension sometimes."

He said it like he might say he goes to the movies sometimes, or to the mall sometimes. Like it was nothing.

"You . . . What do you mean?"

"I know it sounds strange to you, but hear me out." He slid off his bed and moved to his dresser, where he pulled a pen out of a warped clay mug he'd made in art class. "I wanted you to listen to that tape to ease you into some things. These things I'm going to tell you are pretty off-the-wall, but I think you're open to a . . . different way of thinking."

"I'm your sister," I said. "It basically means you can tell me everything."

His chuckle was now a full-fledged laugh. "I'm not sure if that's what it means," he said.

"I love you," I said, because as I mentioned before, I don't say that enough.

"Thank you," Alistair said. "You might not after I'm done talking, but thank you."

Of course, I wanted him to say *I love you too*. I didn't need him to say it, but I wanted him to say it. What I needed was for him to understand what I truly felt.

"I will *always* love you," I said this time, because I've never said that before. Because it's true.

"This whole thing started with a sister named Una who loved her brother," he said. "Actually, before even that, there was the wombat and the waterfall, but you already know that, don't you?"

I did. I knew exactly what he was talking about. Not this Una stuff. The wombat! The waterfall! I can't delve into the exact details right now, because the idea isn't fully formed yet, but as I told you before, it has to do with the ending of Luna's story. How would Alistair know about the ending when I'd only written the beginning? It was scary, even scarier than the dead hummingbird a few weeks ago. I struggled to respond.

"You know . . . about . . ."

"You're uncomfortable," he said. "I can tell. Hear me out. I've seen your wombat. It has strands of glowing fur. I've seen your waterfall. It's in a dark forest, and the wombat is at the bottom of the pool beneath it."

That was it, the exact image. It first came to me early that morning after Kyle's shooting. I was showering, trying to wake up, trying to wash away my frightening new reality, one full of gunshots and missing kids. I know it was only in my mind, but at that moment the image seemed seared into the inner skin of my eyelids. Water crashing down. A shimmering pool. And at the bottom, a wombat, the strands of its fur glowing.

"Where did you see it?" I asked, afraid of his answer, afraid of any answer.

"I saw it in the last scraps of memories I can access from a girl named Una," he said.

I was tempted to walk out of the room then and there. What was my brother doing? Who was Una and how could he see her memories? How could he see mine?

"You're scaring me," I said. "I don't understand what you're saying."

"I'm saying that the idea for the wombat didn't materialize from nothing. It originated somewhere. It found its way to you. Which means you're special."

It was cold outside. It was cold in his room. Yet my skin felt hot, like I was about to sweat. I didn't feel special. I felt sick.

"Ideas like that don't come from an actual place," I said. "They just . . . come."

Alistair shook his head and twirled the pen in his fingers like a little baton. "There's another dimension besides ours. It's a place where only kids go. I go there. I've spent a long time there. I call it Aquavania, but there are other names for it."

"Alistair, stop. You're—"

"No," he said. "I have to ask *you* to stop. Before you say anything else, let me tell you that this is real. This is not something

86

I'm making up. I've stood where you're standing. Actually, I was sitting in the corner in the beanbag chair, but . . . technicalities. Point is, you're going to try to read something into what I'm saying. Don't. What I'm telling you is the plain and simple truth."

"What you're telling me sounds crazy."

"Well, the truth can be crazy sometimes," he said. "Let me explain why you saw that wombat. If you still think it's crazy, fine. If you can come up with a better explanation, then go ahead and believe that. But this is what I believe. This is what I know."

"Go on," I said, because that's what you say to your brother when he decides it's time to bare his soul. His cracked soul.

He spoke slowly and clearly, like he didn't want me to miss any details. "When kids visit this other dimension, this Aquavania, they basically become gods," he said. "Think of it as the ultimate sandbox, but kids can create more than castles and sand sculptures. It all starts with water, and from that water, they build worlds containing anything they can think of. Anything is possible. Ice caverns swarming with flying polar bears. Talking stick figures. Space stations with monster galleries. Anything. And the kids, the daydreamers as we call them, have a long time to create. Because when they go to Aquavania, it's as if the regular world—or the Solid World as we call it—freezes. They can spend countless years in Aquavania and come back and not even a second will have passed at home."

I was staring at Alistair's bookshelf, the spines of classic fantasy tales staring back at me. "Okay," I said. "So it's like . . . What's the book where the kids go to a magical—"

"This isn't a book," Alistair said. "This is where the inspiration for books comes from. Images and sounds and ideas from these worlds seep through the water and into our dimension. And those things inspire people like you. Storytellers."

There was frost on Alistair's window, clinging to the edges. If I held a magnifying glass up to it, what would I see? A web of ice crystals. Molecules. Frozen water—that's all.

"So the wombat is something some kid thought up in Aquavania?" I asked.

"Not exactly," Alistair said. "The wombat is how it all began. It was the original gateway into Aquavania."

"And the image came to me . . . through water?"

Alistair nodded and said, "For some reason, you saw the beginning."

"Why me?"

"I don't know. Maybe so you can help me."

"Help you? I don't even know what you're doing."

Alistair paused. Then he tapped on his teeth with the pen. *Tap. Tap. Tap.* "I'm doing my job."

"Which is?"

"I'll tell you," he said, "but first you have to make me a promise."

Then he slipped the pen behind his ear and put out his hands. I grasped them, and he squeezed back, hard. The bones in my fingers couldn't take this for long, and while I don't think he was trying to hurt me, it was pretty obvious he was showing me how serious he was.

"I need to know what I'm promising," I said.

"You're gonna be tempted to tell Mom and Dad about this," he said, and he squeezed harder. "And you can tell them. But I need you to wait a few days. At least until I hear back from Jenny Colvin."

Keeping stuff from Mom and Dad was sort of my specialty. I guess it's every kid's specialty at one time or another. But sometimes moms and dads need to know things.

"I'll make that promise under one condition," I said.

"Name it."

I struggled for the words. The best I could come up with was, "Tell me you're not . . . that you aren't going to get hurt. Or, I guess I mean that if I keep this secret, you aren't going to hurt yourself?"

"Right now, I'm in more control than I've ever been," Alistair said as he released his grip. I stretched my hands. My fingers felt slightly bent, though not as bent as my mind. I didn't know if Alistair was in control of his life, but at that moment, he seemed so much more in control of things than I felt.

"I promise," I told him. "So tell me. What's this mysterious job that you have?"

"I am the guardian of the images and ideas," he told me. "When daydreamers need the end, then I give them the end. I am the holder of the souls. And once I figure out how, I'm going to release them."

"What? Who?"

"Fiona and Charlie. All of them."

THE KNOCK-KNOCK JOKE

—— ◆◆ ——

IN A SMALL VILLAGE, IN SOME SNOWY MOUNTAINS, LIVED A
joke. She had arms and legs and a face, but she was a joke all
the same. Not in the metaphorical sense. In the literal sense.
When she walked into a room, her very presence told a story.
People would shrug or gasp or sometimes laugh when she was
around, but not only because of how she looked or what she
said. It was because of who she was.

She was, to be precise, a dark and disturbing joke. Not excessively disturbing, but certainly not family dinner material.
Consequently, she couldn't go certain places. To schools, for
instance. To churches, synagogues, and mosques, obviously.
Basically anywhere kids and sensitive folks were likely to be
hanging out.

So she stayed by the railroad tracks, or in dusty old motels,
or at truck stops and in back-alley bars. She was appreciated
in those places, but she didn't particularly like them. They

felt dangerous, and the laughs she found there were nasty ones, full of teeth and halitosis.

"I'd like to be a different kind of joke," she said one night as she slept in her cabin in the mountains. "A pleasant joke. A respectable joke."

The next morning, she set about transforming herself. She traveled to the valley where the puns lived and spied on them and their innocuous wordplay. She exercised, hoping a healthy body would lead to healthy humor. She burned her entire wardrobe, gave herself a makeover, draped herself in primary colors, in vibrant, inoffensive garb.

But she didn't feel any different. She still felt dark. She still felt disturbing.

Then one day, everything changed. She woke up and it was like a switch had been flipped. She felt lighter. She felt . . . wholesome. Maybe all her efforts had paid off, but had needed time to incubate and take effect.

To see if she had truly changed, she decided to show herself in public, so she went to the local schoolhouse. She knocked on the door.

"Who's there?" a voice answered.

"A joke," she replied.

"A joke who?"

"A clean joke," she said.

There was silence for a moment. And then a reply. "Well, that's not very funny. Why are you wasting our time? We've got educating to do here."

The reaction puzzled the joke. If only they had let her in,

they would have realized that she was funny and, for once, agreeable. A simply wonderful joke.

She went home and considered what she had said wrong. Was it the words? Was it the tone? She hadn't even entered the school, so they couldn't have basked in her newness, in her pureness. Perhaps it was a mistake, so she gave it another shot a few hours later.

Knock knock.

"Who's there?" the voice answered.

"A joke."

"A joke who?"

"A joke that children will love."

"Don't waste our time."

It continued like this all day. The joke rethought her approach, knocked again, and when they asked, "A joke who?" she said, "A joke that will brighten your day," and "A joke both witty and wise," and "A joke from the heart." And every time, the voice responded with some variation of "go away."

The joke knocked on the doors of other wholesome places, such as antique shops and petting zoos, but they turned her away too. She didn't understand it.

She fell into a deep depression. All her efforts had been for nothing. She figured she'd just accept her life as it once was. That night, she went down to the local tavern where she'd always been welcome.

Knock knock.

"Who's there?" shouted the tavern keeper.

The joke had been here so many times before, she decided

not to answer. She barged right in. But this wasn't like those other times, and she was not treated to the typical hoots and hollers. Blank, confused faces stared back at her as the door swung shut.

"What happened to you?" the tavern keeper asked her when she approached the bar.

"What do you mean?" the joke replied.

Polishing a glass, the tavern keeper eyed her up and down. "You've changed. You've become a . . . knock-knock joke?"

The joke didn't really know what a knock-knock joke was, but it sounded perfectly pleasant. "I guess I am. So whattya think?"

The tavern keeper lowered his eyes. "I liked you better when you had a punch line."

There were cheers of "Ain't that the truth!" and "You said it!" from the tavern's regulars. The joke was stunned. No punch line? A joke without a punch line was a joke without a soul.

"I . . . I . . ."

"I think it's best if you left," the tavern keeper said. "You're making us uncomfortable."

The joke had no choice. She turned tail and walked out. But she lingered by the tavern door for a moment, contemplating whether to make a more memorable entrance. As she held her hand in front of the door, she realized that she didn't have a clue who she really was. She realized that while she might have cleaned up her act, she was soulless, and for the first time in her life, she was not funny.

So the joke climbed onto the roof of the tavern. She stood there and tried to yell her name into the breeze to test her own existence, but the words that came out made no sense. So she jumped off, which, funnily enough, was pretty dark and disturbing.

Sunday 12/10/1989

MORNING

I spent all day yesterday wondering whether Alistair was joking. If he was, then what was the punch line? That he knows where Fiona and Charlie are? That he was, maybe, responsible for their disappearances? That's beyond dark and disturbing.

Point is, you're going to try to read something into what I'm saying. Don't. What I'm telling you is the plain and simple truth.

When your brother says that, you do read something into what he's saying. You read everything into what he's saying. At least I have. Including that he might be telling the truth.

Here's the thing about believing: sometimes it's a question of will. You work at it. You keep telling yourself to believe in something, and eventually your brain surrenders and lets the belief in. Sometimes it's like a switch being flipped, an overnight thing, a wake up and look at the ceiling and say *This is how the world works now and I guess I'm okay with it* sort of thing.

I want to believe my brother. I want to work hard at it. But I don't have time to work hard. I need belief to simply happen. *Presto chango!*

Still waiting . . . still waiting . . . still waiting . . .

I'm scared. I'm scared that somehow he really does know about the images that pop into my head, that linger in my dreams. I'm scared that he actually believes in magical worlds. I'm scared that this isn't a joke. Because this is not how Alistair jokes. He's not that cruel. I'm scared that this isn't some elaborate lie. Because this is not how Alistair lies. He's a terrible liar—all sweaty and stuttery—and yesterday, he was calm.

If it's not a joke and not a lie, then what is it? Dad has a stack of psychology books that probably explain why my brother would talk like this and why I would want to fall for his nonsense, but explanations don't matter right now. All that matters is that I made a promise, and I like to keep promises. I won't tell our parents. Not yet.

That night, right after Kyle was shot, I made another promise. Alistair asked me to "make sure they know it's not how it looks."

I'm going to keep that promise too. That's what I'm making sure you know, Stella. It looks really, really bad. Insanity bad. But Alistair wants the world to know that it's not how it looks. And by the love of god, I want to believe him.

EVENING

All that thinking about Alistair has been a bit much to handle, so that's why I had to get out of the house earlier today. I had Mom drop me off at Mandy's, and Glen showed up there because even though he walks me home all the time, I haven't exactly been comfortable with him hanging out at my place, especially since Alistair is always there.

So we hung out in Mandy's room, with me and Glen sitting on the bed and Mandy sitting at her desk. Her desk is supposed to be for homework, but mostly she uses it as a station for making collages. She has all these ancient magazines full of pictures of old movie stars and she cuts them up and makes posters with them. Party scenes, usually, with dashing men in black-and-white and va-va-voom women in full color.

"Who are all those people?" Glen asked, checking out the posters on Mandy's walls.

"Well, that's Clark and that's Rita. And over there are Peter and Lauren."

"They're your . . . friends?" Glen asked. I couldn't believe he was seriously asking that, even though Mandy was speaking in a tone someone would use when talking about friends.

"For sure," Mandy said. "Every night is an Oscars after-party, and we gossip until dawn."

"Oh," Glen said. "They're movie stars. Obviously."

"From a long time ago," I told him, and I rubbed his back

to show him I was okay with his mistake. "Most are dead, and so that's why you wouldn't recognize them."

The door to her room was closed and her parents were on the other side of the house, but Mandy still thought she should cup her hands around her mouth when she whispered, "You two should kiss."

"We should . . . what?" I said.

"Look at you," she said. "Being all lovey-dovey like a couple of love doves. You should kiss. I mean, for real kiss."

"Oh . . . we do . . . we do do that . . . all the time," Glen said, which wasn't exactly a lie but was definitely a stretch. We had kissed. Twice. But since they weren't much more than pecks, I hesitate to call them real kisses. Do you count a peck as your first kiss?

"Good," Mandy said. "Then that means you should be cool with it. So . . ." She leaned back in her desk chair with her hands behind her head.

"Now?" I asked.

"No time like the present," she said.

Glen's body went rigid, like he was sitting on the table in a doctor's office. He was obviously . . . raring to go?

"Why do you want to see us kiss?" I asked.

"Because it's romantic," Mandy said.

"It's weird," I said.

"Not if you love each other," Mandy said. "You two love each other, don't you?"

It was hard to tell if she was being genuine or teasing us.

That's Mandy in a nutshell. Existing on an edge that even her best friend can't see.

Now obviously, Stella, I would have told you if Glen and I had used the word *love* yet. We hadn't. Not face-to-face, at least.

But then Glen said, "We do. We do love each other."

And that was suddenly that. We. We? WE! I hadn't agreed to any plural pronouns!

"So romantic," Mandy said. "Let the kissing commence."

I turned to Glen and I could see in his eyes how excited he was. For a moment, I hated Mandy, and then for a moment, I felt sorry for her. The combination of the two made me lean in and kiss Glen. Really kiss him, with my mouth open and everything. His lips were a little drier than I expected, but as we moved our mouths, things got wetter and our tongues touched and our teeth tapped together, and I guess that made it qualify as frenching.

They say that first kisses are supposed to be insanely memorable, and I know I'll remember this moment forever, but the kiss itself was sort of plain. Nice and all, but plain.

"So gross," Mandy said, her body wiggling like she was covered in ants.

"Shut up," I said as I pulled away from the kiss and fell back onto the bed. Glen was instantly red in the face, but his eyes were shooting lasers into Mandy.

"Kidding," Mandy said. "Kidding. That was so adorable. I loved it so much." She gave us a polite round of applause.

"Who have you kissed?" Glen asked with more annoyance than even I could spit out at that moment.

Eyes wide, Mandy bent over her desk and started kissing some of the pictures she had recently cut from a magazine. "I've kissed James and Cary and Rock."

Nobody is the true answer. Mandy has kissed nobody.

"Let's all get out of here," I said, jumping from the bed and reaching back for Glen's hand.

"Fantabulous idea," Mandy said, sliding off her chair and intercepting my hand. "Come on, I have to show you guys something."

We went to her brothers' room. Mandy has two older brothers. Twins. Chad and Dan. They're sixteen and can drive, and so they were out cruising for the day. Their room is actually a converted attic with beds on either side and all sorts of crazy stuff—deer heads, guitars, fishing net—hanging from the ceiling and walls.

Mandy immediately opened a trunk at the foot of one bed and pulled out two sets of what looked like Walkmen, but they had little microphones next to the headphones.

"Holy crap," Glen said. "Are those what I think they are?"

Mandy put one of the headphone sets on. "Roger that," she said, and she handed the other set to Glen.

"What are they?" I asked.

"Walkie-talkies," Mandy said.

"Like, the most high-power walkie-talkies on the market," Glen said. "They're, like, nine hundred dollars."

"Seriously?" I asked.

"Maybe even more," Mandy said. "Chad and Dan saved up for them for, like, a year and they hardly ever use them. Now that they have their licenses, they're too cool for such things."

The headphones were connected by a wire to a little box. Glen used a belt clip on the box to attach it to his waistband and he fidgeted with a knob on the box's side. "There's *nothing* cooler than such things," he said. "I saw these babies in a catalog once, next to some really high-end throwing stars. I didn't think anyone could actually afford them, though."

"So," I said, "what do we do with them? Talk to each other?"

"Or to truckers," Glen said.

"Or we don't talk at all," Mandy said. "We listen."

"To who?" I asked.

"You'll see," Mandy said. "Actually, you'll hear."

We ended up back in my neighborhood, at Hanlon Park, sitting with our legs dangling from a wooden structure. We'd walked nearly two miles through cold, misting rain to get there. Mandy was wearing one set of headphones and I was wearing the other set, sharing it with Glen by turning the left earpiece around.

We had picked up the tail end of a conversation. The voices weren't exactly familiar. Men's voices. Both kind of gruff. Kind of uneducated too, that is if uneducated people leave out words that are supposed to be there. I think they do. Uneducated people seem to use not enough words or too many. Never the proper amount.

". . . and it gets me all worked up 'cause I don't like seeing

101

anything about any kid who ends up like that," said voice number one.

"I hear ya," said voice number two. "But don't ya wonder? Where the armor came from? Like, did someone lift it from a museum? Or a castle? Castles everywhere in Europe and the Mideast, ya know? A kid don't stumble upon armor that fits him and then no one knows who he is."

"Speculating will drive you mad."

"I hear that. I keep wondering about it, though. Someone out there's gotta know something."

"Yeah, well, not my concern. So I'm gonna sign off now."

"Roger that. Be well."

"You too. Out."

Then there was silence. Static.

"Is that it?" Glen asked.

"For now, probably," Mandy said. "But he'll be back on later. He's on all the time. More often than not."

"Who was it?" I asked.

"Duh," Mandy said. "I don't know who the guy talking about the castles was, but the other guy . . . Who else would be all uncomfortable talking about the Littlest Knight?"

I shrugged. My dad. My mom. Alistair. Kyle. Tons of people, actually, who don't like talking about dead kids. Me.

Mandy motioned her head in the general direction of my house, of Fiona Loomis's house, and said, "Someone who perhaps has a guilty conscience about his missing, and presumed dead, niece."

"Oh my god. Was that Dorian Loomis?" Glen said in a tone that most people use for the endings of murder mysteries.

"Bingo," Mandy said. "He's a CB radio junkie. He uses different handles. Luminary. Bush Baby. Red Barry, or something like that. Doesn't matter. The voice is always the same, and I know it's him because he once let it slide that he has a brother named Neal and a sister-in-law named Sarah, and those are totally Fiona's parents' names. He's on the air constantly, always chatting up truckers and dudes that are into building motors and models and things like that."

"I don't get it," I said. "Why can we hear him?"

"Frequencies," Glen said, pointing to the little box that was connected to our walkie-talkie. "We're on the same one."

"Can people hear us?" I asked.

"Only if we're really, really close," Glen said. "These things can pick up signals from much farther away than they can broadcast."

Mandy pointed at Glen. "The kid knows his stuff."

"So, like, Dorian is sitting in his basement or something?" I asked. "Talking on a CB radio, and we can just listen in on anything he says?"

"The airwaves are public domain," Mandy said. "At least that's what Chad and Dan tell me. They bought the walkie-talkies to talk to each other, but soon figured out they could pick up nearby CB conversations on them. Mostly it's dudes talking about dude stuff. Cars. Girls. You know. Chad and Dan grew bored of it after a while, but when Heavy Metal

Fifi disappeared, I pulled these babies out to see if I could uncover some clues. That's when I first started hearing Uncle Weirdo. Remember how I said he seemed really creepy? Like *did some bad, bad things in the war* creepy?"

"You're basically . . . a Hardy Boy," Glen said.

"I prefer Nancy Drew, thank you very much," Mandy said.

"More like Harriet the Spy," I said. "So you listen in on people's conversations? Now *that's* creepy."

"Public. Domain." Mandy tapped my nose twice as she said the words. I guess it was supposed to be playful, but it came off as annoying.

"What clues did you uncover?" Glen asked, his voice cracking a bit. He was scared. He was excited. He was Glen with the volume turned up.

"That Uncle Dorian is one sad sack o' potatoes, that's for sure," Mandy said. "All he wants to chat about is building remote control planes and carving wood. Say something about movies or communists or anything remotely interesting and he changes the subject."

"Like the Littlest Knight," Glen said.

"Exactly!" Mandy hooted. "I mean, this is actually the first time the Littlest Knight has come up, but anyone who's anyone wants to talk about the Littlest Knight. Who's not curious about the Littlest Knight?"

"Jesus, you yourself just said someone whose niece is missing and presumed dead wouldn't want to talk about that," I said as I pulled the headphones off and placed them on Glen's lap. "Why don't you just let him be? He's innocent."

"No," Mandy said. "He's creepy."

"Because he doesn't want to talk about a dead kid in the Dead Sea who's wearing armor?" I said. "Gimme a break. *I* don't want to talk about that."

"It's true," Glen said. "She doesn't."

"How many times have you listened in on him?" I asked.

Mandy shrugged. "Five or six. Mostly when I'm at your place."

"What?"

"In the bathroom," Mandy said with a sigh. "For, like, ten or twenty minutes tops. I bring the walkie-talkie in my purse, but I didn't want to let you know about it until I knew for sure I was onto something."

"But you just admitted you're not onto something," I told her. "You said all he talks about is stupid toys and stuff."

Mandy took her headphones off and handed them to me. "What I'm onto is that your brother is wrapped up in some shady business. With Kyle, with Charlie, with Fiona. And if Fiona's uncle is wrapped up in it too, then you and your family need to be safe. He could come after you. So you keep that walkie-talkie. Dan and Chad won't miss it, and I can't come over all the time to listen and keep you safe. You should do the listening. If this creep slips up and says anything weird, you can tell the cops."

"Or me," Glen said with his chest puffed up.

"Yes," Mandy said. "Or Glenny Boy here. I'll give him the other walkie-talkie. He seems to know what he's doing with these things. Maybe he can fiddle with the switches and knobs and figure out a way to listen from his house too."

Like a mermaid flapping her tail in excitement, Glen flapped his legs. "I'll definitely try! Thanks!" he yelped.

"Yeah . . . thanks," I said, but it was hardly a yelp. It was more of a *Great, now I've got something else to deal with.*

"I want egg rolls," Mandy said as she stood. "Your house is closer. Your mom still buys those microwave egg rolls, right?"

"I guess," I said.

"Good. Let's do this."

Monday, 12/11/1989

---◆---

EVENING

GLEN INSISTED THAT WE BRING THE WALKIE-TALKIES TO SCHOOL today, saying, "When you're in your study hall and I'm in my study hall, we can put them on and chat."

"Won't Ms. Hunkle notice?" I asked.

"She lets kids wear Walkmen all the time," he said. "What's the difference? I'll whisper."

"I don't know if Mr. Gregson will be cool with it on my end."

"Tell him you're listening to one of those books on tape. He won't mind. Kids play cards in study hall. This is no worse than that."

Point taken. I knew I could get away with it. I just wasn't sure I wanted to get away with it. During study hall, I was planning on writing more about the wombat. The whole concept of Alistair's Aquavania was sparking all sorts of thoughts and ideas for the wombat story. A phrase keeps playing over in my head.

Anything is possible. Anything is possible. Anything is possible.

I went along with Glen's plan anyway. I brought the walkie-talkie and tuned it to the frequency we'd agreed upon. I figured I'd let Glen do most of the talking, which I was sure he wouldn't have a problem with, and when I sat at my desk, I propped my math book up so I could hide behind it and appear to be studying.

"So what do you want to talk about?" Glen asked as soon as we connected, which was exactly the wrong thing for him to say. I didn't want to lead this conversation. I hardly wanted to follow it.

"Um . . . I don't know," I said, and let my head fall and rest on my folded arms. "What do *you* want to talk about?"

"Hmm," he said. "Ask me something that you often wonder about me."

Dangerous proposal. I wondered a lot of things about Glen. Not many that I was comfortable asking him about, though. Like, why would he be into a weird girl like me? Did he think I was using him? And if he did, why would he be okay with that? And if he didn't, then . . .

Hmm . . . these are really things I should be figuring out myself, I guess. But I don't want to figure them out now, and I didn't want to figure them out then. All I wanted to do was write my story. I wanted to think about Alistair and Aquavania and . . .

That's when it came to me: the perfect question to satisfy Glen but also indulge my curiosity about Alistair's stories.

"Okay," I whispered through the airwaves. "How about this? If you had the ability to be, like, a god, I mean a real god, a guy who could create whatever he wanted, what would you create?"

"Roger that," he responded, because he's a sucker for official lingo. "It's a weird question. But weird is good. I guess I'd create a world where there were, like, dragons, centaurs, and elves, because those are the coolest kinds of places. Medievaly ones. But maybe there'd also be spaceships, because spaceships are cool. And lions and African animals, because they're awesome as well. And dinosaurs. T. rex, definitely."

"Sorry, hon, but I don't think you'd last long in that world," I said.

The *hon*—as in short for *honey*, as in you, Glen, are my honey—slipped off my tongue without me thinking about it. Really? *Hon?* What is wrong with me?

It didn't weird him out one bit, though. "Oh, I'd have force fields around me," he said quickly. "And I would smite things whenever I wanted to."

"Smite?"

"It means kill."

"I know what it means. I guess I don't see you as much of a smiter."

"Gods smite. That's what they do."

For weeks, there had been a vision in my head: Alistair holding a gun. Now, listening to Glen, my head hidden behind the book and buried in my arms, there was a new vision:

109

Alistair the god. Flowing beard, sitting on a cloud, holding a lightning bolt, and bellowing that totally bonkers, totally creepy job description:

"I am the guardian of the images and ideas. When day-dreamers need the end, then I give them the end. I am the holder of the souls. And once I figure out how, I'm going to release them."

"Smiting is serious business," I told Glen. "You're talking about lives. Souls."

"Hey, you asked me what I want, and that's what I want. Elves, dinosaurs, and smiting."

Glen sounded smug, so my vision of Alistair became smug too, his chin high and eyes squinty. There were now cages surrounding him, at his feet. Little birdcages with wispy souls imprisoned in them. Ghostlike things, specters in the shape of Charlie and Fiona. Before I knew what was happening, my arms were wet. I was crying.

"I've gotta go," I whispered.

"Did Mr. Gregson bust you?" he asked.

"Something like that. Goodbye."

"It's not goodbye."

"Okay then," I whispered, trying to keep my voice from cracking. "See ya . . . later."

"No," he said. "This is a walkie-talkie. You say *over and out*."

"Oh . . . over then. Over and out."

Still hidden behind the book, I pulled the headphones off and laid them on the desk. I kept my face buried in my arms and I didn't cry more than those first few tears, but I did realize something.

Not all promises need to be kept. Someone else has to know.

I'm afraid Glen probably isn't that person.

THE TUBES

THERE WAS ONCE THIS WORLD WITHOUT PHONES, WITHOUT telegraphs or walkie-talkies or any communication devices at all. It was a perfectly happy world, and the people who lived there generally liked one another. They liked one another enough that they often wished they could talk to one another when separated by great distances. Tough luck. In case you missed it a few sentences ago, there was a clear obstacle: no phones.

"Tubes!" a girl named Harriet hooted in class one day. It was one of those *eureka!* hoots, delivered as she stood up on her chair.

"What's this, now?" her teacher asked. "I'm sorry, but we don't follow you, Harriet. Sit down, please."

Harriet didn't budge. "That's how we should talk to people far away," she explained. "I've been thinking about this all day because my friend Georgie lives a few houses down and

I can't ever speak to her when we're not together. But tubes will solve that! Tubes that go through the entire town!"

"I haven't an inkling what you're talking about, Harriet," the teacher said. "Now stop distracting the class and sit down."

But the rest of the class *did* have an inkling, and the rest of the class would be distracted for the rest of the afternoon. Because what Harriet was proposing was like a secret system of communication the kids had already set up. You see, there were these old pipes that ran through the walls of their school but no longer carried water. A few industrious students drilled some tiny holes through the walls and into the pipes. Then, to listen in and to whisper to friends in other classes, they slipped the small ends of funnels into the holes. It basically turned the pipes into a series of megaphones.

Harriet's idea for tubes was more or less the same thing, but on a much grander scale. Instead of rigid old pipes, flexible tubing seemed a better choice, and instead of removable funnels, permanent amplifying cones seemed appropriate. With the help of her friend Georgie, she tested the idea out.

Georgie's parents owned an Italian restaurant, and they had more than enough pasta and cheese on hand. So the two girls cooked up a bunch of ziti—which is a hollow kind of pasta—and they connected the pieces together using melted mozzarella as glue. In no time, they had a cheesy, bendable tube that was about a hundred yards long. They crafted the amplifying horns from sheets of lasagna that were cooked, cheesed together, and shaped to look like tubas.

Harriet and Georgie had tried in the past to communicate using tin cans linked by string, but it had never really worked. They'd scream into the things and barely get a whisper on the other end. Their ziti tube was the opposite. Whisper into it and a clear holler would burst from the other end.

It was more than a success. It was a defining moment in their world.

The girls brought the tube to a local scientist, who was so thrilled by it that he brought it to a banker, who gave them money to develop more tubes. Within a few months, tubes made of pasta were snaking their way through Harriet's town and everyone was chatting with their friends without ever getting up from their beds or hammocks or wherever it was that they liked to laze about.

Harriet had basically invented a telephone system, though that's not what they called it because *telephone* wasn't a word that existed in their world. They simply referred to the systems as the Tubes.

The Tubes started simply enough, as a few dozen strung around town between houses, but soon businesses started making their own. They gave out tubes that connected directly to their shops and restaurants so that everyone in town would have a direct link. Before long, other towns were doing the same thing and the world started becoming a tangle of tubes. Because every time you wanted to connect with a new person or a new business, you needed a new tube. So if you had hundreds of friends, family members, and businesses you wanted to keep in touch with, then you needed hundreds of tubes.

Pasta factories became tube factories and people stopped leaving their houses altogether, because they didn't want to navigate over the tangle of tubes on the ground. To make isolation livable, engineers figured out how to widen the tubes and connect them to vacuums and fans so that objects, and even people, could be pushed through them.

Problems were inevitable. Tubes started to break. Objects, and even people, got stuck. Mischievous teenagers rerouted tubes and spliced them together in different configurations so that when you thought you were talking to one person, you ended up talking to another. False accusations, ruined marriages, and all manners of strife resulted from the mischief.

Harriet began to feel guilty. Her world had functioned fine without the tubes, and while they had made life easier in a few ways, they had made it harder in many others. She considered destroying them, burning them all, but there were too many and it would've been too dangerous. So she decided to leave.

"This is all our fault," Harriet told Georgie through their original tube. "I can't live here anymore. I'm going somewhere the tubes haven't reached yet. You can come with me if you want."

"I don't think I could live without the tubes," Georgie said. "But I'll miss you so much!"

"I'll miss you too," Harriet said. "But I have to do this. Goodbye."

Then she tossed her original tube to the side, packed a bag, and set out into the world. She knew she'd miss her other friends and her family, but she also knew they'd hardly realize she was gone. They were too obsessed with their tubes to notice much of anything.

Traveling was actually easier than she expected. The tubes were everywhere and they were slippery and slimy, and she could ride on top of them like waves, sliding from one town to the next. After a few weeks, the tubes were still everywhere, but they kept her alive. Their composition of pasta and cheese made them edible. Harriet could also cut holes in them and steal bits of food that were being delivered from one place to another.

There were almost no other people outside anymore. Even the installation of new tubes was done from inside other tubes. But during her journey, Harriet came upon a newborn baby, a little girl. She must have slipped into and out of the tubes somehow and was now lost.

Harriet didn't know what to do. She didn't think she could raise the baby. So she slipped the baby back into one of the tubes, knowing it had to end up somewhere. "Good luck and Godspeed," she said. And Harriet journeyed on.

The tubes had taken over so many habitats that she didn't see evidence that there were even animals left in the world, until one morning she heard chirps and howls in the distance. She followed the sounds of the animals, and within a few days, she was finally out of the range of the tubes and in a dense forest. Animals were everywhere, though they didn't bother with Harriet. She still craved companionship, so she tried desperately to communicate with them, but they'd give her a look or a sniff and then move on.

As discouraged by that as she was, Harriet was still glad to have found a home away from the tubes. She built a shelter next to a river and settled in for a new life.

She lived as a hermit for many years, surviving off of fish from the river, berries, and other wild foods. The animals never really became her friends. They tolerated her, but they could sense that she was different and they didn't welcome her into their various societies.

By the time she was an old woman, she was becoming nostalgic. Knowing she didn't have much time left, she decided to travel home to see if she might find her friend Georgie again, or at least discover what happened with the tubes.

When she reached the first tangle of tubes, she cut into one and spoke into it.

"This is Harriet," she said. "Whoever hears this, please let it be known that I have been gone a long time, but I am coming home."

"Harriet?" replied a voice. "The Harriet who invented the tubes?"

"Yes," Harriet replied.

"Stay where you are," the voice said. "We're coming for you."

Harriet didn't need to wait long. Within seconds a giant mechanical claw shot out from the tube and grabbed her and pulled her in. At lightning speeds she traveled through the tube, and when she came out on the other side, she landed on a pile of sticks.

Surrounding the sticks was a group of people dressed in ragged clothes and holding torches. Sitting on a tall throne behind the people and looking down on them was an old woman. She was wrinkled and withered, but Harriet recognized her. It was Georgie.

"Harriet," Georgie said. "You abandoned us long ago. And now you are sentenced to death."

"For leaving?" Harriet asked.

"No, for coming back and using the tubes," Georgie said. "You were right, it was our fault that the world became what it was. A baby was found dead in the tubes, years ago. It was a big wake-up call, and showed us the errors of our ways. So I led a revolution and we made the tubes illegal. We redirected them so they all lead here, and anyone caught using them is brought here and sentenced to death."

"But I only wanted to see you," Harriet said. "I didn't know it was illegal. I only wanted to know what had happened to the world."

"This," Georgie said. "This is what happened to the world."

And Georgie nodded at the people, who lowered their torches and set the sticks aflame.

Tuesday, 12/12/1989

MORNING

I'M HUNCHED OVER MY DESK IN HOMEROOM, WRITING THIS
before first bell because hopefully this is a turning point, and
I need to record it while it's still fresh.

I did it. I told Dad. It wasn't too hard, actually. My parents
have adjusted their work schedules so that at least one of
them can be home at all times while the other is always available to walk me to school.

Dad was on Keri-walking duty this morning, and I figured
it was now or never.

"I'm worried about Alistair," I told him.

"Yeah," he said. "Yeah."

But there was a lot more than *yeah* in those *yeahs*. His
eyes, his posture, his breath crystallizing in big clouds with
each puff into the frosty air, they all told me that the first *yeah*
meant *Aren't we all?* and the second *yeah* meant *We've really
got to do something about this, don't we?*

"He's having delusions, I think," I told Dad. "He says he goes to a magical world. A place that grants wishes. I think he believes Fiona and Charlie are there."

Dad didn't slow his stride. He didn't look at me either. School was visible through the trees in the distance, and he was treating it like a finish line in a race. "When I was a kid—" he started to say, but I couldn't let him take one of his inevitable detours down memory lane.

"Please," I said. "Not another one of your stories. I love your stories, Dad. They make me smile and they make me think, but—"

"I know," he said. "They're not about what's happening now."

"Yeah," I said.

The meaning of my *yeah* could have filled a book.

Dad rubbed his hands together to warm them up and said, "There are things we aren't telling you. Alistair is not in a healthy state. Mom and I know this. Rest assured that he has spoken to some experts. And he'll need to speak to more. We're working on finding the right fit."

"He believes these things, Dad," I said. "I can't begin to describe what he believes."

He stopped and pushed his head toward me like a curious bird. "Did he tell you he was going to hurt himself . . . or anyone else?"

"No," I said, so glad that Dad was worried about the same thing I was. "But . . ."

He nodded, and said, "If he wants to talk to you, listen to him. If what he says worries you, tell us. But realize that you're not going to solve things for him. Mom and I aren't going to solve things for him either."

"But you're an expert," I said.

"Not in this," he said. "These are very specific psychiatric issues that I don't have much experience with. But there are people who do. We'll leave it to them. My job right now is to be a dad. You love your brother, don't you?"

"Yes. Yes. Yes."

I would have said it a million times if I could have, but Dad started walking again and we were almost at school. "Then your job is to be a sister," he said. "All you have to do is this: Listen. Have patience. And love."

EVENING

Leave Alistair to the experts. As in psychiatrists. As in shrinks. As in the wackiest flavor of scientists.

Oh, glorious science. If my family had a religion, it'd be you. We celebrate Christmas and all that—because, come on, *presents!*—but when it comes to explaining things, we bow down to science. When it comes to fixing things, we worship science.

So science will fix Alistair. The science of psychotherapy? The science of prescriptions? Might work. I hope so, but I can't say for sure. I can only say that in the past doctors would cut out parts of people's brains to "cure" them. Oh yes, lobotomies were all the rage, and not so long ago. All in the name of science.

Which is a roundabout way of saying that science is wonderful, but I don't always trust science. Because of those mistakes of the past. Also for personal reasons.

The personal bit goes back about two years. Late springtime. Or maybe it was an unusually warm day in early springtime. I remember I was in a denim jacket, not a down feather anywhere on my person.

Mandy and I were sitting on the swings in Hanlon Park, discussing whatever it was we discussed in sixth grade. Boys? I guess so. I had a crush on Sean Delaney back then, which is pretty insane considering what a rumor-spreading, rattail-having slimeball he turned out to be.

At some point, we got to talking about how middle school relationships are a bit like swings, all up and down, back and forth, which got us talking about middle school science, about pendulums and, I think, maybe . . . Newton's Laws? Newton had laws about how things fall, fly, swing, spin around, and flip upside down in the world, right?

Yes, I realize I should've paid more attention during class.

Anyway, this all led to Mandy grabbing both of our backpacks—mine full of books and hers full of magazines— and placing them in the bucket seat of one of those swings designed for babies. Together, the backpacks probably weighed close to twenty-five pounds. That's one chunker of an infant.

Next, Mandy stood in the gravel, pulled the weighted swing back, and held it about an inch in front of her nose. "The magic of science," she said as she let it go.

You know what a pendulum is, don't you, Stella? It's usually a ball on a string that rocks back and forth. Businessmen often have little ones on their desks—don't ask me why—but pretty much anything on a string, rope, or chain can be turned into a pendulum. A swing, for example. The thing about pendulums is that when you hold them and drop them, gravity will make them move. They swoop down, swoop up, and come back. They end up right where you dropped them from. Or almost as close. They slow down after a while because of . . . wind friction?

Okay, I may have forgotten some of the terms over the years, but the point is if you hold a pendulum in front of your nose, then drop it, it will swing out and swing back, but it won't hit you in the nose. That's science. And that's what Mandy was doing. She was giving science a run for its money.

Hey, we get bored here in Thessaly. Isn't a heck of a lot to do.

Where was I, Stella?

Oh right, Mandy dropped the backpack-baby-swing-pendulum. Then she closed her eyes and clenched her teeth, made her body go stiff as the thing flew down and up, the chains creaking as it went. Then it changed direction and came racing back at her, down again and up. I was tempted to dive in front of it, because it sure looked like it was going to plonk her right in the nose. But I didn't, maybe because I trusted science or because I wanted to see what happened. Probably more of the latter.

Well, hooray science, because it stopped short of Mandy's honker. By a sliver. The force of the movement even caused her hair to blow back like some supermodel standing in front of a fan at a photo shoot. I gasped. She winced. Then she threw up her hands and cheered, "Your turn!"

That's how it goes with me and Mandy. Her first. At everything. The good and the bad. First slice from the pie, first cannonball into the cold swimming hole. Not that I'd call myself a follower, or her a leader even, but we fell into that routine long ago. Which sometimes works to my advantage. If Mandy had gotten plonked on the nose by the swing that day, then I would have called it quits. But since she didn't, I was obliged to take my turn.

I stood in the exact same spot that Mandy stood, in her footprints in the gravel. I pulled the swing back, feeling the weight of it. "Not sure I can do this," I said as I pressed the rubber to the tip of my nose.

"I can do it for you, if you want," Mandy said. And she put her hands on the swing while nudging mine down. I didn't say *yes*, but I didn't stop her. I held my hands at my sides and closed my eyes and went stiff like she did.

"Okay. I'm ready," I said.

Whoosh. Whoosh. Bam.

Oh, science. To go along with your lobotomies, you need to answer for the girl in the denim jacket who ended up writhing in the gravel with a bloody nose. That's right. Booooo Newton and your lousy laws! Because that swing hit me smack-dab in the nose.

Truth be told, I didn't actually see it hit me. My eyes were still closed at that point. But it felt like it probably feels when a gorilla punches you in the face.

"Oh my god, oh my god, oh my god," Mandy cried as she came to my rescue. "You shouldn't have leaned forward. Why did you lean forward?"

"I don't know. I didn't mean to," I babbled, and blood pooled in my hands, which were cupped over my nose.

"Why did you lean forward?" she asked again, rubbing my back.

"I didn't," I said, which I knew to be true and still know to be true. If anything, I leaned back.

Now, two years later, I will do what my dad asked. I will be a sister. I will listen. I will practice patience. I will love. I will let science take its shot at fixing my brother, but if science ends up plonking him in the nose, well then . . . screw science.

Wednesday, 12/13/1989

EVENING

LET ME TELL YOU SOMETHING ABOUT DECEMBER IN THESSALY: it sucks. It's rainy or it's snowy and it's worse than February because in December you know it's only going to get colder. Also it's so dark. It's painful to get out of bed before the sun comes up, and you don't believe your alarm half the time so you're always oversleeping.

Today was the suckiest of sucky December's sucky days. And not because of specific things. Just the general feeling about it. A sucky feeling.

Glen got all depressed because he wanted to chat on the walkie-talkies again during study hall and I didn't want to, so we didn't, which made the walk home today kind of blah with Glen complaining about his grandma and me hardly listening. And Mandy was sick and so I couldn't talk to her about anything. And Mrs. Delgado gave us a pop quiz in Earth Science and I'm sure I got no better than a C.

Not end-of-the-world stuff, but when it all piles on, it piles on high.

So all I wanted to do tonight was zone out in front of the TV with something stupid, and I was flipping the channels trying to find the most brainless thing possible when Alistair came in.

"Stop there," he said, pointing at the TV. "Go back one."

I clicked one channel down on the clicker and there it was: a picture of the Littlest Knight. It was some news special on cable. While there had been plenty of coverage of the Littlest Knight, the media had never shared a clear picture of him. But this one was clear. Maybe too clear.

Trust me, you don't want to see the face of a dead kid. Ever.

Alistair sat down on the edge of the sofa and rested his chin in his hand. "I thought it might be him," he said, "but now there's no denying it."

"Who?" I asked.

"Hadrian," Alistair said.

"Hadrian who?"

"A guy I knew, an unbelievably old swimmer," Alistair said. "I . . . I'm the one who . . . He died because of me."

There was a tremor in his voice that reminded me of the old Alistair, the bumbling kid who used to question things more, who used to get more confused and flustered. Only the old Alistair was usually worried about a stain in the carpet, not a dead kid half a world away.

"What are you talking about?" I said. "He's way off in the desert somewhere."

"I let a monster called the Mandrake get to him," Alistair said. "The vicious, merciless Mandrake ran him through. And the thing that everyone suspects is true."

"What does everyone suspect?"

"That if you die in Aquavania, then you die here too."

"You didn't know that?" I asked. "I thought you were all-knowing in Aquavania."

This was me heeding Dad's words. This was me being a sister. This was me wanting to believe, but not being able to believe, so pretending to believe, because it was dark stuff he was talking about. People getting hurt. Exactly what my parents were worried about.

"I know a lot," Alistair said, finally turning his gaze from the TV. "But there's a lot I don't know. Like about the other swimmers. I'm still working on getting them back too. That's what happened to Hadrian, but it hasn't happened to them, which means there's still hope."

That word! *Hope*. It counts for so, so much. Even more than wanting to believe Alistair, I want to believe that there's hope for him. Yes, I had broken my promise to him and, at that moment, I decided to break it again. But it was in the name of hope.

Hope alone can't do everything, though. Hope needs help.

"Mom!" I called out. "Dad!"

There was no answer.

"What are you doing?" Alistair asked.

"Mom! Dad!"

"They're not here," Alistair told me. "They left thirty

minutes ago. They had a meeting with Ms. Kern. Left some baked ziti in the fridge if you're hungry."

"They're seeing her without you?" I asked.

He shrugged. "I'm not sure they want my input these days. I guess they're doing what they think is best for me."

"And so am I," I said.

"You're going to tell them what I told you?" he asked.

"I'm sorry, but I already have," I said. "At least a little bit. But I can't keep secrets like this."

"I never said these were secrets," Alistair replied. "Only that I needed a little time. I haven't heard back from Jenny Colvin yet, and that is the most important thing at this point. Go ahead and tell Mom and Dad what I told you, but I don't think they'd believe it."

"And why am I supposed to believe it again?" I asked, a question I have asked myself about a billion times already.

"Because you know about the wombat," he said.

"Again with the wombat! Who cares about a wombat?"

"And you know about the waterfall."

"So what?" I said, my voice hopping up a few octaves. "It's weird for you to know that. It scares me that you know that. But it doesn't prove anything."

"Fine," he said. "I'll ask you one more question, and maybe that will change your mind."

"I can't imagine that being possible."

"What does Banar mean to you?" he asked.

Impossible.

THE PHOSPHORESCENT WOMBAT, PART II

THREE YEARS WENT BY.

By the time Rosie had stored her bike in the attic and had started driving a VW bug, Luna was more green than she was brown, and when the sun set, her fur provided the same illumination as a weak streetlight. Hollywood producer Hal Hawson drafted a new contract, and it contained a clause.

Should aforementioned wombat glow any greener, or should her wombat fur glow any brighter, then we reserve the right to void the contract.

Aforementioned wombat did glow greener and her fur did glow brighter, but the contract remained intact. *Pocketful of Hullabaloo* was now a hit, and not because of the skeet-shooting grandmothers or the scat-singing unicyclists who graced its stage, but because of the tuxedoed wombat who sat on a pillar in the back and shone like a Christmas bulb and reminded the world that there are still strange and wondrous things.

And yet all things, even strange and wondrous ones, lose their luster with time. They always do.

Fifteen more years went by.

Rosie and Hamish's parents perished in a freak ballooning accident over the Sahara and their bodies were never recovered. Rosie fell into a depression and then into love. She married a baker named Pedro who was a wizard with sourdough, and they left town to live by the sea. While it pained Rosie to be away from Luna, she couldn't bring the wombat with her.

"We want to have children," Pedro said. "I'm not sure they'd be safe around Luna. She might be radioactive."

Even though Luna had passed countless physicals, Rosie had to agree. They didn't know the source of Luna's light, so they didn't know if it was dangerous to children.

Hamish was not a child anymore, so he took on the danger himself and took over watching Luna, shuffling her back and forth to the studio in a tiny red sports car he bought with money from the Sunfirst bank account. He always insisted that Luna stay in the trunk, because her light was blinding when reflected in the rearview mirror.

Pocketful of Hullabaloo was not the hit it once was. Luna's luminosity, for years the major attraction, was beginning to inspire channel-surfing. She resembled a wombat less and less each day. By spring of her eighteenth year on the show,

Luna looked like a green orb, resting atop the pillar. The fabulous Mr. Nickelsworth, short legs, wiggly nose, and all, was a memory, and there were only so many times people would tune in to see sword-swallowing Siamese twins on roller skates.

The show was canceled that autumn.

It didn't bother Luna. She was tiring of the job, because she was changing. Not her body so much as her mind. Yes, the increasing glow of her fur made her resemble an orb that expanded day by day, but she was like the filament of a light-bulb. Her actual body was still a wombat body, and it hadn't grown even a millimeter. The glow had simply gotten bigger, denser, impenetrable to the naked eye.

The more significant change was happening in her brain. She was becoming curious about the pictures and symbols she saw along roadways, in libraries, and on television screens. She knew they were trying to tell her something. But what? Surely that there was more to the world than being Mr. Nickelsworth.

By constantly listening and watching, she learned what many words and gestures meant. She understood communication, and even though she wanted to respond with wiggles and winks, no one could see her features anymore. The glow was too bright. Of course, Luna could see the entire world as clearly as ever. Her gaze cut through the glow, and it was only when she fixed it on a mirror that she would see herself as the world saw her.

People assumed she was blazing hot, like a coal from a

barbecue pit. Animals trusted their instinctual fear of fire and kept their distance. The truth was, she was cool to the touch. She could be hugged, scratched behind the ear, placed in the shower, and lifted into bicycle baskets and car trunks. Hamish knew this. Everyone else didn't.

After the show was canceled, the government expressed some interest in studying Luna, but Hamish couldn't bear to give her up. So he cleared out the bank account and snuck the two of them off to a farm many miles from the studio. Only Rosie knew where they were, and she came to visit every once in a while—always alone, though, which meant Hamish didn't get to spend any time with her children, his new niece and nephew. There were no other family and friends to speak of, and so Hamish grew fond of Luna in ways he never had before. Even though he couldn't really see her anymore, he knew there was a heart at the center of that glow. He could sense there was a brain.

Luna spent most of her time in the barn, where there were stacks of cardboard boxes full of old letters and magazines. At first, she only liked looking at the colorful pictures, but eventually she was drawn to the black lines that covered most of the pages.

These, she would one day learn, were called letters. She tried to reproduce them by moving stalks of straw with her mouth and dropping them on the floor of the barn. Before long, she could do the entire alphabet. Then she moved on to words. Order didn't matter to her at first. *ART* was the same as *TAR* was the same as *RAT*. These, she would one day learn, were called anagrams. They had different meanings, but she didn't know that quite yet.

While Luna was learning to read and write, Hamish rarely came into the barn. The glow was too much, even for him. He would hover near the door, at the edge of the ever-expanding glow, and he would lob fruit, turkey legs, and cheese balls to Luna.

For a time, Hamish read her bedtime stories, but as the glow expanded, the distance between the two increased. It became too much of a strain to shout such long tales, so Hamish would simply stand on the edge of the glow and holler the same good-night message.

"Miss you, little girl. Be good now."

Luna missed Hamish as well, but being the polite wombat that she was, she stayed away from the house. She knew her presence was far too distracting. Even when she tried to blot out the light—by rolling in mud or covering herself in a ratty old horse blanket—it always found its way through.

It was high noon the day a blindfolded Hamish came for Luna. It had been years since Hamish had even picked her up, since he'd scratched her ear, since he'd given her a shower. It had been nearly as long since Luna had seen Hamish up close. Hamish was old. His skin was painted with brown and purple splotches. His posture was bad.

"Come into my arms, old pal," he said.

Luna did as asked. It felt different from before. Hamish was weaker, but it was more than that. Hamish held on to her as if he never wanted to let her go.

"Lead me to the car," Hamish said, because he knew that Luna understood at least a few things. "Nibble once if I should move left and nibble twice for right. Nuzzle once for forward and nuzzle twice for backward. Can you do that?"

Luna nuzzled once and Hamish was off. She nibbled and nuzzled as the two made their way out of the barn. "Faster, buddy," Hamish said. "The blindfold is hardly working. My eyes won't be able to take it much longer."

So Luna sped up her nibbles and nuzzles as best she could and led Hamish to that tiny old red sports car that sat in the dirt driveway. Its skin was like Hamish's skin, but the blotches were rust.

As Hamish lowered Luna into the trunk, he told her, "We've managed to keep the government at bay, and perhaps they've forgotten about you, but I can only imagine what they'd think of you now that you're so bright. I've done my best to hide you, but you're bound to be detected here. We'll get you somewhere safer, old friend."

The car rumbled down the country road, and Luna tried to imagine what the landscape outside of the trunk looked like. She tried to conjure memories of sitting in the bike basket. And as she was lost in thought, she felt the ground drop out beneath them and the car take a plunge.

For years, she would think about what caused it. Had her

glow penetrated the trunk and filled the car with a blinding light? Had Hamish's eyes given out? Had Hamish himself given out and decided to let go of the wheel?

When all was said and done, though, it didn't really matter. What mattered is the car fell hundreds of feet, tumbled like a toy into a deep ravine, tore apart, caught flame, and killed Hamish in an instant, crushed him, burned him, and made him unrecognizable.

But it didn't do a thing, not a single thing, to hurt Luna.

TO BE CONTINUED . . .

Wednesday, 12/13/1989 . . . Continued

NIGHT

I KNOW, STELLA. NOT A WORD ABOUT A WATERFALL IN THERE. Not a word about Banar. Calm down. They're coming. And that's what's freaking me out. A lucky guess? Can't be. The waterfall was strange enough. But Banar?

"What does Banar mean to you?" is what Alistair asked me earlier.

Well, the Spanish student in me knows it means *to bathe*. But the writer in me knows it as a name. The name of a character that will appear later in Luna's story. A bush baby named Banar who has secrets to tell. Powerful secrets.

You don't just guess a name like that out of thin air. Or maybe you do. Because that's where I got it. Well, out of *wet air*, I guess.

It was on Sunday, when I was with Glen and Mandy, walking to Hanlon Park in the misting rain. I was thinking about Luna's story and wondering if I should change it, edit it so that she wasn't a wombat anymore. If I ever wanted people to read the story, would it make more sense if the main character were an animal that everyone could relate to more? Like a chimp or a dog? Or should I go even wilder than a wombat? Something totally original. A tapir? A coatimundi? A capybara?

I couldn't decide, but the name *Banar* plopped into my head like a lump of clay tossed down on a table by an art teacher. *Make something out of this* was the message, but it wasn't until later that I decided what to make. It was when Mandy mentioned that one of the names Dorian Loomis used on the CB radio was Bush Baby.

Banar the bush baby, I thought. *He should be a character in Luna's story.* He wouldn't replace her, but he would represent the turning point, the moment when Luna's life would truly change.

I haven't written a word about Banar, so for Alistair to know that name is . . . disturbing. So disturbing that it makes me seem crazy too. I'm not crazy, though. You'd tell me if I were crazy, right, Stella?

Mom and Dad came home about ten minutes after Alistair mentioned Banar. Ten minutes earlier and I would have told them everything. So much more than I said to Dad during yesterday's walk to school. I would have told them what I knew about Aquavania, the creepy things Alistair was saying about Fiona's and Charlie's souls. I would have told them about Jenny Colvin, the Littlest Knight, and the Mandrake. I would have urged them to stop trying to find "the right fit" and just get the boy some help already. Not tomorrow, but right that very second.

Banar changed things. I was stunned into silence.

"I'm glad you're home," is all I told them.

And Mom said, "We all need to have a little chat."

We all sat in the kitchen, and Mom poured glasses of milk and laid out some cookies, while Dad leaned against the refrigerator, looked at Alistair, and said, "First thing we're going to tell you is that they haven't identified any bodies."

"What are you talking about?" I asked.

"They've made an arrest," Mom said. "They think the person might be involved in both Charlie's and Fiona's disappearances."

If Alistair's eyes could have gotten wider, then they would have wrapped around his face. "Seriously," he said. "Who?"

"His name is Milo Drake."

THE CONFESSION OF MILO DRAKE

Many will question why I am doing this. Even I am having second thoughts. I know how the system works, however. The state will assign a lawyer to defend me and that lawyer will tell me to keep my fool mouth shut. After all these years, I cannot do that.

My brother, Luke, fell into the Oriskanny ten years ago, and we never saw him again. Most people around here remember when that happened, but they do not think about it every day. I do. My parents do. I have

139

tried to push the details into the back of my brain, like locking a dog in the basement, and while I still hear the barking, I had begun to forget what the dog looked like.

A few days ago, that all changed. That is when I saw things clearly again. Police officers arrived at my door with new information about Luke. I will avoid details about what they told me, because it concerns innocent people dealing with their own pain, but I will tell you that it brought back disturbing thoughts. There are things I cannot lock away anymore.

People remember me as a boy, so they think of me as a boy. I am no longer a boy, but I am not sure what kind of man I am. As soon as I deliver this confession to the various news outlets, I will turn myself in to the police. Because I am the one they are looking for.

I am the reason Fiona Loomis is missing. I am the reason Charlie Dwyer is missing. I am not going to use this as a forum to explain myself, because I do not think I can ever do that. I am going to use this as a way to provide closure to families that need closure.

Look no further. Because I did this.

I do not want to cause any additional pain.

I am sorry.

Thursday, 12/14/1989

AFTERNOON

THEY FOUND BONES. LOTS AND LOTS OF BONES. THE POLICE and FBI have been digging in Milo Drake's yard all night and all morning, and the local news is keeping us up-to-date.

"Another set of bones," the TV reporters keep saying as they stand on the street next to the police tape. "That's all we can confirm at this point."

Milo Drake lives in some broken-down house in some tiny town I've never heard of, though apparently it's only twenty miles or so from Thessaly. A place called Oran. From the pictures they've been showing on the news, his backyard isn't that big, the size of a couple of driveways maybe.

The bones keep coming up, though.

I don't know tons about biology, but I know that Charlie wouldn't be a skeleton already, especially if you buried him. Neither would Fiona. Too cold and not enough time for decomposition. So everyone is holding out hope. But things are not looking good.

I agreed to talk to Glen on the walkie-talkies in study hall again because I needed to talk to someone.

"Whatta sicko that guy is," was the first thing Glen said as soon as we were connected.

"How are you today?" I responded, hoping he'd get the hint that this is how you start a proper conversation.

His hint-taking could use a bit of work, because all he said was, "I wish they'd show TV in class."

"It's too morbid," I said. "I don't know why we have to hear every detail. Find out the facts first, then report it. The *Sutton Bulletin* should never have published that confession. Not without corroboration. That's what my dad says, anyhow."

"Well, *my* dad says it's essentially an op-ed, and op-eds have different rules," Glen responded.

Awesome, I thought. *Is this going to turn into one of those my-dad-can-beat-up-your-dad situations?* Since Glen's dad manages the company that sells many of the local newspapers their rolls of newsprint, Glen figures his views on the media are beyond question. Arguing with him wasn't worth the effort.

"I'm sad for all the families," I said. "Including Mr. Drake's. Haven't they already had enough pain?"

"Maybe," Glen said. "But come on, if this man Drake has done half the things they think he's done, then he isn't getting my sympathy."

"What?" I said, cupping my hands over the headphones.

142

There was some noise in study hall, kids chatting, probably about the same thing we were chatting about, so I wasn't sure if I'd heard Glen right.

"He should burn in hell," Glen said.

"Did you call him the Mandrake?" I asked.

"Well, his name is Drake. And he's a man. Though have you seen his hair? He might be part porcupine. That stuff is a mess. I bet he hardly bathes."

"I've gotta go," I said. "Mr. Gregson is motioning for me to talk to him."

"Crap," Glen said. "Okay. No detention for you, because I want to walk you home and maybe we can watch the news together. Over and out."

Another lie. Mr. Gregson didn't motion to me. I actually don't think he even cared that I was wearing a walkie-talkie. He was too wrapped up in the *Sutton Bulletin*. Probably analyzing Milo Drake's confession like everyone else.

I wanted to snatch the newspaper out of his hands and look at it again. I had pasted the clipping on one of your pages, Stella, but you were all the way in my locker, and I needed to see immediately if there was anything to indicate that the Littlest Knight was connected to this.

Weird. So freaking weird.

A dead kid in armor halfway across the world. A man with a backyard full of bones a few towns away. My brother has made a connection between the two. *I let a monster called the Mandrake get to him,* Alistair had said yesterday, before

Mom and Dad had even come home and mentioned Milo. The man, Drake.

How could that possibly be another coincidence?

EVENING

Alistair is focused. He didn't even come to dinner tonight. Mom fixed him a plate and he ate in his room. His excuse is homework. Since he's missed so much school, the teachers have sent catch-up assignments and reading for him to do. It's a lot of stuff, but it's not like he can't join us for a meal or two.

At the table, all I wanted to talk about was Milo Drake, because really, how could we talk about anything else? Mom and Dad weren't thrilled about it. That confession seemed like a revelation last night, but as more and more bones are being unearthed, more and more hopes are being buried. Still, there were—there are!—so many unanswered questions.

"A couple of weeks ago, you asked something about Luke Drake," I said to Mom as soon as she sat down. "You said Alistair had seen something, right?"

"I did," Mom replied, and she spooned another scoop of scalloped potatoes onto my plate, the international gesture for *Fill that mouth with taters and not questions, my dear.*

"Well," I said, pushing the plate to the side for a moment, "if I'm going to understand what's happening in our family, then I deserve to know the details."

Dad sighed. "You certainly do. And I'm sorry we haven't been more forthcoming."

144

"Hallelujah!" I threw up my arms, and Mom dropped the spoon into the serving dish, the clang of metal on ceramic saying what she wasn't willing to say herself: that she hated being overruled, that she hated that Dad always decided when it was the right time for me and Alistair to know anything.

Dad either didn't notice or didn't care. Because he turned to me and asked, "Do you remember the Luke Drake disappearance?"

Milo's confession had brought some recollections back, but only hazy ones. Feelings more than anything. "Sort of," I said. "I was really young, right?"

If Mom was going to be overruled, at least she was going to get a few words in. "You were four, almost five," she said. "Luke fell into the Oriskanny when he was out playing with Milo. Luke was twelve, I think. A good-looking kid. Milo was probably fourteen. Always seemed a bit weird to me."

"And what did Alistair see? If I was four, then he was, like, two . . . or three?"

Dad nodded at my guess and said, "Alistair claims—"

"Claims," Mom echoed. "Important word."

"Yes," Dad replied. "Memories, especially from when you're young, aren't always reliable. And what Alistair remembers is seeing Luke Drake's body. In the river, near Uncle Dale's cabin. Do you remember that cabin?"

"Of course," I said. "It was . . . rustic."

"Well," Dad said, "Alistair claims he didn't realize what he was seeing until recently. He rode a bike out there to find out if he could confirm his memory. And while he was searching the riverbanks, he says he found the gun, buried and hidden in a metal box. An ammo can."

I turned from the table to check the hallway that led to Alistair's room. It was empty. "But he lied about the gun. Kyle confessed. It was Kyle's gun all along."

"Most stories, especially difficult ones, are a mix of truth and lies," Dad said.

"But why would Alistair lie about the gun?" I asked.

Mom raised her eyebrows. Like mother, like daughter. Same thoughts, same concerns.

Dad might not be a psychiatrist. He might not know all the science. But he is a guy people with problems talk to. He's supposed to have answers and he tries to have answers, but sometimes, it's obvious that he's grasping at straws. Like this time, when he said, "He's scared. He's confused. He's seen things he can't unsee and he doesn't know what to say."

Scared and confused were the opposite of how I'd describe Alistair these days. He was confident in the things he was telling me. The only time he seemed flustered was when he was talking about the Littlest Knight. And that wasn't really doubt. That seemed to be guilt. When he was silent, it was for a reason.

"You think he was covering up for Kyle because he was scared? Because he's confused?" I asked.

Mom sighed. Dad shrugged and nodded at the same time.

"And Milo Drake?" I asked. "Why him? Why now?"

"The police weren't sure whether to believe Alistair's story about seeing Luke's body all those years ago," Dad said.

"We all want to believe your brother," Mom added. "But, as you know, he's been saying strange things. And if he's telling one lie, then he's probably telling more."

Dad jumped back in and said, "To confirm Alistair's story, the police visited Milo Drake. Alistair told them what clothes Luke was wearing when he saw his body, so they asked Milo if he remembered what clothes Luke was wearing the day he fell in the river."

I took a bite of potatoes and peered over Dad's shoulder into the living room at the TV, which was off. We were in the dark. We had no idea what other discoveries the police had made since we'd sat down for dinner.

"So did they?" I asked.

"Did they what?" Mom replied.

"Confirm?" I asked. "About Luke's clothes."

Dad shrugged again, but didn't nod this time. "Never told us whether they did or didn't. Once Kyle gave his more believable side of the story, I suppose it didn't matter what Alistair said. The gun was Kyle's. Luke is long gone. And now with Milo . . . Well, this is how police work goes. You poke around, ask questions, and sometimes you dredge up something you don't expect."

"Sometimes someone leads you to a suspect that you didn't even realize was a suspect in the first place," Mom added.

I imagined for a second a monster rampaging down the

hallway, salivating, snarling, knocking family photos from the wall. Not a mud monster like the Dorgon in my story about Princess Sigrid. A ferocious demon of a thing, barreling toward Alistair's door. The Mandrake.

"Wait, wait, wait," I said. "Are you saying that Alistair led them to Milo Drake for a reason? That he knew something about Milo but was too scared to tell anyone? And this was, like, his way of pointing a finger without actually pointing a finger?"

"Maybe. Maybe not. We're as confused as you are, honey," Dad said.

If only. I wanted to bring up Banar and the wombat stuff. I wanted to tell them that not only was I worried about my brother, I was worried about myself. But that would only confuse things more, wouldn't it? I had to slip it in somehow, though. Test the waters.

"Have you ever known anyone with the name Banar?" I asked them.

They both shook their heads. It didn't spark any sort of reaction other than indifference.

"Why do you ask?" Dad said.

"No reason," I said. "I'm thinking about using it as a character name in a story, but I want to make sure it doesn't sound too weird."

"Honestly," Mom said with a sigh, "that's the least weird thing I've heard in ages." Then she got up from the table and, without asking us whether we wanted to watch it or not, she turned on the TV.

THE McCLOUDS

HIGH IN THE SKY LIVED A FAMILY OF CLOUDS, AND THEIR NAME was McCloud. They were Scottish clouds. The father, Horace, was a wispy cloud, a cirrus cloud if you want to be technical about it. The mother, Electra, was a storm cloud. There were two daughters. The older and gentler one, Lorna, stayed close to the ground, hovering over hilltops and often masquerading as fog. The younger and more boisterous one, Stella, was thick and puffy, the type of cloud that inspired people to say, *That's a frog . . . or maybe duck . . . or a Studebaker.*

For many years, they weren't a sad family or an angry family (even though the mom was stormy). They weren't a happy family either. They were merely a family of clouds, called the McClouds, and no one, outside of meteorologists, paid them much attention.

That is, until Lorna disappeared.

One morning, she told her parents she planned to linger

over a valley and provide some shade for picnickers, which was something she often did. Good deeds made her feel, for lack of a better word, good. She practiced kindness as much as possible, but she was always home by dinnertime.

Except on this day. The next day too.

The McClouds were understandably worried. They asked friends to help them find Lorna, and a search party of clouds swept across the land. When that many clouds come together, it's called a storm front, and this one turned out to be a doozy. It flooded the coasts of every continent, leveling towns, killing millions, and causing mayhem.

And it was all for naught. Because they didn't find Lorna.

The other clouds gave up after a while. Then the McClouds gave up too. Lorna was gone for good, they figured. It was best to focus their energies on Stella.

Stella loved the attention. With Lorna out of the way, she was the star of the family. Her parents kept a close watch over her, but they also spoiled her. They did whatever they could to keep her close and happy. They couldn't bear to lose another daughter.

Meanwhile, down on the ground, leaders had gathered together.

"We must put an end to this catastrophic weather!" shouted the secretary-general of the United Nations when they held an emergency meeting of the world's top scientists. The scientists agreed. So they teamed up to create the greatest machine ever. It was basically a giant fan designed to blow all the clouds out of the sky.

The McClouds had no idea that this was happening, because they were spending all their time indulging Stella. Stella would puff into different shapes and her parents would flatter her.

"You look like a palace of pillows," they'd say. Or, "You look like a bucket of popcorn."

Keep in mind, compliments in the cloud world often revolved around fluffiness.

When the humans finally finished their machine, which they called the Ultra-Blow, they put it on Mount Everest and fired it up. All the other clouds in the world had already grown wise to the humans' plan and had slipped off and hidden in caves.

Not the McClouds, though. When gusts from the Ultra-Blow reached Scotland, it was nighttime and they were asleep. The force of the wind pushed the three clouds together and they melded as one. All their thoughts and emotions became intermingled. They became a singular soul.

It's an odd thing to share someone else's soul and an even odder thing to share it with your family. But because of this, the mystery of Lorna was solved. Lorna had been there all along. Her sister, Stella, had absorbed her and had been hiding her deep in her billows.

Why did she do this? Simple. Stella was greedy and wanted all of her parents' love.

Damn you, Stella! her parents were tempted to say, but saying that was essentially damning themselves. They were a single entity now, and the Ultra-Blow kept blowing them up and up and through the atmosphere and into space. And so it was that the cloud named McCloud hurtled into the void, disgusted with itself, bewildered by itself, in love with itself, like every family since the beginning of time.

Little-known fact: clouds freeze in space. And when McCloud froze, it stopped thinking and being. It ended up in suspended animation.

For eons, the frozen cloud traveled through space, until it came upon a young planet. As it was pulled in by the planet's gravity and hit the planet's thin atmosphere, McCloud melted and broke into thousands of little pieces, until it wasn't a family anymore, or even individual personalities. It was aspects of personalities: anger, confusion, compassion, and so on.

Back on Earth, there was no weather, for all the other clouds were forced to stay in hiding or face the wrath of the Ultra-Blow. However, on the young planet, where the remnants of the McClouds fell from the sky, there was always weather. Except it was thoughts and emotions that rained and snowed. It was the essence of a family that once was and would never be again.

The animals on the planet weren't much more than blobs in the sea, but they absorbed the precipitation and became intelligent and swamped by feelings both good and bad. They evolved, slimmed down, and grew arms, legs, and eyes. After a while, one feeling dominated their hearts and minds: anger.

Because in the end, that's what dominated the cloud named McCloud. Stella was angry with Lorna for being so kind and generous, something Stella couldn't manage herself. Lorna was angry with Stella for absorbing her. Horace and Electra were angry with the entire situation, but mostly with themselves for letting the situation come to pass.

The aliens channeled their new intelligence and anger. They built spaceships and set coordinates for Earth with one directive in mind: destroy everything. The land, the animals, the humans, the clouds. Everything.

Damn you, Stella. Damn you.

Friday, 12/15/1989

AFTERNOON

I COULDN'T HELP MYSELF. I TURNED ON THE WALKIE-TALKIE this morning. Not to talk to Glen, but to spy on Dorian Loomis, to find out if he knew things I didn't already know about Milo Drake. I figured the Loomis family probably had some inside information that hadn't been shared with the public. So I sat on my bed, headphones pressed to my ears, and I fiddled with the knobs and got nothing but static. Disappointed, I trudged through two inches of fresh snow to school.

At school, everyone was talking about bones. The news hadn't released any updates, and if my parents knew anything, they weren't telling me.

"I heard there's bones for at least five bodies out there, so my question is this: whose bones are the other bones?" Mandy asked with a cough as we sat on the benches in the locker room, lacing up our sneakers. She had spent the last couple of days at home with a cold, watching game shows and soap operas and every news update that interrupted them. "There are tons of other missing kid cases. Remember that boy last year on Long Island? Or that girl in California all over the news last summer? What's-her-face?"

"I don't know," I said. "My only question is this: if everything went down like people think it went down, then how does Milo Drake snatch up Charlie? There's maybe fifteen minutes between when Alistair left the Dwyers' backyard and when the ambulance showed up."

"Plenty of time to stuff a kid in the back of a van."

"So what? Milo's hiding in the swamp? Or out in the street hoping to find some kid? It was pouring rain."

"Well, if he got Fiona, then maybe she told him about Charlie too and he was hanging out near his house," Mandy said as she hopped up and closed her locker. "Listen. I'm not a psychopath so I don't think like a psychopath, but I do know a few things about the yakuza."

"The yakuza?"

"Come on," Mandy said. "The yakuza? Ruthless Japanese swordsmen mafia types who you don't mess with? Everyone knows this."

A few other girls had been listening in on our conversation and they provided the appropriate shrugs.

"Jeez," Mandy said. "Forgive me for being educated. What I was trying to say is that the yakuza commit their crimes when it's raining so that all the evidence is washed away."

"Fiona disappeared when it was snowing," I said.

"Rain, snow, it's all water," Mandy said.

Phaedra Moreau was one of those girls listening in and she tapped me on the shoulder. "Aren't you happy?" she asked.

"What? Why?"

"No one will ever think your brother did this ever again," she said. "Not now that they've caught the real guy. Your brother won't be a scary weirdo anymore. He'll be a harmless weirdo."

Phaedra is the type of kid who will tell you that your shoes are out of fashion and act like she's doing you a favor by saying it.

I spun the dial on my locker to make sure the combination was scrambled up. "Why do people think they know anything?" I said. "Just because someone told a story? They're stories. People pick the stories they want to be true and they believe them. It doesn't make the stories true."

Phaedra smirked and said, "Well, I'm only trying to put a positive spin on it and let you know that even if people keep saying that your brother—"

"They're stories," I said again. Then I stormed out of there.

EVENING

A few minutes ago, I put on the walkie-talkie. Again, I'm not sure what I was hoping to hear. Dorian Loomis relaying inside information about the case, announcing conclusively that Milo Drake is indeed the monster we all think he is, that Fiona and Charlie will never come back, and that my brother can give up his weirdo talk for good? Did I expect to hear all the answers to everything tied up in some devastating, stereo-phonic bow?

Again, all I got was static.

We must have been lucky that one time we caught Dorian on the CB. Knowing Mandy, I'm sure she exaggerated how many times she's actually heard him. I tossed the head-phones in the corner and went into the other room.

My parents were on the couch and they were hugging.

"What's the matter?" I asked.

"Animal bones," my mom said, practically giggling. "They're all animal bones."

Saturday, 12/16/1989

AFTERNOON

MILO DRAKE IS AN INSANE PERSON. IT MIGHT NOT BE A NICE thing to say, but we all know this. We just don't know what type of insane person.

This morning, the sheriff held a press conference to discuss the case. Dad taped it, because he wants to keep a record of everything. Now I'm watching it for, like, the fifth time and writing down what the sheriff said.

Milo Drake is no longer considered a suspect. We have ruled him out in both the disappearances of Fiona Loomis and Charlie Dwyer. There is indisputable evidence that he could not have been involved in either occurrence. He was nowhere near the victims at the time periods in question. In addition, the bones recovered from his yard are animals' bones. Mostly deer and raccoons, though there are cats, foxes, and a few dogs as well. It appears that no crimes have been committed in relation to these bones, but we will continue our discussions with Mr. Drake. I will not be taking questions at this time, but should new information come to light, we will share it with the public. We encourage various news outlets to be judicious in their reporting. Thank you.

"Judicious in their reporting." That means don't print every insane person's confession! That means you, *Sutton Bulletin*! My parents had canceled their subscription to you a while ago and only recently renewed so they could know what their neighbors were reading about the Loomises, the Dwyers, and us. I'm pretty sure they're regretting that decision. I know I am.

Last night's relief transformed into something new this morning. Fear. Heavy, heavy terror. I've been scared for weeks. For Fiona. For Charlie. For Alistair. For myself. I've been scared about the how and the what. How do we find them? What are we going to do to help Alistair . . . and me? But this morning was when I really started worrying about the why. Why so many lies? Why so many stories? I realized that I don't understand what motivates people. Somehow, that scares me the most.

"Why would a guy confess to something he didn't do?" I asked Mom as she drove me to the mall in Sutton to buy Christmas presents, which she had insisted on doing even though it's something I know she hates doing.

Mom paused when I asked her. I could almost hear her

saying, *Isn't this a better question for your father?* But that's not what she said. Because I think we both knew why I asked her. I didn't want the professional answer. I wanted the mom answer.

"Well," she said, "people feel guilty about a lot of things. Sometimes all they want is to be punished. So they confess, to almost anything."

Is that what Milo Drake wanted? Is that what Kyle wanted? Is that what Alistair wanted?

"Why were there so many animals buried in his back-yard?" I asked.

This pause was longer. She was either speculating or wondering if she should share the truth. I couldn't tell. "He wanted to give them a proper burial."

"Because he killed them?"

"Because he found them," she said. "They were roadkill."

As Mom said this, I spied a dead squirrel on the side of the road. A coincidence, sure, but only a small one. Streets around here are covered in death. From deer all the way down to baby birds.

Baby birds. Baby birds.

At the stoplight next to the memorial tree, I was still staring out of the window, trying to conjure the image of the dead hummingbird from a couple of weeks ago, trying to make it seem real again, trying to reassure myself it was real.

"Everything okay?" Mom asked.

"What are coincidences?" I replied.

"Sorry? What do you mean?"

"I mean . . . if there are all these coincidences piling up in your life . . . where do they come from? What do they mean?"

Mom turned her eyes from the road for a second, which is a big no-no when driving, but I think she wanted to say this to me face-to-face. "I haven't the first damn clue."

That's not what you expect from your mom. I wanted her to tell me that coincidences were signs that good things would happen. Or a sign that bad things would happen. Anything but what she said, which was basically, *Why don't you tell me, because I'd like to know myself.*

Mom turned her eyes back to the road, loosened her grip on the steering wheel, and stretched the fingers on her right hand. It almost seemed like she was preparing to make a fist so she could punch the dashboard or the windshield.

But she didn't. She put the hand back on the wheel and she began to cry.

What do you do when your mom cries? Well, I know what you'd do, Stella. Something comforting, like hug her and tell her you're there for her, right? Well, I'm not you, Stella. I'm me. And what I did was this: I stared out the window some more, hoping that if I kept staring then when I finally turned back, her tears would be gone.

Mom turned on the radio. A song crept into the car. The lyrics were all about how birds suddenly appear whenever the singer's boyfriend is around. It's a love song, but it didn't feel like one to me. It felt icky, eerie, wrong.

Mom started humming along, which I thought meant she wasn't crying anymore, so I turned back. She still had a few tears on her face, but she seemed almost content. I guess she likes the song. I've heard it before, but I never gave the lyrics much thought until that moment.

Seriously, why do birds suddenly appear?

Baby birds. Baby birds. Baby birds.

SUNDAY, 12/17/1989

MORNING

ANOTHER WEEKEND ALMOST OVER. NEXT WEEK IS A SHORT week of classes and then we have Christmas break. Then Alistair is back at school.

Yesterday, Mom and I bought him some new shirts for Christmas. We want him to look nice when he returns. Better than he did before, so people might actually think he is better than before. In the past, Alistair would have opened a present like new shirts and he would have said, *Oh, these are . . . fine.* Because, really, what kid wants new shirts for Christmas when there are video games, bikes, model rockets, and all that fun stuff?

I don't know how he'll react this year. It's hard to know anything. I'll admit that the coincidences, and all the things my mind is struggling to believe, are starting to weigh me down. I know my parents try to put on their best faces for me and my brother, but I'm beginning to see all the weight on them too.

So at breakfast, I asked Dad if maybe we should go to church today. He didn't laugh, but I think he might have been tempted to. As I told you, we're a science family. Religion is barely mentioned around here, though Mom and Dad did tell me once, when I was about eight or nine, that I could start going to church if it was something I wanted to do. It was my choice. Which seemed great. Freedom! Glorious freedom!

Looking back on it, I see it wasn't really my choice at all. My parents didn't go to church. I didn't really know what church was like. So why would I choose to go, especially at eight or nine when I could watch cartoons instead or go mess around at Mandy's?

"Getting in the Christmas spirit, are we?" Dad asked me this morning when I started talking like a born-again.

"I want answers," I said.

Alistair was at breakfast too (we all were, though Mom was loading the dishwasher). I could tell he was listening, but he wasn't offering any opinions.

"Well," Dad said, "some people find answers there." The *but certainly not the Clearys* was implied.

"I'm going," I said, and I stood from the table.

"What? Where?" Mom asked as she finally pulled up a chair. We're usually done with breakfast by the time she sits, though she never complains about it.

"Church," I said. "I'm going to church. What's a good one?"

"Hmmm," Dad said. "That's an idea fraught with—"

"There's St. Mary's," Mom said. "Sacred Heart. There's the

164

Lutheran one. It's new, over by Prescott. If you're serious, you might want to try the Unitarian Universalist Church in Willomac."

Mom went to church as a kid because that's what everyone did around here back then. She grew up in Thessaly, and even if she couldn't tell you the history of every building in town, she could definitely tell you a story that took place in each one.

"What's a Uni-whatever Church?" I asked her.

"It accepts all faiths," Alistair said.

"Since when did you become an expert on churches?" I asked.

He tapped himself on the head, as if to show me how big his brain was.

"He's basically right," Mom said. "They're Christians more or less, but they welcome anyone into their services."

"This is something you want?" Dad asked in the same way someone double-checks whether you're really choosing fruit for dessert instead of chocolate cake.

"You don't have to go," I said. "I'll go alone. Drop me off."

The conversation turned at this point, from one with words to one where Mom and Dad used their eyes, which is always hilarious because they think we don't pick up on their signals.

Is this a good idea? asked Dad's eyes.

What will it hurt? said Mom's eyes. *Things are screwed up enough as it is. Maybe it's what she needs. There are worse things.*

Shouldn't someone go with her?

It sounds like she might want to go alone. She's fourteen.

She won't become some weird religious person who's always quoting the Bible, will she?

So what if she does? You told her a few years ago that this was her choice. She's our daughter. We love her.

Of course we do. But how is this going to affect Alistair? He looks up to her, and if he sees her struggling to—

Okay. Maybe their eyes didn't say that much, but Dad's mouth eventually said, "I've got some shopping left to do. If you want to go, I'd be happy to drop you off."

AFTERNOON

It was about a fifteen-minute drive to the church in Willomac, which is a town we sometimes visit if we want to go for a hike or have a picnic because it's thick with postcard-worthy lakes and creeks. I don't know anyone who lives in Willomac. Or at least I don't think I do. I didn't recognize anyone in the church.

It turns out going to church alone isn't all that weird. There are other people who come alone. And everyone is either super quiet or super friendly, even when they don't know who you are. Maybe *because* they don't know who you are. Since Alistair is a kid, they haven't shown his face in newspapers or on TV. All the people in Thessaly know what he looks like, and probably know what I look like too. Outside of our hometown, though, we're utter strangers.

Of course, Fiona, Charlie, and Milo did come up in the sermon. Not by name, but these days when you talk about missing kids, confessions, and heartbreak in a sermon, then we all know what that sermon is about. At least I think it was a sermon. It wasn't one of those speeches with fire and brimstone, there wasn't any singing, and the woman (a woman!) who was delivering it wasn't dressed in black with a white collar. She had on slacks and a blouse and she stood in front of us and talked like a teacher, but a teacher who's also a friend. I sat near the back, but not all the way in the back. I figured church is like a classroom or a school bus. Where you sit tells the world something.

Many of the people seemed happy to be there, and I don't know if they cared where they sat, but there were fidgety kids sliding off their seats like they were coated in butter and their parents kept pulling them up. I guarantee if there were a movie star or a monkey up on the stage, their butts would be glued to the wood.

I've noticed before and I noticed this morning that adults can be as fidgety as kids, but they're not as obvious about it. They pretend to stretch their necks or scratch their backs, but the message is basically *Get me on the next train outta here*. I could relate. I fidgeted. But it wasn't the entire time. Sure, some of it was boring, but occasionally there were some words of wisdom from Debra.

That's right. The preacher wasn't Reverend Something or Deacon Whatchamacallit. She was Debra. Just Debra! And she didn't spew a bunch of Bible passages, though she did make fun of herself at one point, joking that she went to high school with Methuselah, which is the name of a guy from the Old Testament who was pushing a thousand years old. I don't remember everything else she said, but I remember what she said about being confused.

"Sometimes confusion feels like pain. Sometimes it feels like falling."

Falling. She got that *exactly* right. She also talked about choices. Again, my memory isn't perfect, but one thing stuck with me.

"We are a sum of our choices. We are not our single choices."

I liked that bit the best. I wanted to tell it to everyone as soon as I got home. It's an important thing to remember.

Afterward, Debra gave people an opportunity to speak to her directly. I waited in line, which reminded me of years ago when I was a flower girl at Uncle Dale's wedding and everyone got less than a minute to talk to the bride and groom. *No time for chitchat. Get to the point, Grandma!*

That's why when I finally had my moment with Debra, I got right to the point. "What does God or the Bible or religion in general say about coincidences?" I asked.

"Whoa," she said. "That's a big subject."

"Yeah, the thing is, I've been noticing all sorts of coincidences and I'm not sure what they mean. I write these stories and I guess they're inspired by life and whatever, but then something happens and I don't know if I'm noticing it because I wrote the story or the story is actually causing it but . . ."

I was out of breath. I didn't realize how excited I'd gotten, but Debra certainly did. She put a hand on my shoulder. "This is your first time with us?"

I nodded.

She nodded. "There are writings on coincidences. But I'm guessing you're not looking for an academic answer."

"What sort of answer am I looking for?"

Debra laughed out loud, but not in a mean way. "What's your name?" she asked.

"Kerrigan," I said, because that technically is my name, even though everyone calls me Keri.

"Kerrigan, I'm guessing you're looking for a personal answer. I can't tell you why you're noticing so many coincidences, but I think it probably speaks to whatever it is you're looking at these days."

I shrugged. "I just look around."

Debra motioned around the church with her hands like a ringleader at a circus. "What do you see when you look around here?"

I checked out the wooden seats, which had butt marks worn into them, and the view through an open door that led to a cluttered office. I searched for crosses and stained glass, but I didn't find any. It wasn't that sort of church. Almost all the other people had left, and so the place was mostly empty. Dad was there, though, standing in the doorway waiting for me. The reason I didn't say "waiting patiently" is because he was looking at his feet, which was a dead giveaway that he didn't want to be there. Fidgety. Like I told you, Stella.

"I see . . . worry," I said.

"Worry? In general or in specific?"

I shrugged. "People come to you because they worry, right?"

"I suppose some people do, but the main reason people come here is for community."

"Is that what faith is about?" I asked.

"How do you mean?" she replied.

"When you believe something that you don't have solid proof of, that's faith, right? But faith is. hard to do alone. You need others to believe the same things you do, or else you're gonna go a little nutty, aren't you?"

Debra smiled and said, "An interesting way of putting it."

By that point, Dad had made his way through the church and was slipping his hand in front of Debra. A classic Dad sneak attack. "Richard Cleary," he said. "Keri's father."

"Kerrigan is a lovely and inquisitive young woman," Debra said. "I'm glad she joined us today. And I am pleased to meet you."

It seemed as though she *was* pleased to meet him. Really and truly. Her eyes said it. Her mouth. Her shoulders. Everything. Not that Dad is unpleasant or anything, but she was so graceful in her greeting that I think he was caught a bit off guard.

He smiled a crooked smile and said, "It's . . . Keri decided to come on her own this time. Maybe next time . . ."

"Any and all are welcome," Debra said. "Whenever."

"I'm sorry," he said. "Am I interrupting?"

Debra's eyes moved to me. Her eyebrows went up. *Your call,* she was telling me.

"No," I said. "I was bugging her with my crazy philosophical questions. That's all."

Dad tussled my hair and said, "Sometimes I wonder if she's an ancient Greek reincarnated."

Yep. Thanks, Dad. *Exactly* what a girl wants to hear.

"Answers aren't always easy," Debra said. "But I always encourage questions."

"Hear hear," Dad replied in a voice probably too loud for a church. Loud enough to echo.

Indoor echoes are always followed by silence, and we all stood there for a few seconds not saying anything. Then Dad dug into his pocket and pulled out some crumpled money and tried to hand it to Debra.

"Oh, no," Debra said. "Not necessary."

"Please," Dad said, pushing the cash at her. "For the collection plate."

"Buy Kerrigan an ice cream," she said.

Dad shrugged and put the cash back in his pocket. We said our goodbyes to Debra and she said her *hope to see you again* and when we were in the parking lot, with the frosty wind blowing against my face, Dad took the cash out of his pocket and handed it to me.

Twelve dollars.

EVENING

As we ate dinner tonight, Mom asked me about the sermon. I repeated the quote about choices, which she appreciated. She turned to Alistair and said, "Something to consider. Something to talk about with Dr. Hollister tomorrow, right?"

Dr. Hollister is the name of the psychiatrist my parents found. She's a woman Dad occasionally works with at the hospital, and Alistair is scheduled to see her in the morning. That's all I know because that's all I've been told. Things are moving along, or so my parents believe.

And so Dad moved the dinner conversation along, asked me more about my morning in church. I said that it was sort of like school and sort of like the one-woman show we saw that time we all went out to the theater in Ovid. Which steered the conversation in another direction, toward talking about drama club and Dad telling me and Alistair that it would be a good thing for both of us to do, especially when we got to high school. For friends. For fun. For college transcripts. I'm not against drama club, but you don't do drama club because your parents tell you it's a good thing to do. I informed them of this.

"I gotta follow my muse," I said.

My muse, whatever it is, is leading me to write stories. Of course, my parents don't really ask me about my stories. Which is weird, because Dad is always telling stories himself. Not writing them down necessarily, but always yapping about something that happened back when a double feature and a Coke would cost you barely a dime.

It's no surprise that Alistair is still curious about my stories, though. As we were clearing dishes, he whispered, "I wanna help you with the wombat story. Come to my room at eight."

At this point, I wasn't going to object. Mom and Dad were on top of getting Alistair help, and I still had my responsibilities of being a supportive big sister. However, I will say that when I knocked on his door at eight and he opened it without a word and pointed to the beanbag chair in the corner, I felt . . . little. Once again, he wasn't treating me as an elder, or even as an equal.

"Just so you know, I'm not looking for a coauthor," I said as I moved over and sat on his bed instead.

Alistair shut the door and held up the cordless phone. "You want to follow your muse," he said. "It leads to Jenny Colvin."

"From the tape?"

"Exactly," he said. "She must have it by now, but she hasn't responded or shown up at the fountain, and there's no time to waste."

"Why is there no time?"

"Because in Aquavania, years have gone by and Chip and Dot might give up soon." He slapped the phone in my hand like it was the hilt of a sword. "I dialed everything but the last digit. Press nine and you'll be connected."

I don't think I'd ever called someone who lives that far away. I'm not sure I've even spoken on the phone to someone in another country. "What time is it there?" I asked.

"Ten thirty a.m. on Monday," he said. "But it's her summer break, so I'm hoping she's home."

"And if she isn't?"

"We keep trying." He nodded at the phone. "Dial nine. Say you're you. Keri Cleary."

"And?"

"Ask her if she's listened to the tape. See what she says. Then once you have a moment, say this." He handed me a slip of paper with a few sentences written on it, and as he did, he pressed nine on the phone.

"I don't see why you aren't talking to her," I said as the rings pulsed softly in the earpiece.

"Like I said, she'll be terrified of me. She'll hang up immediately."

Before I could object anymore, there was a voice on the other end, and I instinctually raised the phone to my ear.

"Hello," said a woman with an accent. I guess it was an Australian accent, but I don't know if I could tell that from a New Zealand accent or even an English one. In any case, it sounded . . . fictional.

"Um, hi," I said. "This is, um, Keri. Keri Cleary. Calling for Jenny."

Silence.

"Jenny Colvin?" I said, my lungs tightening.

More silence. Then the woman called out, "Jennifer! Telephone!" And as I caught my breath, she returned to the line. "It'll be a minute, dear. She's pounding away on her computer, as always."

"As always," I said, like I had a clue.

It was at least a minute, an excruciating sixty seconds of waiting for Jenny to pick up the other end, a lifetime of staring at my brother, who was giving me a thumbs-up like I was about to go down a hill in a soapbox racer. I probably should've hung up, but I'll admit I was curious. Who was this person?

A breathless voice finally came on the line. "Hello."

"Hello."

"Who's this again?" she asked. Her voice was similar to the woman's, but it was lighter, airier. I'm guessing they were mom and daughter. Which made me think of my mom, my voice.

"This is Keri," I whispered. "Keri Cleary."

Another pause, and then, "You're American?"

"Yup," I said. "So . . . what . . . did you think of it?"

"It?"

"The tape."

A longer pause. A painful pause. "What is your problem?"

"I don't . . . I . . ." Alistair saw me floundering and he pointed at the paper. I raised it up.

"You still there?" Jenny asked. "Who was that boy on the tape? What exactly is your game?"

I hadn't even read the paper yet, so as I said the words, I was in the same boat as Jenny. Experiencing them for the first time. "I'm still here," I told her. "It's just . . . Fiona Loomis was my neighbor. Fiona Loomis was your friend. She believed in you. And you failed her. But you have a second chance. The portal at Steerpike Fountain will open again at two p.m. If the Riverman wanted your soul, he would have taken it already. He wants your courage. Your genius. So stop hiding. And don't be a coward, and don't be an idiot. Find Fiona. Bring her back."

"I am not a coward," she replied. "I am far from an idiot.

175

You must be crazy to think I'll listen to this rubbish. I am not going anywhere because some boy on a tape tells me to. I am not going to end up like Sigrid. I am happy with my life how it is for once. And I don't ever want to forget that. That's all that matters to me."

I didn't have any more of Alistair's words to draw from, so I improvised. "Sometimes it's about more than your own happiness. Sometimes you have to think of other people."

Dial tone. I didn't even notice it until I stopped talking. And the name Sigrid? It didn't register until I hung up.

"Yikes," I said as I placed the phone on the bed. "That was . . . intense."

"What did she say?" Alistair asked.

"Who the heck is Sigrid?" I responded. "And why does Jenny not want to end up like her?"

Alistair bit his lip. He closed his eyes and put his hands over his face. Either he was thinking deeply about something or wanted me to believe he was thinking deeply. When he pulled his hands away and opened his eyes, he finally answered. "I don't know."

"You don't know?" I barked. "You pretend to know everything!"

"Sigrid is not a name that comes up in all the memories I've absorbed," he said. "She could be someone Jenny once knew from Aquavania. Maybe a Riverman before me released her."

"The Riverman again! What does that mean? Who the hell is this Riverman?" I asked.

"I am," Alistair said plainly.

Now it was me who was putting my face in my hands. "This doesn't make sense. None of this makes sense."

Alistair placed a hand on my shoulder. I don't know what it was about it, but it felt like an old man's hand. Feeble and spindly. So I recoiled, and Alistair put that old man hand up in surrender. By the light of his halogen lamp, it looked like a standard-issue twelve-year-old-boy hand.

"I'm sorry," he said. "Usually Aquavania works in a simple, logical way. Daydreamers create. When they're done, the Riverman sends them home and guards over their worlds. It's when people make mistakes that things get . . . confusing."

"You're kidding me, right?" I said with a gasp. "This is so, so beyond confusing. Help me, because I don't have a clue what you're saying."

"Should I start at the beginning?"

"You better."

And so it was that Alistair told me a story.

Only this wasn't just any story. This was the *first* story. An origin story for Aquavania. It was the tale of a sister and a brother. It was rather long, and I don't have the time to delve into all the details, but I'll give you the highlights. To keep you in the loop, Stella.

The sister in the story was named Una. And the brother? Well, he was named Banar. How about that?

And how about this? Poor Banar died. In a creek. Tragically, because there's no other way for a boy to die. It was partly his sister's fault. And so the heartbroken, guilt-ridden Una ran away from home and came upon what? Well, a waterfall, dummy. Are you writing this down? Oh yeah, I'm the one that's doing that.

At the bottom of the waterfall there was glowing fur, and when Una touched it, she went to Aquavania. She was the first person to go, and while she was there, she created what she thought was a perfect world. She filled the world with replacements of her brother. Numerous figments of her imagination, and she named them all Banar.

Problem was, none of the replacements were good enough for her. Her perfect world wasn't good enough for her. She decided to abandon it and all her creations.

The other problem was, her creations weren't ready to abandon *her*. And so it came to be that one of the replacement Banars captured Una's soul. He sucked it out of her ear and into a hollow reed. Her soul became liquid. Her memories and ideas were like ink. Banar knew he was supposed to release her soul. Because by releasing it, he would have sent Una home and given her back the life she once had. He also would've shared the images and ideas she created with all of us storytellers in the "Solid World."

But that's not what he did.

Instead, he climbed into a lonely tower where he hid her soul. The tower was surrounded on all sides by . . . a waterfall. Are we noticing a theme, here?

One day, Banar made a mistake, because mistakes are always made. Things got, as Alistair said, confusing. He spilled

Una's soul, like someone spills a drink. Some of her soul fell in the waterfall. Some of it fell on Banar.

"The parts of Una's soul that fell in the waterfall leaked into the Solid World and inspired the world's first storyteller," Alistair told me. "A guy named Cabal. He saw Una's images and ideas and incorporated them into his own stories."

"And the rest of her soul?" I asked. "The part that got on Banar?"

"It changed him," he said. "It turned him into something else. The same thing I am now."

"The Riverman," I stated.

"The Riverman," he confirmed. "Or the Whisper. The Bugbear. The Boogeyman, if you like. There are a lot of names for what I am, but I am not the first to have these names. Banar was the first. Each Riverman absorbs the soul of the Riverman that came before. It's a calling. It's a job, really."

"A job? Like being a . . . mailman?" I asked. Which was Mom's job occasionally, especially when the post office was short-staffed and desk workers had to pick up some delivery routes.

Alistair smiled at the comparison. "Sort of," he said. "Only the Riverman delivers inspiration from Aquavania and returns souls back to their homes. But some have abused that power. They've absorbed souls they shouldn't have and failed to deliver them home."

I'm not sure if it was due to Alistair's skills as a storyteller or the lingering shock of the phone call, but I was fully invested in the absurdity by this point. "So how'd you get the job?" I asked. "Doesn't sound like something you interview for."

Alistair turned toward his dresser and stared at the fishbowl that was sitting on top of it. "I'd like to say that I was chosen, but I suspect it has more to do with the fact that I was willing."

"Willing to do what, exactly?"

"Guard over the inspiration. Take on all the burden of all the souls that have been absorbed. To be a home to all the daydreamers who went to Aquavania and never came back."

"How many is that?"

"Too many."

"Fiona? Charlie?"

Alistair nodded.

"So they're . . . part of you?" I asked.

Alistair nodded again. "Just like Una was part of Banar."

"Una never went home, then?" I asked.

Alistair massaged his scalp and said, "She did, actually. Years later. She washed up on shore. There were issues with her memory, but she essentially made it home."

"How?" I asked. I'm not sure if I wanted a logical or magical explanation. I simply wanted something to believe.

Alistair seemed to want the same thing. He shrugged and said, "I think . . . I hope . . . that someone put her back together."

OPPOSITE DAY

Kids used to kid about Opposite Day. There was no rhyme or reason to it. On some random day, some popular person would decide, *Hmmm, let's make today Opposite Day.* Then everyone would go around saying things like *I love you!* when what they meant was *I hate you!* Or they'd say *Want to share my lunch?* when what they meant was *Get your own lunch, you lousy creep!*

Of course, no one ever *truly* meant these things. It was all harmless fun. And it wasn't real. Until it was.

One sunny morning in April, Felicia Bromley woke up underneath her bed instead of on top of it. *This is odd,* she thought. *Perhaps I was sleepwalking.* But it wasn't that. It was that things were flipped. Opposite. Not everything, of course. But enough things that it caused the world to go haywire.

In Felicia's closet, all her clothes had changed to the opposite colors. Reds were now greens, blues were now orange, and so on. In the kitchen, instead of cereal in her ceramic bowl, there were pieces of ceramics in a bowl made of cereal. They did not taste good. They were sharp.

A kid was driving the school bus that morning, while a bunch of bus drivers were sitting in the back. Felicia thought it best to walk. When she reached school, she found that school was inside out, with the desks and blackboards all surrounding the building and the grass and sports fields inside of it.

"Can you believe it?" Felicia's friend Marcy said. "Opposite Day has become a real thing!"

"Well," Felicia replied, "if you say that's true, then wouldn't it make it false, and if it's false, then . . ."

It was a confusing time, to say the least.

As the day went on, madness was the norm. Felicia failed a test in math (she always aced them), dunked a basketball in gym (she'd never even been able to dribble), and ate the most delicious meal of her life (from the school cafeteria, of all places). Some kids loved the changes. Others hated them. No one could deny that the day was interesting at least.

School schedules must have been immune to Opposite Day, because classes let out the same time they always did. But instead of going straight home to do homework (which was her daily obligation) and to sew sock puppets (which was her daily hobby), Felicia spent the afternoon making out with Lance Garrison under the bleachers at the football field. Lance Garrison was the coolest kid in school, not the type of guy who would normally give Felicia the time of day.

"I love you," Lance told her as he caressed her face.

"I hate you," Felicia told him as she stroked his chest.

"What?" he said.

"It's Opposite Day," Felicia said. "We mean the opposite."

"So I don't really love you?" Lance asked.

Yep. Confusing.

"Let's just appreciate this moment for what it is," Felicia said.

"So, we're not supposed to appreciate it?" Lance asked.

"I don't know, just—" And instead of talking, Felicia went back to kissing, because she knew if she woke up the next day and things were back to normal, then she might never get this chance again.

That realization led to other realizations. All the things that used to not go Felicia's way had a chance of going her way today. So she went to the bank, where she had an account with $142.85 in it.

"I'd like to deposit a million dollars," she told the teller.

"Very well, ma'am," said the man behind the glass, and he walked into the back and returned a few minutes later with a bag full of cash. "One million dollars. Please don't come again."

He handed the bag to Felicia, who said, "A bad day to you, sir," and she walked out whistling a tune. She'd never been able to whistle before.

She planned to use the money to buy the one house in town she had always loved, a mansion that looked like a castle, with a moat, a parapet-lined tower, and a steel gate at the front. But when she showed up at the gate, she didn't even need to negotiate with the owner, an old man with a big puff of white hair and a mustache that was so long that it drooped.

"It's all yours," he said, handing her the deed and grabbing the cash as he sped over the drawbridge, his mustache flopping as he ran. Delighted, Felicia went inside, only to find that the place was jam-packed with awful things. The moat was made of stinky pea soup. The beds were covered in poison ivy. The showers sprayed blood.

Her dream house was a house of horrors. That was the problem with Opposite Day: bad things became good, but good things became bad. Some things stayed the same. All in all, there was a balance, like in the normal world. Only this world was much, much weirder.

Felicia decided it wasn't worth experimenting and trying to get exactly what she wanted. There were too many contradictions involved. She decided to go about the day and hope for the best. Or hope for the worst? Even the most basic things were beyond confusing. Which gave her one more idea.

What would happen if she tried to kill herself?

If it truly was Opposite Day, would she end up immortal in the end? Immortality lasts more than a day. Was it worth the risk?

She decided it was. She climbed to the top of the tower in her new mansion. It was at least fifty feet to the ground. Jumping would normally have killed her. But now? There was only one way to know for sure.

Felicia was not a risk taker. At least not on an ordinary day. But today was Opposite Day, and she was impulsive and more than a little bit nuts. Without hesitation, she ran across the top of the tower, handsprang off of one of the parapets, and threw herself into the air.

The opposite happened. But the opposite of falling from a tower isn't immortality. It's flying upward. So that's what she did. Felicia shot straight to the clouds, straight through the clouds, and into the atmosphere.

It being Opposite Day and all, the change in temperature and pressure didn't bother her. It made her joyous, euphoric, happier with life than she'd ever been. But when she was beyond the atmosphere and beyond Earth's pull of gravity, something strange happened. Without gravity, there was no up or down. No east or west.

Opposite Day got confused. Which way was Felicia supposed to go now?

Felicia bounced around in space like a rubber ball. Contradictions kept piling up. If this really was Opposite Day, why wasn't everything opposite? Why only some things? What was the opposite of outer space? What was the opposite of Felicia?

Even the most omnipotent of entities couldn't answer these questions. And so, Opposite Day was pronounced over.

Felicia's body froze in the cold air of outer space and she floated there for a while, until she was struck by a frozen cloud and sent on a trajectory that led her straight into the Sun.

Which is the opposite of having a nice day.

Monday, 12/18/1989

MORNING

Part of me would like to think that yesterday was Opposite Day, to chalk it all up as a moment when the world got turned upside down. But here I am, having slept on things, and I feel the same as I suddenly felt last night.

I believe my brother.

It was the wombat. It was the waterfall. It was Banar. And, finally, it was Sigrid. Sigrid is not a common name. Well, perhaps in Norway or Sweden it is. But not here. And not in Australia. Or at least I don't think it is in Australia. Australia seems like the type of place where everyone has names that end in Y. Billy. Bunny. Marty. Jenny.

Jenny Colvin. I still don't understand who she is or what exactly Alistair wants her to do. I don't know if Alistair's tactics convinced her of anything. But they convinced me. She convinced me. Simply by saying the name Sigrid.

The name Sigrid came to me on Thanksgiving morning.

Through the water? Maybe. Water is everywhere. So ideas are everywhere, I guess. I only remember that an image and idea popped into my head. A princess named Sigrid in a lonely tower. Like a fairy-tale princess—Rapunzel is the obvious comparison—only this princess didn't need saving. She's the one who *did* the saving.

Was Sigrid the name of one of these kids who went to Aquavania? One of the kids, as Alistair said, the Riverman released? I don't know. I only know that Jenny mentioned Sigrid and it flipped a switch in me. I'm not sure what will flip it back.

AFTERNOON

The switch stays firmly in place, flipped over to the part of my mind that is willing to believe unbelievable things. School today did nothing to switch it back. Actually, it did quite the opposite.

We have a few days of school left before Christmas break, and I went this morning hoping that there wouldn't be any pop quizzes, group projects, or classes where we had to talk or actually think about things. Because my mind was occupied with Jenny Colvin. Aside from her mention of Sigrid, I wanted to understand what Alistair needed her to do. *Aqua* means water, and Jenny was supposed to go to a fountain. A portal between this world and Aquavania? Seemed like it. Jenny was also supposed to be "a swimmer" and needed an atlas and a spacesuit to reach some people named Chip and

Dot. So she needed to navigate Aquavania by swimming from place to place? But she'd end up in outer space?

It's safe to say there's so much I still don't understand. I could ask Alistair questions, and I did ask Alistair questions, but they led to more questions.

The most important one I had last night was, "What can I do to help?"

"Remember what I tell you," he said. "In case I forget."

So today, I've been trying to remember, trying to put all the pieces in their right places and keep them there. Which meant I was distracted, so distracted that I'm surprised I didn't walk into the lockers during the migrations to and from classes. Glen certainly noticed. Between third and fourth periods, he joined me on my way to math and said, "You're not talking much today."

"I've got a lot on my mind," I said.

"My dad says that psycho's mind blacks out," Glen replied.

"What? Who?"

"Milo Drake," Glen said. "My dad talked to an editor at the *Bulletin* who said that Milo Drake told the police that he 'loses time.' He'll get in his car and drive somewhere and then end up at home and have no idea what happened. That's why he confessed. He really did think he snatched Fiona and Charlie, but then forgot about it."

"He's not well," I said.

"*Sufferin' succotash!*" Glen said with a cartoony lisp. "That might be the understatement of the century. Any guy who scoops up roadkill and buries it in his yard is as nutty as a

188

fruitcake." He put a finger near his temple and spun it around and whistled the sort of tune that plays at a circus when a clown rides in on a tiny tricycle.

"Does your mind have a filter?" I asked.

"Like a pool?" he replied. "Don't think so. If it does, I should probably get it cleaned." He laughed as if this were incredibly funny, which it wasn't.

"I mean, do you say everything that pops into your head?"

"Hmmm . . . yes," he said. "It's called honesty."

"It's called annoying," I responded.

He'd been cheery up to that point, but I must have hit a nerve, because his tone got distinctly peeved. "Hey," he said. "Why are you talking like this? You'd better tell me today is Opposite Day."

I stopped midstride. "What?"

"Up is down. Dogs are cats, that sort of thing."

"Did you really bring up Opposite Day?"

"Yeah, so? It's not a real thing, in case you didn't get the memo."

My backpack was hanging off one shoulder, and it was so heavy that all I had to do was shrug a little and it slid down my arm to the floor. I unzipped it and pulled out my diary.

That's right. You, Stella! Out there and exposed in the hall at Thessaly Middle! I opened you up to the page where I had written my latest story, the one titled "Opposite Day."

"Look," I said with my index finger crushing the title.

Glen squinted. "So?"

"I wrote this *last freaking night*!" I said. "You don't

understand, I'm writing about Opposite Day, you're talking about Opposite Day, and there has to be a reason why and—"

He snatched the book out of my hand. "So it's, like, a story?" he said. "You write stories?"

"Yes," I said. "But not for you." Then I reached to rescue you, Stella, but he blocked me with his back and hunched over so he could give the story a closer look.

"We're in a relationship," he said. "All of this stuff should be for me too. We should be sharing everything with each other."

I didn't realize how strong Glen was until I was trying to wrestle you away from him. He bobbed and spun and bumped me with his shoulders as he tried to read more.

"Come on!" I shouted. "Give it back!"

You'd think a crowd would have gathered or a teacher would have stepped in, but it must not have looked like a big deal. Maybe it looked like we were having fun. A game between a boyfriend and girlfriend. Maybe that's how it felt to Glen. But to me it felt like life and death.

I don't think Glen had the chance to read more than a sentence or two of the story, but then he started flipping through the pages and seeing other things I'd written. "Wait a second, wait a second," he said. "Is that my name in here?"

I'd like to say I had no other choices, but I probably did have other choices besides the one I made. Still, the one I made worked, and that's all that counts.

"Gimme that!" I shouted. Then I bit him on the shoulder.

He dropped you on the ground while howling "Gawww!"

and I scooped you up, Stella, and into my backpack, which I threw over my shoulder.

As I sped off down the hall, I called out, "Don't ever try crap like that again!"

And he cried back, "We're not breaking up, are we?"

Tuesday, 12/19/1989

EVENING

I'M WORRIED. WHAT ELSE IS NEW? MY GRIP ON SANITY WORRIES me. These coincidences worry me. What I did to Glen worries me. The fact that I'm not funny anymore worries me. I used to joke with you more, Stella, didn't I? There are always punch lines to be found in life, and my inability to find them these days worries me. But you know what worries me the most? The same thing that worries everyone. They're not back yet.

It's been six weeks since Fiona up and vanished. One month since Kyle was shot and Charlie went missing. Lies. Stories. Speculations. They've all muddied the waters. And nothing is worked out. Not really.

What has Alistair been waiting for? What has he been doing? My switch is flipped. He needs to keep it flipped!

Actually, I'll tell you what Alistair has been doing. Seeing Dr. Hollister. I don't know what they talk about because my parents aren't even supposed to know that. Not unless lives are at risk.

But lives *are* at risk, aren't they? And yet I can't exactly go up to Dad and say, "So Alistair told me that Fiona's and Charlie's souls are trapped somewhere inside of him and I sorta, kinda, maybe . . . believe him."

I'll be the one seeing the psychiatrist. I'll be the one locked away, because at least Alistair has an excuse. At least he's seen some disturbing things. Me, I'm simply willing to suspend some disbelief.

But for how long? If something doesn't happen soon, my switch might be flipped back. So this morning, when I bumped into my brother coming out of the bathroom, I asked him, "Any more word from Jenny Colvin?"

"No," he said in a low voice. "I'm exploring another option."

"What can I do to help?"

"Remember," he said, just like he'd said before.

I guess I have your help with that remembering part, don't I, Stella? And what I'll remember about today is that it's the day Kyle returned home. In a wheelchair. His parents pushed him quietly and slowly up the snowy driveway and bumped him into the door frame as they entered a house where there'd been two cold and empty bedrooms for the last month. At least, that's how I imagine the scene.

Mom was the one who saw it. Driving by on her way home from work, she watched the Dwyers put one broken piece back into their broken family.

"He may walk again someday," Dad said. "Let's hold out hope on that account."

We were in the kitchen when he said that, just my parents and I. Alistair had shut himself away in his room again. They hadn't told him that Kyle was home yet. We all knew there was a good chance that Kyle wouldn't be coming home on his own two feet, but we didn't want to accept it until one of us saw it. Now one of us had.

"How do you know he might be able to walk?" I asked.

"Word gets around the hospital."

Word didn't get around the school. Or at least it didn't get to me today, because I didn't really speak to anyone. Ever since I bit Glen, he's been keeping his distance. Mandy has been too, which is a bit weird, but then again, she's Mandy. When I saw her in the cafeteria today, she waved me off and said, "Sorry, I don't have time to annoy you right now," and headed to the exit with half a cellophane-wrapped sandwich in her hand.

When you spend a day not talking to people, you begin to see its appeal. You don't have to explain yourself. You don't have to ask questions or seem interested. You don't have to listen to your brother tell you stories about alternate dimensions and then call random girls in other hemispheres and wonder constantly what the hell is happening to your brain, which you were pretty sure was a pretty good brain, once upon a time.

What you can do, and what you will do, is this: you will write more about the wombat.

THE PHOSPHORESCENT WOMBAT, PART III

HAMISH LAY DEAD AT THE BOTTOM OF THE RAVINE.

His little red sports car burned, but it didn't glow as brightly as Luna did. When the ambulance, fire trucks, and police cars arrived, they had no idea what they had found. They stood on the edge of the ravine, scratched their heads, pulled off their sunglasses, rubbed their eyes, and put their sunglasses back on.

"Let's call in . . . Who do we call in?" the sheriff asked.

"The government?" the fire chief asked.

"Do either of you have the government's phone number?" the ambulance driver asked.

"I know a guy who knows a guy, I guess," the sheriff said, and he went back to his car and got on the radio.

Luna, meanwhile, started to crawl from the wreckage and up the ravine. She knew that Hamish was dead and she was weeping uncontrollably, but she also knew that she needed to hide somewhere. For years, Hamish had been hiding her. Because she was no longer the harmless, dimly lit Mr. Nickelsworth. She was now a force of nature, a radiant dynamo, and surely there would be people who would want to exploit her.

When the helicopters arrived an hour later, Luna was near the top of the ravine and the police and first responders had fortified themselves behind some boulders—some with their hands shielding their eyes, others with their shaking guns drawn.

Men in protective suits came out of the helicopters. They wore dark goggles and carried guns with tranquilizer darts. They fired into the glow, basically without aiming, but eventually they hit Luna. When she stopped moving, they closed in with nets and a cage.

Since her glow was so bright that it would blind a pilot, it would've been dangerous to transport her in the helicopter. So they called in a tank with an enclosed compartment in the back. Even the tank wasn't entirely effective. As it rolled away from the scene, thin beams of light leaked from the tiny cracks around the screws and seams of the machine. It looked like a rolling Chia Pet, with light for hair.

The tank took Luna as far as the nearest port, where she was loaded into an airtight shipping container and placed on a barge. A tugboat pulled the barge to an oil rig about one hundred miles offshore.

Only this wasn't a regular oil rig. It was designed to look like one, but it was actually a place where the government performed its most top-secret experiments. Submarines, war-ships, and fighter jets circled the place to keep it secure. And in a chamber near the bottom, about fifty feet below the surface of the sea, they stored Luna.

"They" were a collection of the nation's best scientists, who lived on the oil rig and employed the world's best technology. Using infrared cameras mounted in the chamber, they examined Luna from afar. Luna's glow was not on the infrared spectrum, so she didn't look like an orb when viewed through the cameras. The scientists could make out her true shape from her body heat.

"I'm not sure this is an alien," remarked the chief scientist, Gladys Gershwin, as she examined the very distinctive creature that waddled around the chamber.

"Looks a bit like a wombat to me," said the second in charge, Hogan Hogoboom, a man who had spent a chunk of his childhood in Australia.

"Isn't that Mr. Nickelsworth?" said the youngest in the group, an awkward but brilliant young geneticist named DeeDee Delaney.

"Who's Mr. Nickelsworth?" everyone asked.

And DeeDee brought them all back to her cabin, where she had a VCR and a bunch of videotapes. She showed them episodes of *Pocketful of Hullabaloo*.

"It's from seventy-five years ago, at least," she said. "I'm surprised none of you have heard of it. I guess I'm the only junkie for the classics."

There was a zoologist named Yan Yeager on the rig and

they called him in for his expertise. The infrared cameras could only show so much, but the thing that puzzled Yan Yeager the most was Luna's age. "How could this possibly be the same wombat from your television show?" he said. "A wombat can live twenty-five years tops. Maybe this is an offspring."

DeeDee begged to differ. Even in infrared, Luna looked exactly the same as when she was on TV. The shape of her nose, the size of her ears, every bump on her body. "That's the same wombat, only she didn't glow this much back then," DeeDee said. "If you're such an expert, maybe you can explain the glowing."

Yan scratched his chin. "We might have to call in a chemist for that."

They called in a chemist. "Beats me," she said.

They called in a physicist. "Beats me," he said.

They called in almost every scientist on the rig and got a chorus of *beats me*.

Still, every scientist wanted to study this curious specimen. Together, they constructed a robot with infrared cameras for eyes and they sent the robot into the chamber to run tests on Luna.

They poked, prodded, shaved, bathed, jiggled, wiggled, and even tickled the wombat. They took blood, hair, and droppings and looked at them under the microscope. They showed inkblots to Luna and they put a microphone in their observation room that transmitted all of their conversations to a speaker in Luna's chamber. They wanted to see how she would react to voices and sounds.

198

They were especially curious to know how she had survived the car crash. So they got rough. They tried to see how far they could push and punish Luna. Why not, right? They didn't really have any hypotheses. They were throwing paint at a canvas and hoping to come up with art.

For years, they recorded their observations, but couldn't determine anything significant other than the fact that Luna was a wombat who glowed and whose body was impervious to the following things: dry ice, acid, flamethrowers, lava, bullets, chain saws, bubonic plague, and those machines that crush cars at the junkyard.

Meanwhile, Luna was listening to their voices through the speaker and figuring out quite a lot about them. She was growing brighter in more ways than one. On the surface, she was sedate, enduring whatever tests they put her through and waddling around without complaint. But that was only because she was formulating a plan, and when her plan was finally ready, she put it into action.

She did something the scientists found particularly strange. She starting drinking water, lots and lots of water. For years, she only went through a hamster bottle a day, but all of a sudden, the robot had to refill her bottle once every few hours.

Which was strange enough, but here's the strangest thing: she wasn't peeing.

The scientists could write off the glowing and her ability to withstand death as mutations, but the ingestion of liquid without the expulsion of liquid seemed impossible. From the infrared, they could tell she wasn't overheated and sweating the liquid out.

"So where did all the water go?" DeeDee asked after the fifth day of constant drinking and not a drop of pee.

"I guess she's got a big bladder," Yan said.

Gladys, Hogan, and all the other scientists laughed, but it was actually the most accurate observation anyone had made about Luna. She did have an exceptionally large and exceptionally flexible bladder. Also, she was exceptionally determined.

Because on the sixth day, she let loose. When she did, she had what it took.

She got up on her hind legs and peed on the walls. But she didn't pee like some dog that wasn't housebroken. She peed with purpose.

The thing about infrared light is that it displays heat. Luna's glow did not produce heat, and other than the robot, she was the only thing in the chamber. The only hot writing source she had was pee. And she needed enough to write the message:

I AM LUNA, A PERFECTLY FINE WOMBAT, AND I HAVE A SOUL.

A stunned silence gripped the scientists. No one had expected this.

DeeDee spoke to Luna through the microphone. "Luna. Can you understand us, Luna?" she asked.

Luna had enough pee left to write *YES*.

The scientists gasped. "Get that wombat a drink!" Gladys commanded.

For the next few months, they spoke to Luna. To give her bladder a rest, they devised a gadget that looked like a pacifier with a laser on the end. Luna could hold it in her mouth and write on a board that would absorb the heat. The scientists could see the writing using their infrared cameras.

Luna's vocabulary was limited, but she was able to tell them her basic story, confirming that she was indeed Mr. Nickelsworth and explaining that she didn't know where she was originally from or why she was the way she was. She was just Luna, a phosphorescent wombat.

There were many discussions—in private, of course, away from Luna's ears—about what to do with her.

They had studied her about as much as they could and they observed that her glow was getting even brighter, so bright that it was penetrating the walls of her chamber. She would have to be moved, but they couldn't imagine where.

"I have an idea," said a marine biologist named Hiroto Hangawi.

Hiroto blabbed on and on about the importance of the oceans and how that related to the survival of the planet— *blah, blah, blah, science talk, science talk*—but what his plan for Luna basically came down to was this:

Luna might've been a wombat, but she was also the brightest light source anyone had ever encountered on Earth. Not to mention the fact that she seemed to be immortal, or exceptionally resilient, having lived at least one hundred years and having survived a horrific car accident and their rigorous tests. Hiroto wanted to send her to the darkest corner of the Earth: the bottom of the ocean.

"When she returns, we can find other uses for her," he said. "But for now, we are sitting on top of the ocean. If we can't learn anything more about her, let's see if we can learn more about our planet."

There was a vote and Hiroto's plan won by a hair. A hair was enough.

"We should at least inform Luna about what she's getting into," said DeeDee, who had grown quite fond of the wombat and had voted against putting her in such obvious danger.

"Of course," Hiroto said. "It's essential. Because she must tell us what she sees."

So they explained to Luna that they'd be sending her into the deepest part of the ocean, the Mariana Trench. The Mariana Trench is nearly seven miles down, over a mile lower than Mount Everest is high. It is terrifyingly cold and dark, and the pressure would crush almost every living thing on Earth. At one point, a heavy-duty exploratory submersible had been sent to the bottom to collect data. The two men inside reported they actually found signs of life at those seemingly inhospitable depths, but what they didn't tell the general public was that they also found a hole.

They only revealed the information about the hole to a small collection of scientists, Hiroto Hangawi included. This was because the hole frightened them. Its shape was not natural. It was the shape of a body, with arms, legs, and a head. Like a little human. Which probably meant that they weren't the first intelligent beings to reach such depths. They didn't know what was in the hole, or how deep it was, but they knew it was too deep for their submersible to withstand, and that didn't matter anyway, because it was also too small for any submersible, even a tiny one, to fit through.

But it wasn't too small for a glowing, indestructible wombat.

"Will you see what's in that hole for us, Luna?" Hiroto asked.

"I will," Luna said by writing with her laser pacifier.

"Only if you want to," DeeDee said.

"I want to," Luna replied.

This was the truth. For years, she had stayed hidden in that barn. For years, she had been locked in that chamber. When she was Mr. Nickelsworth, at least she gave the world some smiles and laughter. She still felt the need to contribute in some way. This was the best she could do.

They designed a harness constructed from the world's most indestructible materials mixed with bits of Luna's fur and skin for extra strength. They made multiple thin cords out of the stuff too, each one at least fifteen miles long. They wove the cords into a tether, attached it to the harness, and put the harness on Luna.

On account of the fact that, even underwater, Luna was too bright to provide photographic images, they had to rely on her telling them what she saw when she came back. That is, if she came back. They'd do their best to get her down as far as they could. The submersible that originally found the hole would be her guide. They clipped her to it, set the coordinates, and turned on autopilot.

"The submersible will unclip you as soon as you hit a depth of thirty-six thousand feet," Hiroto said. "Once you reach the hole, you're basically on your own."

"And you're okay with that?" DeeDee asked.

"I've always been on my own," Luna said. "This is what I was meant to do."

"Good girl," Hiroto said, and he sent the robot in to attach Luna's harness.

Without thinking, DeeDee hurried after the robot, and the other scientists didn't know what was happening until she was in the chamber, hugging Luna.

"You're a wonder, Mr. Nickelsworth," DeeDee cried. "Worth a billion dollars, at least."

She couldn't say anything more, because the light was so bright that it knocked her unconscious. And by the time DeeDee woke in the rig's medical center, the submersible was unclipping Luna at the body-shaped hole.

DeeDee was blind.

Luna was as far away from humans as she'd ever been.

TO BE CONTINUED . . .

Wednesday, 12/20/1989

AFTERNOON

LIKE JUSTINE BARLOW, THAT HUMAN MAGNET FOR DEAD BABY birds, I, Keri Cleary, have decided to start jogging. Supposedly, it's good for your head as well as your heart, and both of mine need a bit of help. School was uneventful, and the news is yet another crapfest (we're fighting with Panama now?). So I put on a sweat suit, hat, and gloves. I grabbed what I thought was my Walkman and hit the slushy streets.

It wasn't my Walkman, of course. It was the stupid walkie-talkie. I put it on anyway. I don't understand a lot about frequencies and I thought maybe I could get a radio station if I fiddled with the knob. All I got was static.

Instead of bringing it back and swapping it for the Walkman, I just wore it. I didn't want to go inside and have Dad see my outfit and ask what I was doing. It was better to jog and find out if I liked it and shower the sweat off and then only answer questions if absolutely necessary. Besides, static isn't so bad to listen to. Beats listening to your thoughts when your thoughts are a scramble of stories and you're having trouble telling what's real and what's a dream and what's a coincidence and what's basically what.

If you never jog and you suddenly jog, it's not easy to jog. Didn't help that it was below freezing out and the slush was now ice and my lungs were burning because they were working so hard trying to stay warm. I also had to keep watching the ground because I didn't want to slip and I definitely didn't want to see any more dead baby birds.

It all added up to surrender. I was ready to quit almost as soon as I reached the Loomis house, which isn't very far at all. There was a pickup truck in the driveway, the first vehicle I'd seen there in a few days. The back was weighed down with bags and boxes that were held tight with bungee cords. I changed my pace from a slow jog to a fast walk, which is basically the same thing for me. And that's when it came through the headphones. A voice.

"Knock knock . . . knock knock . . . knock knock . . ."

There was no reply, so the voice replied to itself, in a slightly nasally tone.

"Who's there?"

"Dorian Loomis."

"Dorian Loomis who?"

"Open the door, Ian, Lou misses you!"

It wasn't funny. I'm not sure I even understood it. I mean, who the hell are Ian and Lou? Is that even a punch line?

"Yep," the voice said. "It's Dorian Loomis. I go by Luminary or Bush Baby. The Red Baron sometimes. But right now this is me speaking as me, as Dorian. Speaking to anyone who cares to listen."

I cared to listen. I hurried a little farther down the road, past the Loomis house and the Carmine house, because Mrs. Carmine is a total busybody who's always sticking her nose into things. To catch my breath, I sat on a big rock next to the sign for Seven Pines Road at the corner of Harriman. I listened.

THE RECOLLECTIONS OF DORIAN LOOMIS

---◆---

SOMETIMES YOU GOTTA TALK. TO ANYBODY. TO THE AIR, IF that's what it takes. I know this ain't my regular routine, but routine can drop you so deep in a hole that you can't dig out, and you can't live in a hole your entire life. It's all my way of saying that I'm done. I'm gone. I tried to do life the regular way, with family and an address. What good did that do?

None. Absolutely none.

I can't talk to my brother. When we were both really young, we were all right. Got into adventures. Ran all around town causing a ruckus. He was funny. He could be fun.

Not these days. Not these years, actually. Ever since we both went and grew up. Ever since before that.

And his wife? Oh boy, beautiful woman, but I hesitate to even call her my sister-in-law, 'cause she don't exactly act sisterly. She's strange. I've seen all sorts of darkness in my day, so I know she has a darkness. Anyone who knocks 'em back like she does has gotta have a darkness. Anyone who hides things like she does has gotta have a darkness. Only I don't know what her darkness is, or where it's from.

The fact that the two of them could pop out such beautiful children is a testament to . . . hell, I don't know. Flowers grow from manure. Best way I can explain it.

I should shut up, though. Talking ill of people who took me in is no way to talk at all. But then again, I also can't stay with them anymore. Not with the way they handled Ma's passing, like it wasn't nothing at all. Not how they dealt with her suffering, like it didn't matter at all. Not with the way they ignored my niece, with the way they've handled everything since she . . . left.

Yes, *left*. Call me naïve or clueless if you want, but I don't think she was taken. I think she left. I know her brother and sister think that too, because they've told me. And if we find her . . . when we find her . . . I hope that we can figure out what's best for—

Look at me. Now I've gone and said too much. Gotten too personal. I bet many of you can relate, though. Veterans. Guys on the long haul. Family is never easy, but it's extra tough for ones like us. We live our lives the only way we know how to live 'em. Alone.

Not an excuse. An explanation.

Which makes me think of this other guy. He's younger, but maybe he's a bit like us. Maybe he's more alone than even we could imagine. He had a brother, like I got a brother, but he lost him. It wasn't his fault, losing his brother, but I know he feels like it was his fault. That's how it always feels when someone you love is there and then gone. You coulda done something different, something better. It'll drive you up the wall thinking about the possibilities, and that no doubt got the best of him.

I used to talk about this stuff with my niece. She clued me in to the idea of alternate realities. Like, there are infinite versions of the world. Each a bit different. Existing, I don't know where . . . somewhere. And an alternate reality is created every time we make a choice. The choice might be simple. Eggs for breakfast or pancakes? Even that can determine your reality, the entire course of your life.

Not to get all philosophical, but that sort of thinking gets me remembering this day when I was eight and my brother—Neal is his name—was about thirteen and we did one of the stupidest things a coupla kids could've ever done. I'm guessing it was his idea, but I don't know for sure. I wouldn't put it past me to think up such insanity.

It was summertime, but we got dressed up in our winter clothes. Snowmobile suits, hats, gloves, the whole nine. Even ski goggles. Basically covered every inch of our skin. Like we were wearing armor. Then we went into the garage.

In the garage, there was a bucket of old tennis balls from when Ma took up the sport. She wasn't using them anymore because she learned pretty quickly that none of the other ladies in Thessaly were into games that make you sweat. So the bucket was sitting there, untouched, right next to the barbecue gear.

My brother and I took a can of lighter fluid and we sprayed a bunch into the bucket, all over the balls. Then we took a candle and attached it with a C-clamp to a sawhorse at the other end of the garage. Then we lit the candle.

This was gonna be a game. A competition. We were five years apart, but still very competitive. Boys will be boys, as Ma used to say.

The point of the game was to throw a ball soaked in lighter fluid through the candle flame and make it catch fire. For every ball that caught fire, the thrower would get a point. After each throw, we'd fetch the flaming ball and smother it. To be clear, we did have a hose nearby to keep things safe. That's also what all the clothes were for. To keep things safe.

Well, we started chucking the balls and having a great time. The game was to ten points, and after a few minutes, the score was something like four to one, with Neal in the lead. It was my turn and I had this perfect throw. Knocked the candle right from the clamp and set the ball ablaze. I woulda cheered too, but there was hardly any time to do a thing. 'Cause the ball came bouncing back lickety-split and landed right in the bucket. The whole thing went up like flash paper.

You do smart things and stupid things in the thick of a moment, and the first thing I did was pretty damn stupid. I kicked at the bucket to try to put out the fire. Doesn't take a genius to guess that this tipped the bucket over and sent flaming balls bouncing all across the floor. We started chasing them because we didn't have any idea where they might end up. Lots of flammable stuff in a garage, ya know.

In all the running around, Neal probably didn't notice that his pants leg caught on fire. I sure as heck noticed, though. There's that old rhyme about *liar, liar, pants on fire.* I don't know where that comes from, but I think about my brother every time I hear it. The flames were on his legs like ivy on a tree, creeping up and wrapping themselves around. Looking back at it, wearing a whole mess of winter clothes was probably the stupidest part of this stupid game. Sure, it protected our skin a little bit, but it also made us a lot more flammable.

With my brother on fire, I could have run away. I kinda wanted to. To be honest, it scared the dickens out of me. But I did what instinct told me, and instinct this time was smart enough. I jumped on top of him. These days they tell kids to stop, drop, and roll if your clothes are on fire. Not sure if they told us that when I was young. All I knew was that I had to smother the flames.

I was a big guy. A strong guy, even at eight. I managed to tackle Neal and wrap myself around his legs. It worked. The flames were out in a second or two.

But right away he pushed me away and started shouting, "What the hell are you doing?"

"Saving you," I told him.

He looked down at his legs and he had to've seen the charred fabric. Impossible to miss. But he didn't thank me or say *sorry* or nothing. He jumped up and hurried over to the garage door and threw it open. Then he ran around the garage kicking the flaming balls out across the driveway into the front yard, where the grass was still wet from a sun shower.

When all the balls were put out, he pointed at me and said, "Why are you so stupid? Why'd you have to go and ruin a perfectly good game?"

I shrugged and said, "Because I'm an idiot."

Not that I really thought I was an idiot, but he was my big brother and I hated disappointing him.

And that's when he spat on me.

Right in my face. Right on my cheek.

Which is the most disrespectful thing you can do to a person. Worse than even punching him in the nose. Even an eight-year-old knows that.

Neither of us said anything for a few seconds. Then Neal sneered and stormed off into the house.

I don't know if he ever thinks back on that day. Probably not.

I do. More often than I'd like. I'm thinking back on it now as I finish packing up the truck. An alternate reality split off that day. But it wasn't the alternate reality where I let my brother burn. Where I ran away. Because that would've never happened, even if the thought had entered my mind.

The path was about what he did. It was about his choice to spit on me.

Life is a series of paths. To helping people. To hurting people. To leaving certain places and certain people behind. For better or worse.

That's what I'm doing now.

That's what I hope my niece did.

So I'm gonna go looking for her. She's too young to be out there alone, and I'm gonna do whatever it takes to find her. When I do find her, I'm gonna listen to her. Really listen. Try to understand her path. Which is maybe what no one has ever done.

Sunday, 12/24/1989

MORNING

Sorry, Stella. It's been a few days. I needed a breather. A time-out.

No one responded to Dorian Loomis after his . . . I'm not entirely sure what you would call it. I called it recollections, but maybe it's something different. In English class we read *Romeo and Juliet*, and in that play there's something called a soliloquy, where characters yap away for a few minutes even if no one is listening. Maybe Dorian's speech qualified as one of those. Whatever it was, I might have been the only person who heard it.

He drove off shortly after he said it. I was still sitting on the rock, though I'd taken off the walkie-talkie. I waved at him, which caught him off guard. He waved back, but it was an *Am I supposed to know who you are?* sorta wave.

Here's the thing: I probably didn't get it exactly right. I haven't gotten a lot of it exactly right. What am I talking about, Stella? Well, let's just say I've read books before. Nonfiction, they call it, otherwise known as "true stories." But they'll have long passages of dialogue or speeches that weren't recorded or written down on the spot. So they're drawn from memory. Let's face it, our memories aren't perfect. We don't get anything exactly right.

Which is why when I wrote down *The Recollections of Dorian Loomis*, I know I didn't get it exactly right. How could I remember all of that? But I'm a storyteller, and it's a storyteller's job to take on other people's voices. To present as real a picture of things as possible. Every storyteller will write a different story. Ask Dorian's brother, Fiona's dad, about that day in the garage, and he'll tell you something different. Is one a better truth than the other? I don't know.

So are stories alternate realities? Jeez, I'm not sure I want to break my brain with that sort of thinking, but I guess they are in a way. And the stories they tell about Fiona, the things people in this town think might have happened to her, the places she might have ended up? Each is a different reality.

And look at me, I choose to believe the reality that puts her down the hall from me, somewhere inside the brain of my weird brother.

AFTERNOON

The last few days have been a slog. Glen and Mandy still aren't talking to me. Glen, I understand. I did bite the guy, which isn't exactly model girlfriend behavior. Our last day of school before break was Thursday, and today is Sunday. Christmas Eve. So I'm sure he's busy with family stuff, and it's not like there have been a lot of opportunities to run into each other. Still, I thought he might call, and the fact that he hasn't makes me think that maybe we're not boyfriend and girlfriend anymore. I can't tell if that's a relief or not. It doesn't feel like a relief.

Mandy's silence is more puzzling, but of all the puzzles in my life, it's the one that can stay scrambled for a bit. Our friendship goes up and down. Not like a roller coaster, because the downs are fun on a roller coaster. Like a plane in turbulence, I guess. No, that's not right either, because that means the ups are bad too, which they aren't. I know I rag on Mandy a lot, but there are so many great things that she's done for me.

Like last year. I was going through a rough patch. Phaedra Moreau was giving me a lot of crap about my zits, which were in full bloom. She was stopping me in the hall and handing me Oxy pads and saying stuff like, "You know, it's all about the grease in your pores. Wipe off all the sweat and slime and say buh-bye to the constellations on your face. You can thank me later." Or she'd come up to me after every social studies class and just say a number. *Six*, or *eight*, or *four*. No, she wasn't rating my outfits this time. She was counting my zits and telling me how many I had each morning.

More of that typical Phaedra BS. I knew then, like I know now, that I should've ignored her, but Phaedra is impossible to ignore. She's magic. Like a warlock. Like a ponytailed leprechaun. Only her power is the power to annoy the piss out of you. That's not an exaggeration either. She makes me so angry sometimes that my body clenches up and I have to run to the bathroom. I know, Stella. Gross. What do you want? I'm being honest.

And honestly, I don't think I could deal with people like Phaedra without Mandy's support. During the zit incidents, Mandy would sit with me and plot intricate revenge scenarios that always involved Phaedra's running naked from the locker room covered in spiders while her clothes hung from the school flagpole. We never followed through with the plans. The planning was enough.

I'd also sleep over at Mandy's house sometimes. Apparently, I'm a bit of a sleep talker, and Mandy would hear me grumbling about Phaedra at night. So she'd sing to me to calm me down. I'd wake up hearing her off-key voice whisper-crooning a wacky song. Sometimes I wouldn't even let her know I was awake. I'd listen with my eyes closed.

Don't you know you're beautiful?

Don't you know you're a shining star?

Don't you know you light up the room?

In whatever place you are.

Shooby dooby, bow wow wow.

Dooby shooby, wow wow bow!

The lyrics were always different, always composed by Mandy, always silly, sappy, and exactly what a friend is supposed to say to you when you're feeling awful. They helped.

In short, Mandy paid attention to me. Paying attention

matters. That's all I can say about that. So the fact that she isn't paying attention to me now worries me a bit, but, yeah, there are plenty of other things to worry about too.

EVENING

It's Christmas Eve. Which means certain things. In our neighborhood, it means everyone puts out luminaries at the ends of their driveways. Yep, luminaries. As in the plural of luminary. Which is one of Dorian Loomis's CB nicknames. Another coincidence? They're hardly worth mentioning anymore.

As for these luminaries, they're basically white paper bags with jars and candles in them. When you light the candles, the bags glow in the dark. Very beautiful, actually, and my family usually goes for a walk to check them all out. It's always best when it's snowy, and it's been snowy for the last few days. As I write this, there's at least a foot on the ground.

Be jealous, all you surfers out there in sunny California and Hawaii. We don't have to dream about a white Christmas here in Thessaly. Pretty much guaranteed. Sometimes there are white Halloweens and white Easters too.

As far as my parents are concerned, things are getting back on track for Alistair and therefore back on track for our family. At least that's how they're acting. We went out for our Christmas Eve walk after dinner and Mom hummed carols and Dad chucked snowballs at me and Alistair.

Alistair seemed to enjoy it. "I've missed this," he even said, which I guess meant he missed being a normal family.

We all miss that, but I'm not sure we're a normal family again. I'm not sure we ever were one.

Mom was leading the way and she was careful to steer clear of the Loomis and the Dwyer houses, which was ironic, because when we were rounding the corner by Hanlon Park, we ran into them walking down the plowed street.

Mr. Dwyer and Mrs. Dwyer, with Kyle in the middle in his wheelchair.

Snow starting falling as soon as we saw them. If Dad wasn't there, the silence might have lasted for hours, but he's allergic to silence. "Merry Christmas," he said in as close to a jolly voice as he could muster.

Mr. and Mrs. Dwyer nodded in response.

"Right back atcha," Kyle said, and he reached up and pretended to doff his cap, even though he wasn't wearing a cap. Snow was dusting his dark, slicked-back hair, and go on and strike me with lightning, but I'm gonna be honest again. Cleaned up and sitting down, by the light of the moon, the streetlights, and the luminaries, Kyle Dwyer looked cute.

"I'm sorry," Alistair said to no one in particular. To the entire Dwyer family, I suppose.

Kyle shook his head and started to reply. "Buddy, don't even worry about—"

But Alistair cut him off. "No. I'm sorry for everything that you're going through. All of you. I'm doing whatever I can to help get Charlie back."

A sour look swept across Mr. and Mrs. Dwyer's faces, and

Mom leaned over and whispered something about "what Ms. Kern said" into Alistair's ear.

"Maybe Santa will drop him down the chimney for us," Kyle said.

It was so inappropriate that I cracked a bit of a smile, and I could tell Kyle appreciated the reaction, but I was the only one who found this amusing.

"Merry Christmas," Mrs. Dwyer said in a voice barely louder than a whisper.

"And Happy New Year," Mr. Dwyer added.

Then they got the hell out of there, pushing Kyle past us and through the fresh snow, leaving a trail of wheel marks that some gullible little tyke will probably end up mistaking for evidence of Santa's sleigh. I didn't hear anyone in my family heave a sigh of relief as the Dwyers left, but I know there was relief. Sleighloads of it.

"Let's head back," Mom said.

So now we're safe in the cozy Cleary home, away from the assorted awkwardness. Mom and Dad let us open one present before bed. We do this every year. It sort of eases the pressure, like squeezing a little liquid out of a blister, only the blister is our raging desire to rip into packages. Which is nearly un-bearable. Every year. Except this one. I haven't thought much about presents. So when I opened my Christmas Eve one, I was caught off guard.

I figured it was a book, because it was shaped like a book. And it was a book, but not one to read. Another diary.

"We know you've been writing a lot lately," Mom said. "Stories and all that. You should keep at it."

"Seriously," I said, running my hand across the leather cover. "How did you know?"

"We're parents," Dad said. "Doesn't mean we're clueless."

It was only a diary, probably worth about five bucks or so, but the thought really did count in this case. There were so many responses I could have had to that, but my response was to hug them. Both. So tightly.

"Thank you, thank you, thank you," I said. "I'm more than halfway done with the first one."

Alistair smiled at me, and man, did it feel like a big brother smile. Again, I don't know how to explain it, because I've never had a big brother, but I have to think that's how one would smile at me. Tilted head. Raised shoulders. Adoring? Yeah. Kinda *aw shucks, look at you, kid.*

When the hugging and smiling was through, Alistair opened his present. It was a Sega Genesis. I get a book of blank pages and this kid gets an entire video gaming system! The world's *best* video gaming system at that!

"Holy snikeys," I yelped. "Aren't those impossible to find?"

"I know people," Dad said. People who work at Sears or the toy store, I suspect, which aren't exactly celebrities and politicians, but certainly help when Christmas rolls around.

"It's for both of you," Mom told us. "We figured . . . well, Alistair used to play the Nintendo over at . . ."

She didn't want to say "Charlie's house" and she didn't have to. We could all fill in the blank.

"Where are the games?" I asked as I pulled the box from Alistair. I was definitely more excited about it than he was.

"You have to wait until tomorrow for those," Dad said.

"What a gyp, right, bro?" I said as I handed the box back to Alistair.

He smiled again, only this time it seemed forced. "Thank you," was his only response. It was a tired thank-you, a polite one.

"No violent games," Mom said. "That's my one condition."

Hilarious. Mom obviously knows nothing about video games.

NIGHT

I'm settling in for the night. A month ago, I could never have imagined this would be how things would end up. I'm wondering about Glen and Mandy, home in their beds, probably excited for Christmas morning, probably not thinking about me *at all.* I'm wondering about Dorian Loomis, unpacking his truck somewhere, setting out on a mission, probably down the wrong path. I'm wondering about Kyle, who needs his parents to lift him in and out of bed now, who needs his parents to help him onto the toilet. I'm wondering about Debra, the preacher. How much of the original story of Christmas does she really believe? Does she ever doubt her faith? I'm wondering about Jenny Colvin down there in Australia, more than fourteen hours ahead of us Americans. Her presents are probably all unwrapped. That is, if she celebrates Christmas. They celebrate it all over the world, but plenty of people don't. I'm wondering about all these other kids Alistair mentioned on that tape to Jenny. Boaz was one of them. That's a peculiar name. Chip and Dot? Sound like cartoon characters to me.

I'm wondering about Fiona and Charlie, but the problem with wondering about them is my mind goes to the darkest places. I'd rather my mind go somewhere beautiful. So while other kids turn to thoughts of Santa, I'm going to turn my thoughts to Aquavania. I was willing to believe in Santa once. It's not so strange that I can believe in something else.

THE KID WHO BELIEVED

———— ·⟡· ————

THERE WAS ONCE A BOY NAMED IAN WHO WAS BORN WITHOUT the ability to doubt. If you said something to him, anything, he would believe you. "The sky is made of strawberry ice cream," you might tell him, for instance.

"Sounds perfectly reasonable," he would reply. "Thanks for the tip. I'll be sure to carry a waffle cone."

The thing about a kid who believes everything is that he's never disappointed. Because when something turns out to be a lie, he simply believes the next thing you say.

"Sky ain't made of ice cream," someone else might tell him, for instance. "It's made of molecules and blue junk. Sky stuff."

"Hmmm," he would reply. "Blue junk. Sky stuff. Works for me."

Some people called what he had blissful ignorance. It wasn't that, though. Because he knew a lot of stuff. He was hardly ignorant, only sometimes misinformed. Others called it optimism, but it wasn't that either. Because he believed bad stuff too. Gullibility was close to what he had, but gullible people often discover their mistakes and wallow in shame. Ian had no shame. Only pure faith.

It led to some tricky situations. When people had rumors to spread, no matter how vicious or ridiculous, they brought them to Ian. Ian would tell the rumors to everyone he knew, because he liked to share the information he learned. Innocent people were hurt. Lives were thrown off course. Ian became an outcast, someone not to be trusted.

And yet he trusted everyone.

One day, Ian was walking down the street when he ran into the Devil. The Devil didn't introduce himself as the Devil, but he wore a red suit and had hooves for feet. A tail was tucked into his pants leg and flopped and wiggled beneath the fabric like it wanted to escape. Anyone with half a brain would've guessed this man was the Devil, but when Ian said, "Hello, sir, my name is Ian. And who might you be?"

The Devil replied, "My name is . . . Lou. Lou Cipher."

"Nice to meet you, Lou," Ian said. "What are you up to this fine afternoon?"

What the Devil was up to was buying souls. That's what the Devil does. He goes out and offers people whatever they want and then takes their souls in return. But this is not what he told Ian, because the Devil isn't the most straightforward fellow. "I'm out shopping for . . . presents," he said.

"Christmas presents?" Ian asked.

"Sure," the Devil said. "Why not?"

"There's a lovely store around the corner," Ian said. "They sell all sorts of wonderful things."

"I'm terrible with directions," the Devil said. "Do you mind showing me?"

"Not at all," Ian said, and he led the Devil around the corner. Onlookers kept their distance. They didn't want to be associated with either the gullible, rumor-spreading Ian or the soul-shopping Devil.

The store was a lovely store indeed, selling gifts and fine foods, but the Devil stopped before they could go inside. "You know what?" he said. "I left all my money at home."

"Oh," Ian said. "That's a shame. Would you like me to lend you some?"

"You are so kind," the Devil said, "but I can't ask you to do that. If only the store would let me pay in something other than money."

"Maybe they will," Ian said. "What do you have?"

"Wishes," the Devil said.

"Should I go inside and ask them?" Ian said. "They may accept wishes as payment."

Usually, this was the point when most people would become intrigued. *So, this character has wishes to spend,* they would think. *I'd like a few wishes myself. Maybe I'll buy his wishes so that he'll have the cash to buy presents. A wish is worth more than any cash I have. I'll come out the winner in the end.*

But Ian wasn't like most people. When you trust everything and everyone, it's hard to be greedy. The reason most people are greedy is that most people don't trust everything and everyone. They fear that if they don't snatch up all the wealth they can, someone else will beat them to it.

Ian didn't have that fear. He didn't have any fears, actually, because fearing is about doubting. Which should have made the Devil's job easier, but actually had the opposite effect. The Devil expected greed, fear, and doubt. He relied on it.

"I don't think we need to ask if they accept wishes as payment," the Devil said. "In fact, I know they don't because it says so right here."

He pointed to a CASH ONLY sign on the door. The sign wasn't there a moment before, but the Devil is known to be a skilled conjurer and he can certainly conjure a CASH ONLY sign.

"Well, look at that," Ian said. "You are certainly right. Now we're in a bit of a pickle, aren't we?"

"If only someone needed my wishes," the Devil said softly, "and had the cash to pay for them."

Ian pondered this. What use did he have for wishes? Life for him was quite fine, thank you very much. "I bet there are some kids down at the hospital who could use a wish or two," he said. "I'm sure their parents would buy them."

The Devil was astonished. How was Ian not taking the bait? Surely the Devil could move on to someone else and buy another soul, but this soul was unique. He had never met anyone like Ian. The Devil now wanted his soul more than anything else.

"You know what?" the Devil said. "My wishes are about to expire. I don't think I have time to make it to the hospital before they become useless. I need someone nearby or else they'll go to waste. Hmmm . . ."

"Hmmm . . ." Ian replied, and then, "I got it!"

"Yes."

"Use them yourself!"

"Oh, but they don't work that way. I must sell them to someone to make them work. And those Christmas presents I hope to buy? I haven't told you yet, but they are for the children in the hospital. If only someone nearby would give me money for the wishes, I could buy the children presents and that person could use the wishes however he or she likes. To help the children in the hospital, for instance."

"Well, that's quite an intriguing predicament. If only there were someone . . ."

At this point, the Devil was gritting his teeth and scuffing his hooves on the ground. He had never met such a clueless person. His cool demeanor cracked for a moment. He grabbed Ian by the collar and gave him a good shake.

"Your soul, you fool!" he snarled. "I was going to sell you the first wish for all the money in your pocket. Then when you got a taste of how fantastic wishing is, I was going to sell the second wish for your soul! Most people wish to never grow old or to be always rich or to find love. They'll sacrifice their souls for such things."

"Is that so?" Ian said calmly.

"But you're such a simpleton that you didn't even buy the first wish!"

"So I'm a simpleton," Ian said, without even a hint of sarcasm. "News to me, but makes sense."

"Oh, for crying out loud," the Devil said. "I'm the Devil, you moron. I need your stinkin' soul. But I can't have it unless you agree to it. I should just tell you to give me your soul and be done with it. You're probably so stupid that you would agree."

Now, you probably thought this is one of those stories where the hero outwits the Devil, didn't you? Well, there are too many of those stories already, and the Devil wouldn't be the Devil if he were constantly outwitted. So no, this isn't one of those. This is one where the Devil wins.

"Why didn't you just say so?" Ian said. "If you need my soul, then you need my soul. I'm happy to give it to you. Only I don't know where I keep it."

The Devil grinned. "Don't worry about that," he said. "I'm sort of an expert."

Then the Devil transformed into a vapor that swirled in the air and went into Ian's mouth and up and around to where his soul lived. It tickled Ian's nose and he sneezed out both his soul and the Devil.

The Devil transformed back into the hooved man with the red suit, bowed to Ian, and said, "I'd like to say it was a pleasure doing business with you, but . . ."

"But what?" Ian asked.

The Devil shook his head in sympathy and said, "See you in Hell."

"Until then," Ian said, and tipped his hat.

And the Devil was gone.

Flash forward to seventy years later. Ian lived a long and healthy life. He married a kind, caring, and tolerant woman named Sophia. They had kids, who had their own kids, all beautiful and with only average gullibility. Ian had done some dangerous things over the years—jumping off bridges, driving too fast, and so on—because of bad advice and peer pressure, but he had also listened to plenty of good advice. He was lucky that the bad didn't outweigh the good, that most people are honest people if given the chance.

Sophia was an honest woman, and when she sat by his deathbed, she told Ian, "You'll do so well in Heaven. Everyone tells the truth there."

"But I'm not going to Heaven," Ian said. "The Devil owns my soul. It's Hell for me, it seems."

Sophia sighed. And smiled. "Me too," she said.

"Is that so?" Ian said.

"It is," Sophia said. "When I was a young woman, I met the Devil. I was in the hospital and very sick. He sold my parents a wish, a wish that made me better. When I found out how well the wish worked, I wanted another. I sought out the Devil and he sold me a second wish. But this one cost me my soul."

"What was the wish?" Ian asked.

"That I'd fall in love with a man who was honest and

listened and always believed in me," she said as she petted her dear husband's head.

"*Always* believed in you?" Ian asked.

"In this life and the next," Sophia whispered as she embraced her husband.

He whispered back, "I believe you."

And that's when Ian passed away.

Monday, 12/25/1989
((Christmas)

AFTERNOON

I GOT MY BEST NIGHT'S SLEEP IN MONTHS LAST NIGHT. WHICH IS funny. I never used to sleep on the night before Christmas. Yes, yes, you guessed it. Too many reindeer hooves on the rooftop causing a racket.

Did you know that *Satan* is an anagram for *Santa*? Of course you did, because you're smart, Stella. Did you know that an anagram is when two words or phrases share the same letters? Like *ART, RAT,* and *TAR*? Or *SATAN* and *SANTA*?

Of course you did. How could you not?

We started opening presents around nine this morning, which is insanely late for us, and it took Mom, already munching on cookies, to get things going. "Well, I've never seen such a bunch of lazybones in my entire life," she said. "There are presents, people. Presents!"

Mom isn't one of those people who wears Christmas sweaters all year and has stacks of Christmas records, but the holiday gives her a different kind of joy than it gives the rest of us. For me and Alistair, it's always been about presents. For Dad, it's been about watching us get all excited. For Mom, it's about forgetting. She doesn't seem to remember any problems on Christmas. At least she pretends not to. Her bedroom could be on fire and she'd close the door and shrug it off with "Let's have some eggnog."

In case you were wondering, Stella, my haul for the year consists of: two sweaters, five books, four tapes, eye shadow (what!), a pocketbook, Rollerblades, a jacket, four Sega games (to share with Alistair), socks, and at least a pound of Sour Patch Kids.

Alistair got books, tapes, games, and candy too, along with those clothes Mom and I picked out. He seemed to like the clothes just fine. "Snazzy duds," he said, which is something Dad would say.

As we were getting to the end of the pile, there was a badly wrapped present sitting near the back of the tree. The box was small and the paper was orange and black, more Halloweeny than Christmasy.

"Who's that one for?" Mom asked.

Dad practically leapt from his chair and snatched it up. "This," he said as he handed it to me, "is for Keri."

I looked at the tag, which was another piece of wrapping paper, cut small and crooked, folded, and taped on. Written on it was: *FOR KERRIGAN, LOVE GLEN.*

"How'd this get here?" I asked.

"He stopped by a few days ago," Dad said. "Asked if I could slip this under the tree. He's a thoughtful guy, that Glen."

He was. Most of the time. And I wasn't. Most of time. I hadn't gotten him anything. I'd like to say I forgot to get him something, but that isn't true. I considered buying him a videotape of old cartoons—Bugs Bunny, Daffy Duck, and that big rooster, whatever his name is. He'd like something like that, but I didn't follow through. Because I'm lazy. Because I'm mean. Because I hold grudges. Why was I holding a grudge? So he wanted to know about my stories. What's so wrong with that?

I felt even worse when I opened the present. It was one of those necklaces with fake diamonds and a heart pendant. There was a little heart-shaped card inside as well. It read: *YOU HAVE MY HEART, YOU HAVE MY SOUL.*

Now, I'm well aware that those pendants are tacky and I know that notes like that are usually a bunch of bull. But I'm going to be honest, Stella. I got choked up.

"Put it on, put it on," Mom urged, which totally caught me off guard. Not that she hates Glen, but she was never *this* enthusiastic about him.

I slipped it around my neck. Mom's mouth twisted up, but not in a bad way. In a *gimme a moment because I'm feeling a lot of things right now* sorta way, and she put a hand on Dad's shoulder. Dad raised his mug of coffee in a toast, though no one else had a drink so he was toasting alone.

Alistair stared at the pendant for a moment, then he started collecting his presents in a big box. "I have to go to my room," he said. "I have more work to do."

"No," Mom said, in a tone that was probably harsher than I think she intended. "It's Christmas. We spend Christmas together."

There were dark splotches under Alistair's eyes, almost like bruises, but I knew they weren't the result of a night in bed speculating about presents. Something bigger was taking a toll on him. You could see it in the way he moved, like his limbs weighed tons.

"You're right," he told Mom. "I'm sorry. Being home is about being with all of you."

"Don't apologize," Dad said.

"No," Mom said. "He should apologize. I know it's been tough for him, but it's been tough for all of us. *Being home? Where else has he been?*"

It had to be the pendant that set him off, and I suddenly remembered there was something about a guy named Chip wearing a pendant. Something Jenny Colvin was supposed to ask about. Something in Aquavania.

"You're right, Mom," Alistair said. "I get so preoccupied with stuff that is . . . Well, family is the most important thing. Being home means not being trapped in my own mind for a bit. I know it's been difficult talking to me and that's my fault."

"It's not a matter of whose fault it is," Dad said.

"It is," Alistair said. "I feel a bit like a stranger here, but not because of anything you guys have done. I really should be honest with you about what's going on."

Holy crap, I thought. *Is he going to spill the beans on Aqua-vania and Jenny Colvin and the whole thing? How much do our parents already know? How much will they be able to handle?*

"Honesty is all we need," Mom said.

"Fiona is not dead," Alistair said, enunciating every word like English was our second language. "Neither is Charlie."

"Oh, Alistair," Dad said. "Speculating like that may feel like the right thing to do, but we have to be realistic."

Alistair's voice remained firm and clear as he said, "I'm being more realistic than you could ever realize. Everyone is hanging their heads and acting like there's no hope anymore. We all pretend like they're gone for good, and when the subject comes up, we change the subject. But there aren't any bodies. Milo Drake didn't do a thing, and the reason I spend so much time alone, the reason I don't seem to be interested in things around here, is that I'm spending all my time trying to get them back."

"You don't even know what happened to them!" Dad shouted. The outburst was so sudden that I flinched. I've never heard Dad that loud before, but it wasn't an angry loud. It was a befuddled loud.

It didn't spook Alistair at all, and still cool, still calm, he said, "I know what happened, and I know they will be back. Turn on the TV."

Mom crumpled up a piece of wrapping paper and tossed it in the fireplace, where some glowing embers sparked it up and set it aflame. All eyes turned to the fire. "It's Christmas," she said. "No TV."

"Something should be on the news," Alistair said. "Or I should hope it is."

"What news is worth interrupting Christmas?" Mom asked, and she pointed at the fire. "This is your TV today. Your news today involves what time the ham will be served and how many pieces of pie your dad can eat."

"I'm talking about proof," Alistair said. "Another one is back. Like the Littlest Knight. Only alive."

EVENING

They're calling it a Christmas miracle. Sunita Agrawal was an exceptional young woman who, at the age of thirteen, was already studying engineering and psychology at college in her native Nepal. Until one night in 1983, she vanished. Early yesterday, on Christmas Eve, she returned home. She has no memory of where she spent the last six years, but she was wearing the same clothes as the day she disappeared. Many questions remain, but her family and the entire community are very thankful to have her home.

That was the gist of the news report. It was one of those heartwarming little stories they play at the end of newscasts. A Christmas miracle, though? I'm only fourteen and even I know they don't celebrate Christmas in Nepal. Do they? I'm pretty sure they're Buddhists. Or maybe Hindu. In either case, not into decking the halls.

Aside from that obvious blunder, the news report was actually quite creepy. It featured video of the girl, Sunita, hugging her joyous family, paired with a picture of her taken in 1983, shortly before she disappeared.

She looked the same in both images. *Exactly the same.* Not only the same clothes, but the same hair, same face. Like she hadn't aged at all. Maybe it was something with the lighting. Maybe she was actually taller but the camera didn't show it. Maybe in person she looked different, but on TV she resembled a time-traveler from six years before.

Our mouths weren't agape as we watched it, but they might as well have been. "How . . . Did you see something about this last night? Were you up late watching TV?" Mom asked Alistair.

"Sunita Agrawal is a brilliant girl known as the Astronomer," Alistair said. "She was where Charlie and Fiona are now. I brought her back. And I'm working to bring them back."

Dad turned off the TV. "Buddy," he said, "we can't do this anymore. We can't play games like this. You need to talk this through with Dr. Hollister. You need to address what's making you tell these stories."

"You're talking about your friends," Mom added. "These are *real* lives here."

Alistair nodded solemnly and whispered, "Fiona appreciated what you said to her, Mom. When you saw her riding her bike that day a couple months ago and asked her if everything was okay at home. I'm sorry if I doubted you. You were listening. It's not your fault what happened."

Mom pulled back, stunned.

"Wait," Dad said. "What are you talking about?"

"And Charlie," Alistair said, turning to him. "He appreciates that you said you'd buy him a new rabbit after the one he got for his birthday disappeared and his parents decided not to replace her. That was your secret, between you and him, and I know it might not seem like he kept that secret, but he did."

Now it was Dad who recoiled.

I finally decided to say something because it couldn't get any weirder than it already was. "How exactly did she get home? This Sunita girl?"

Alistair pointed to my pendant. "I put her back together."

"Like the candy cane girl?" I asked, forgetting that no one else has actually read my stories.

"I don't know about that," Alistair said. "But I extracted her from her creations. Her figments."

"Keri," Dad said in a tone as serious as I'd ever heard him use. "Can you please go to your room? We need to talk to your brother alone."

And so that's where I am. In my room, wondering what comes next.

NIGHT

I was lying in bed a few minutes ago, with the heart pendant in one hand and the phone in the other. Mom, Dad, and Alistair were still in the family room talking, so I used the opportunity to call Glen.

If I were a character in one of my stories, I'd be the most annoying character in the world. Characters are supposed to have understandable motivations. The reader is supposed to be able to relate to them. But then there's me, the master of questionable decisions.

For instance, I decide to make Glen my boyfriend out of the blue. Why? For attention, I guess. For distraction. Then what happens? He's very nice to me. Isn't that awful? Of course it isn't, but I act like it is. Because I'm not very nice to him. If I'm not a villain, then I'm something pretty damn close.

I can change, though, can't I? Redeem myself? If Glen is a romantic lead in my story, then I can be one too. This thing I set into motion—this weird relationship—I can make it work. That's why I had to call him, even if it meant facing an awkward conversation. I needed to set things straight between us, because my life is twisted enough already.

On the second ring, his mom picked up. "Merry Christmas," she said.

"Merry Christmas," I responded, because that's what you say, even if you're not particularly merry. "Is Glen home?"

"My goodness," she said. "Is this Keri?"

"Yes, ma'am."

"Oh, Keri," she said. "So wonderful to hear your voice. Are your ears burning? Because we were all just talking about you."

"You were?" I said. God. What a terrifying notion. A bunch of strangers sitting around on Christmas discussing *me*.

"We were hoping we'd all get to see more of you this holiday break," she said.

"Oh, I . . ."

"I'm sorry, honey, you didn't call to talk to me," she said. "You want to talk to Glenny, don't you? I'll fetch him."

Out of the frying pan, into the fire. As uncomfortable as I was talking to Glen's mom, talking to him was going to be much, much worse.

"Ho, ho, ho," he said when he picked up, which sounded a bit like an insult, but I don't think he meant it as one.

"I'm sorry," I said. "For biting you. For being . . . bitchy. All the time."

"Oh, no," he said. "You weren't. You aren't. I'm sorry too. That's why—"

"It's beautiful," I said. "I'm wearing it right now."

"Oh. Good," he said. "I thought it might be too . . . shiny?"

"It's a good shiny. A beautiful shiny. I'm sorry, but my present to you is . . . coming."

Once I figure out what to get him, that is. Man, am I a jerk.

"That's okay," he said. "I've got another present for you coming too."

"No, Glen," I said. "You don't have to do that." Because he didn't. Because two presents basically puts more pressure on me to get him something extra special. Or *two* extra special somethings.

"Already done," he said. "It's nothing, really. I didn't do much."

More than me. So much more than me. I had to change the subject. "So how's your Christmas been?" I asked.

"Awesome," he said. "I got a Sega."

"So did we!"

Then we talked about games for a while and then we said Merry Christmas and then we hung up. It sounded exactly like a conversation between a girlfriend and a boyfriend is supposed to sound.

Tuesday, 12/26/1989

MORNING

DR. HOLLISTER, ALISTAIR'S PSYCHIATRIST, MUST BE A BIG FAN of Boxing Day. In other words, she doesn't work on the day after Christmas. Or at least my parents can't afford to pay her to work on the day after Christmas. I heard Mom and Dad discussing it early this morning. Not everything they said, but certain words came up. Words like *disturbing* and *not working* and *new environment* and *coincidence*.

Coincidence!

They must have thought I was still sleeping, but I was in the bathroom, and sometimes you can hear what's going on in their bedroom through the vents above the sink. Not that you want to hear everything that goes on in their bedroom. Gross. Me. Out.

That girl in Nepal. Sunita. The Astronomer, right? That stuff about Charlie and Fiona. I know it freaked my parents out more than they'll admit. Coincidence is one thing but . . .

Magic. How about magic?

I knocked on Alistair's door again.

"Jenny Colvin?" I asked when he opened it. "Is she part of this? She helped bring this girl back?"

He shook his head and ushered me in. "It was me and me alone," he said. "Well, not alone exactly, but . . ."

"So what we did, the call and tape and all that, it was useless?" I asked.

"The opposite," he said. "Talking through things with you made me realize that Jenny and Chip and Dot were never going to cooperate. I am the Boogeyman to them. You don't cooperate with the Boogeyman."

"So what did you do?" I asked as I flopped into the beanbag chair.

"I absorbed them," he said. "I took what they know, what I know, and what the ones who came before me know, and I used that knowledge to extract Sunita from her creations."

"Well that didn't take long," I said.

He chuckled and sighed at the same time. Chighed? Shuckled? "Depends what you consider long," he said. "Like I told you, time is different in Aquavania. It was hard and precise work, involving draining all of Sunita's figments of their memories of her, but keeping their bodies and other memories intact. Thankfully Chip and Dot had already gotten things started. So it only took a few decades."

Decades. As in tens. Of years! I didn't even bother pressing for more information on that. I needed to know one thing. "And what about Fiona?" I asked. "She's next?"

"I'm working on it."

"Mom and Dad are—"

"I know."

"Do you?"

With a voice that threatened to go hoarse at any moment, he said, "They talked to me last night about my options for the future."

"What?" I asked. "Like options other than Dr. Hollister? Something else? Something more?"

"Don't worry," he said. "Things might change around here, but they won't stand in the way of what I'm doing. Their concerns will hardly be an issue once Fiona comes back."

"And when will that be?"

"Soon. Or at least it will seem soon."

"What about Charlie?"

"Charlie is another matter."

The Sega Genesis was sitting, still in the box, on Alistair's dresser, next to that fishbowl. Now, I know Alistair has never been a huge video game buff, but he played them enough at Charlie's to have an appreciation for them. There's no doubt he knew how big a deal it was to have a Genesis. I can't think of a kid who wouldn't have at least plugged the thing in by now. But there it was, unopened.

I would have opened it and plugged it in myself, but it's been in Alistair's room since Christmas morning, and I'm not about to burst in and grab it. Which is yet another reason why I hesitate to disregard anything that he's saying. A boy who ignores video games is a boy with humongous things on his plate. I don't know if you could call him a boy at all.

Remember? Decades. As in tens. Of years!

"I hate that I believe you," I said.

"I love that you do," he replied.

"Tell me something," I said. "When did it start? When did you first become the . . . Riverman?"

I've been rereading some of the stories I've written in the last month and some of the things I've been telling you, Stella. Even though Alistair has said there are different names for, well, this *job* he has in Aquavania, the name that keeps coming up is the Riverman. It seems the best name of the bunch, because who are we kidding? I can't very well refer to my little brother as the Boogeyman. I certainly can't call him the Whisper. That sounds like something out of a cheesy comic book, some supervillain who's always putting a finger to his mouth and shushing you before he does something dastardly.

"I became the Riverman on the night I shot Kyle," Alistair told me.

I nodded. "So you did shoot him?"

"Yes."

"Why?"

"Because I wasn't who I am now," he said. "I was a scared, confused kid."

"And you became who you are now because of what?" I asked. "Because you shot him?"

He considered this, then said, "In a way. But I had the

chance to become the Riverman a long time ago. I've had different holes in my life. Portals have opened for me before. That night was the first time I actually went through one and into Aquavania."

"So the first time you went was barely a month ago?" I asked. "And yet you've been back and been there for . . . decades?"

"Centuries, actually. I inherited a big mess, a place full of monsters, and I had to clean it up. Took some time. But like I said, when I'm there, time stands still here. Since I'm the Riverman, I control when people from the Solid World get to come and go. Like the host of a party or the engineer of a train that people get on and off of, when I'm not there, no one else is either. Then it's Aquavania that's frozen."

"So you could stop going to Aquavania for fifty years and no one else would get to go? And nothing would happen there?"

"Yeah," he said. "Pretty much. Other Rivermen in the past have gone long stretches without calling kids to Aquavania. Everyone approaches the job differently."

I pictured those wispy souls again, only this time, they weren't in cages at my brother's feet. They were in a train, a train my brother was driving. In this image, he had an excessively wrinkly face, like a withered piece of fruit.

"Okay, Methuselah, let's get it all out there," I said. "You claim you absorbed Fiona and Charlie, as in, they're part of . . . your brain? So that's how you know private things about them? Their thoughts and memories, for instance? Like the things you said to Mom and Dad."

"Exactly," he said. "I did the same thing with Chip and Dot. And Jenny. I'm not *them*, really, but I can access their thoughts and feelings if I need to. I prefer not to delve into the personal stuff if I can help it. They deserve their privacy. They deserve some secrets."

"You know, Mom and Dad will just think that Fiona and Charlie told you those things. Before they left."

"I know."

"So what's the point? If you're trying to convince them about Aquavania, then you're doing a craptastic job."

"I'm not trying to convince them," he said. "I'm trying to convince you."

"I'm convinced, I'm convinced," I said. "But why would that matter? How have I been any help? What have I done?"

"You've listened," he said. "You've written things down. You will remember. You will tell the story."

"Why do I need to tell the story?"

"Because one of the things that might happen to me is I might forget it."

"How could you predict what you're going to forget?" I asked. "And how can I remember a story that I only know bits and pieces of?"

"Fair enough," he said. "How much time do you have?"

I looked at my wrist, as if to check my watch. I don't wear

a watch, so I shrugged and replied, "We're not back in school for another week."

"Let me fill in the blanks," he said.

And he did. Boy, did he. But I'll have to tell you about that later, Stella. And why's that?

Because I've got blanks to fill in of my own.

WORLDS COLLIDE

PRINCESS SIGRID (REMEMBER HER?) HAD A SECRET THAT NO potion would ever make her forget. She didn't like being a princess, not even when she was young, at the age when she was supposed to be enamored of pink dresses and tiaras. Back then, long before her trusted advisor, Po (remember him?), had started putting a potion of forgetfulness in her evening stew (remember that?), she wished that she could live somewhere else, in another world where she could lead a simpler life.

Guess what? Someone, or rather something, could grant her this wish. Sigrid knew local legends that told of a horrible beast that lived in a forest bog and was called the Dorgon (remember the Dorgon?). This beast was a master of potions that could do almost anything you could imagine. Sigrid knew her parents would not approve of her visiting the Dorgon, and she knew her trusted advisor, Po, always reported back to her parents. And so, one foggy night, she snuck out of the onyx tower in which she lived, disguised herself as a peasant with a head wrap and a ratty dress, and she made her way alone to the forest.

Almost immediately, she found herself lost in the fog. When a wagon pulled up beside her, she asked for a ride.

"Certainly, miss," said the driver. "What's yer name, if ya don't mind me asking?"

She climbed aboard, over a blanket in the back that covered a lumpy mass that she assumed was a fresh harvest of carrots and squash. "My name is . . . Henrietta," she said.

"Tom," said the man, tipping his hat and grinning widely. "Tom Rondrigal. Where might you be going?"

"You won't take me if I told you," she said.

"Try me."

"The Dorgon."

Rondrigal cackled and took a sip from a bladder that hung from a strap over his shoulder. "Are you plannin' to kill me, then, so that you might toss me into that bog?"

"Um . . . no, sir," she said. "Why would I ever?"

"Because if you're wanting a potion, the Dorgon will be wanting a dead body," Rondrigal said, and he reached over and tapped her nose with a knobby, scabby finger.

"Oh heavens," she replied.

Rondrigal cackled again. "You're no killer, I can tell that much."

"What am I to do?" she said. "I need a potion."

"You could sell me your soul," he told her. "And I'll give you a dead body in return."

Her soul? Could such a thing be for sale? Surely not, she thought. It wasn't a physical object, so how could someone else buy it? And after she was dead and gone, what use was there for it? Sigrid believed in science, not in an afterlife.

"That's all you'd want?" she asked. "My soul?"

"Yes, your everlasting soul," he said. "You do realize this means that if I happen to perish before you, then I'll be taking your soul to the afterlife with me?"

"Fine by me," she said. "It's a deal as long as the dead body you give me is already dead. I do not condone killing."

Another cackle burst from Rondrigal's mouth, and then he peeled the blanket away from the back of his wagon to reveal a pile of dead bodies. Fish, reptiles, mammals . . . people. "Pick one," he said.

Horrified, Sigrid reached in and grabbed the smallest thing she could find. A hummingbird.

A few hours later, Sigrid was collecting her potion. A hummingbird was usually not a large enough payment, but since Sigrid was a young girl, the Dorgon made an exception. "Drink this and you will go to other worlds, you will live different lives," the Dorgon said as it handed her the potion. "It will be a difficult journey, so you best be prepared."

"I am," she said. "I'll do whatever it takes."

"It'll take a lot," the Dorgon said, and it slipped back into the bog without another word.

Sigrid asked Tom Rondrigal to bring her back to the spot

where he'd found her, and he happily obliged. "Enjoy the potion," Rondrigal said as Sigrid hopped down from his ghastly
wagon. "I'll be enjoying your soul."

Then he took off into the fog, cackling as he went.

Back at the onyx tower, Sigrid climbed into bed and took a sip
of the potion. "Another life," she whispered. "Another world."

And . . . *Poof!*

The potion worked. She instantly traveled to another
world, where she found herself lying in a bathtub in a dirty
tiled room. A man hovered over her, cursing and sweating.

"I love you, Candy," he said.

She looked down at her body, which was shades of red and
white and not quite complete. She wasn't really a person yet.
He was building her. Out of candy canes. She tried to move,
but nothing happened. She tried to speak, but her lips were
too sticky.

For weeks, she lived in a body made of candy canes. It was
a strange life. She sat on a couch and looked at people acting
out plays on something called a TV. Meanwhile, the man nibbled on her arms and legs. After a while, so too did his wife.
Luckily, it only hurt a little, but Sigrid worried what would
happen if they ate all of her.

Before long, she was nothing more than a head, and that's
when her lips finally came unstuck. She was able to speak, or
to try to speak.

"Gur Ferm Griggid," she said, though what she was trying

to say was *I am Sigrid*. She hoped that if they understood she was an actual person, then maybe they'd help her out.

She said it over and over again, but it was of no use. They didn't understand. They simply argued with each other as saliva melted away what was left of Sigrid's candy cane face.

When she was nothing but a puddle, something happened. *Poof!*

She was in another world, another body. Not home. A weird place. A place full of tubes. They looked like tentacles from sea creatures, and they were everywhere. An ocean of tubes, a landscape of tubes. Everywhere!

Again, Sigrid couldn't move. Or, to be more specific, she couldn't control her movements. Because this time she was in the body of a newborn baby. This time, when she tried to speak, only cries came out of her mouth.

She flailed and wailed upon the slippery surface of the tubes until a young girl spotted her. "Oh, you poor thing," the girl said. "Who are you?"

Sigrid tried to say *I am Sigrid*, but only cries emerged.

"Oh, you poor thing," the girl said again. "My name is Harriet, and while I'd love to take you with me, you'll be safer back in civilization." Then Harriet ripped open one of the tubes and slipped the baby Sigrid inside.

"Good luck and Godspeed," Harriet said.

Air blew through the tube and *whoosh*, Sigrid was transported all the way to a bedroom. She landed on a bed.

In the corner of the room, a girl was talking into the ends of other tubes. "Hello," she kept saying. "It's Georgie. Talk to me, people. Talk to me."

She didn't even notice the baby on her bed. Sigrid cried, but Georgie didn't turn around. She was too occupied with talking into the tubes. After a while, Sigrid felt thirsty. And then tired. And then . . .

Poof!

She entered another world, another life. Now she was a creature with six knuckles on her hands and five eyeballs, and she lived on another planet. In other words, she was an alien. Only this wasn't to be a brief visit. For many years she lived here, so long that she eventually accepted it as her permanent home.

When it rained on her planet, which was pretty much every day, it caused all the aliens, including Sigrid, to be angry. So angry, in fact, that they eventually decided to invade another planet, which was the source of all their anger. Clouds from the other planet had invaded their atmosphere and had rained negativity all over them.

Sigrid joined the mission to the other planet, which was treacherous indeed. They sent a fleet of spacecrafts, but only one made it the entire way. Luckily, it was the most important one. It was the one piloted by Sigrid and it contained a bomb that could destroy an entire solar system.

Sigrid landed her spacecraft in an overgrown field next to

a house. Before they detonated the bomb, she and her copilot went inside the house to confirm that they had the right planet. They weren't sure what they were looking for, but in a bedroom, in a drawer, Sigrid found a strange object. Shiny. Metal. With a handle and a round tip. It appeared to be a weapon.

And on the bed, in the room, Sigrid discovered a skeleton.

Sigrid had lived for years in that alien body, with that alien mind and that alien language. So long, in fact, that she had almost forgotten who she really was. But not entirely.

For in that skeleton, she recognized the form of a human. Sigrid was a human. Deep down. Back in her original body, at least. And in that moment, in her alien body, she realized what was about to happen. She had come to her home planet, full of humans, and she had come to destroy it.

Instinctually, she lifted the weapon in her hand and pointed it at her copilot.

Bam!

Her copilot fell to the ground.

She screamed in triumph, "I am Sigrid!" but it must have sounded like nonsense to any human because she screamed it in her alien language.

Then she turned the weapon on herself and . . .

Poof!

She was now in the body of a joke. How can a joke have a body, you ask? All good jokes have a soul, and every soul needs a body in which to live, do they not?

They don't? Okay, can you suspend disbelief for a moment, at least? Thanks.

So yes, Sigrid was in the body of a joke. A dark and disturbing joke, in case you hadn't already guessed. It was a shameful existence, even though she was actually quite funny. She set about to change herself and embarked on a regimen of self-improvement.

It appeared to work, for all of a sudden, one random day, she became a respectable joke, a good old-fashioned knock-knock joke. She thought it was because of all the toil and sweat she had put into becoming respectable. But it was something else entirely. It was because of Opposite Day.

Stupid Opposite Day!

It made her respectable, but it stole her punch line. Without a punch line, she was nothing. She climbed onto the roof of a tavern and tried to shout *I am Sigrid* into the wind, but the words made no sense because she made no sense.

So she jumped off.

Poof!

She was a bird. A baby bird. In a nest in a tree. Waiting for her mother. She strained her neck to look out over the edge of the nest, and she fell.

She landed on the pavement right in front of a jogger. A woman named Justine Barlow.

Poof!

* * *

She was another baby bird. In another nest in another tree. Also waiting. Also straining. Also falling. Landing right in front of a jogger. You guessed it. Justine Barlow again.

Poof!

Poof!

Poof!

On and on this went. Sigrid kept on changing into baby birds and kept on ending up at the feet of this Justine Barlow person. Why? She didn't have a clue. She only knew that this was definitely not a preferable existence to life in the onyx tower.

I am Sigrid, I am Sigrid, I am Sigrid, she kept trying to say, but she couldn't because she kept on ending up in the body of baby birds. And baby birds can't talk. Especially dead ones. She seemed doomed to life caught in a perpetual loop.

Until . . .

After thousands of *poofs* and thousands of baby birds, she emerged in the body of a hummingbird, buried beneath a pile of avian corpses.

Things had come full circle, in a weird way.

Sigrid the hummingbird dug herself out of the pile and hovered in front of Justine Barlow's face. She recognized the pain and confusion in Justine's eyes.

"What does it all mean?" Justine asked.

It was a question Sigrid had been asking herself constantly. Finally, she had the answer. Sigrid realized that the only place she belonged was home, in the onyx tower. The fortune she had in life was a fortune she needed to share. That's what it all meant. Be good. Be kind. Do whatever you can to help people. Be the best you that you can be.

Simple. Obvious. But true.

She hovered in front of Justine, telling herself, *I am Sigrid, I am Sigrid, I am Sigrid* . . .

Until she ran out of energy and she crashed to the ground. *Poof!*

This time she was finally home. She was Princess Sigrid again. The dose had only been a drop, but she had lived numerous lives that stretched out over hundreds of years. Back home in the onyx tower, not a second had passed since she had tried the Dorgon's potion.

It had been a harrowing and horrible experience, one she wasn't sure she wanted to repeat. So she hid the potion away in a hollowed-out book in her room and she vowed to make the best of her first life, her real life, her *solid* life. She didn't need to be someone else. She needed to use her power to make the world a better place.

From that moment on, she was kind and she was generous. Her resolution was to help people as much as she could.

Until one day, her parents decided she was being too kind and too generous and, without realizing it, they set into action a course of events that would rob their daughter of both her memory and her soul.

Wednesday, 12/27/1989

---◆---

MORNING

I GAVE YOU "WORLDS COLLIDE" BECAUSE I CAN'T GIVE YOU Alistair's story yet, Stella. I hope you understand. Back when Alistair told me the story of Una and Banar, I knew it was just the tip of the Aquavania iceberg, but I had no idea how small a tip it was. I'd need to write an entire book to tell you what he told me last night. He did more than fill in the blanks. It was . . . epic.

Highlights? Will that be good enough for now, Stella?

We'll call Alistair's story *The Whisper*, and all I can say is that when he first went to Aquavania, he traveled among many worlds. From a land full of cavemen to an underground lair where an armor-clad boy named Hadrian commanded a battalion of tentacles. From a realm of ice, polar bears, and a penguin, to a space station full of monsters. From a school full of idiots, to . . . well, on and on and on, until he came to Thessaly. Only it wasn't the real Thessaly. It was a twisted version of our home, and he lived there for many years.

Charlie was in Aquavania. Fiona had been there too, once upon a time, until Charlie stuck a pen in her ear, sucked her soul into the pen, and poured her soul over his head like ink. Then Alistair did the same thing to Charlie. That's how he became the Riverman. Or, as he is sometimes known, the Whisper.

Um. Whoa?

Of course, Alistair filling in the blanks of his story inspired me to fill in the blanks of my stories. Which is why I gave you "Worlds Collide" instead. I wrote it in a whirlwind late last night, channeling that Aquavania magic, using Alistair's experiences to inspire Sigrid's. Like Alistair, Sigrid would travel from world to world. Like Alistair, she would confront skewed versions of reality. Like Alistair, she would struggle to know who she was. And like Alistair, she'd return home at the end as a new version of herself.

While I wrote, I thought about all the wild things Alistair said he saw in Aquavania and I realized that the coincidences between his journey and my various stories are so many that I can't even begin to mention them all.

Birds. Tubes. Towers. Clouds. Candy. Monsters. Schools. Stars. Oceans. And on and on and on.

Alistair says I get my inspiration from Aquavania, but it's almost as if the opposite has happened, as if Alistair has gotten his inspiration from me. If I didn't know any better, I'd think he'd been reading my . . .

Son. Of. A. Cricket!

Thursday, 12/28/1989

AFTERNOON

Mandy met me at Hanlon Park this morning because I asked her to, because it felt like she was maybe the only person that I could talk to. You're great and all, Stella, but sometimes a girl needs friends who aren't made of wood pulp.

Next to the snowbanks by the basketball courts, we hugged for the first time in what felt like forever and I handed her a plastic bag with her brothers' walkie-talkies in it.

"Merry Christmas," I said.

"Keep 'em," she said. "Chad and Dan don't even know they're gone."

She tried to hand them back, but I scuttled over the icy snow to the swings, sat down on one, and rocked back and forth a bit. "I don't need them anymore," I told her. "Dorian Loomis left. And it's my brother who I should really be afraid of."

"What'd he do?" she asked, unable to hide her glee. Then she put the bag down and hopped on the swing next to me.

"I have a diary," I said. "I write about life and I write stories in it sometimes. It's private. I think he's been secretly reading it."

Mandy leaned her head against the swing chain and her face went hangdog. "I'm sorry to hear that," she said. "That sounds positively jerkish of him. But maybe he has a good reason."

"I can't think of one," I said. "He tells me these outrageous things. He gives me hope that Fiona and Charlie are still out there. He's picked me as a sucker because he knows I want to believe in magic."

"I'm not sure I get what you're saying," Mandy replied. "But consider yourself lucky. It must be nice to have the sort of mind that still believes in magic."

"Magic doesn't solve anything," I said. "Because eventually, you see the strings. At least if you're even a half-smart person."

"You are a *whole* smart person, Keri Bear," she said. "The smartest I know."

"Not recently," I said. "I saw all these coincidences in my life and I began to think they were magic. But coincidences are usually the sign of something else. Tricks. Alistair was tricking me."

"How would he do that?"

"With stories," I said. "Such as, Alistair told me about a monster called the Mandrake shortly after I'd written a story about a monster named the Dorgon. He told me about a brother who absorbs his sister right after I wrote a story about a family of clouds that basically do the same thing. He told me this long adventure that is jam-packed with ideas and images that are drawn *directly* from my stories. And he does this to convince me that I'm being magically inspired, that the coincidences mean something, when all they really mean is that he's been reading my diary and telling weird, twisted versions of my stories back to me. Jesus, he even has some girl, who may or may not be in Australia, conspiring with him."

"International conspiracies?" Mandy said. "Sounds a bit elaborate, and I'm still not sure I get it. But you said he's trying to give you hope, right? At least hope is a good thing."

"Not false hope," I said. "Fiona and Charlie are dead. We all know this. They are dead. Dead. Dead. Their souls, gone. All of who they are and who they will ever be . . . G. O. N. E."

As the tears welled up in my eyes, Mandy got up and put her hands on my shoulders. She said, "We don't know that. No one knows that."

"Someone does know that," I said as I stood up and fell into her. "And I'm scared that it's my brother. He's been distracting me for some reason. Why have I been so willing to believe him?"

"Because you love him," Mandy said, hugging me tighter than she'd ever hugged me but still not nearly tight enough.

"Making Jenny Colvin mention Sigrid was bad enough," I said. "But you know what's been bothering me the most? The waterfall and the name 'Banar.' He knew about those before I wrote them, right? I haven't even written them yet and he knows about them, right?"

Mandy released the hug, but still kept her hands on my shoulders. "I'm with you, baby, even if I really don't have a clue what you're talking about."

"But you do," I said. "Because it's you that helped me figure that one out. I'm a sleep talker. I talk in my sleep."

"That I can confirm," Mandy said. "You yammer away all night."

"And Alistair is often up all night," I said. "So he probably heard me talking about the waterfall, heard me mumbling about Banar. Because I dream this stuff, you know? And then he used what he heard to rope me in. But why? That's what's really bugging me now. What exactly is he trying to accomplish?"

"All I know is this," Mandy said. "Just because he read about your knock-knock joke and your tubes and all that, it doesn't mean he's out to get you. He's probably a fan and—"

"Wait a sec," I said, gently pushing her hands off my shoulders. "How do you know about the knock-knock joke? How do you know about the tubes? I didn't say anything about those."

"Um, sure you did." Mandy took a step back. Her arms were straight and her fists were tight at her sides.

"No. I didn't. I mentioned the Dorgon. I mentioned clouds. That was it."

Mandy took another step back and slid on the icy snow. Her arms flew out and spun in the air. She fell, but only to her knees. Looking up at me, she said, "Your brother is probably a fan. Like I'm a fan. Like Glen is a fan."

"How are you fans?" I asked. "What are you talking about? Wait! The only way you could be fans is if you read my diary."

"If you didn't want Glen to see it, you shouldn't have given him your locker combination," Mandy said, still on her knees. "It was supposed to be a surprise. A Christmas present. He borrowed the diary. I just did the Xeroxing. You'll understand soon enough."

"I . . . won't. I . . . can't."

But I did. Suddenly I understood something about Mandy. I turned so I didn't have to look at her, and my eyes fell on the baby swing that, two years before, weighed down with backpacks, had smashed into and bloodied my nose. And I made a silent apology. To science.

Sorry for doubting you, science. You were right all along. Pendulums always do end up where they started. Unless some extra force is added to them. Unless . . .

"You pushed it," I said.

"What?" Mandy asked.

I stepped over and grabbed that baby swing like I was grabbing a handful of hair. And I threw it straight at Mandy's face.

She flinched and fell back on the snow, but the swing didn't even come close to hitting her. It swung up and around the top bar of the swing set, then crashed down, now a few links shorter. Ironically, I was the one it almost hit, but I dodged it just in time.

"What the hell?" Mandy yelled.

"What the hell?" is right! What the hell was she trying to

do to me? What the hell was everyone trying to do to me? I didn't answer. I ran. Out past the basketball courts, my feet sliding on the snow. When I hit the pavement, I sped up.

"You don't deserve him!" Mandy yelled at me. "You don't deserve me!"

I kept running. Faster. Faster.

She kept yelling. Louder. Louder.

"Why does everything always have to be about you, Keri? Go on and write all the mean things you want about me, instead of doing something nice for me for a change!"

The walls of plowed snow that lined the road made it feel like a maze, a tunnel, a hole I was digging myself deeper into. Alone. Alone.

The cold air squeezed me as I ran.

THE PHOSPHORESCENT WOMBAT, PART IV

ASIDE FROM ITS STRANGE BODY-LIKE SHAPE, THE HOLE AT THE floor of the ocean was perfectly hole-like, and Luna let herself sink into it with the fifteen-mile-long tether, her only link to the world above, unspooling behind her.

Down. Down. Down. Two more miles. Three more miles. Down a long passageway toward the center of the Earth. Luna illuminated the walls and she could see they were smooth. No markings. Not even scratches.

When she finally reached the bottom, seven miles below the Mariana Trench, she found what maybe, perhaps, possibly created the hole. It was certainly not what she expected to find, and she knew right away that she had to report the strange discovery to the scientists.

She spent a total of five minutes at the bottom. Then she yanked a cord on her harness that sent a signal through the tether that told the scientists to pull her to the surface. Amazingly, the tether hadn't broken and the scientists received the message. A machine cranked the tether and brought Luna up through the briny deep.

"What was at the bottom?" chief scientist Gladys Gershwin asked when Luna was safe in her chamber again.

"A message," Luna told them using her laser.

"From who?"

"A bush baby," Luna told them, because that was the truth. A little bush baby was sitting at the bottom of the hole, its butt wedged in a crack. And when Luna got close enough to touch the bush baby, it whispered a message into her ear. Using her laser, she wrote the message phonetically on the board for the scientists.

The scientists couldn't make heads or tails of it at first. Neither could Luna. It was a series of sounds and, well, gobbledygook. So they sent Luna down on more missions into the hole. For explanations.

The additional missions yielded only one new thing: a personal message from the bush baby. The second time Luna touched him, he said, "My name is Banar. I am an entirely suitable bush baby. I came from where you came from."

Luna couldn't figure out how to ask Banar where that place was, and Banar didn't bother to tell her.

"Our destiny is the same," he went on. "To be alone. This will help you be alone."

Then Banar repeated that original, indecipherable message.

Luna didn't tell the scientists what Banar had said about his name, about being from the same place, about being alone.

It felt like it was a message that was meant exclusively for her, and she deserved at least one thing for herself. Besides, Banar never mentioned those things again. Each time Luna visited him after that, he simply repeated that indecipherable message. Over and over again. It seemed an impossible code to crack.

Until one day, they cracked it. It was DeeDee who did most of the work, actually. Her encounter with Luna had left her blind, but her mind was as sharp as ever. Instead of sending her home, chief scientist Gladys Gershwin gave DeeDee a small room and time to think. For months, she pondered the message and spoke it out loud to herself. She rearranged the sounds in the dark corners of her mind. Since she was trained as a geneticist, she knew a lot about DNA, and there were patterns in the message that reminded her of genetic code. But it was slightly different.

After months of going over it with no luck, she tried to rethink her approach. This message was found on the bottom of the ocean. Why was it there? Why did it take such efforts to find it? Maybe because it was related to water? Maybe because only people with the technology to find it would know what to do with it?

Those ideas were the key. She called in chemists and physicists, and they all pooled their expertise. Until they finally figured it out.

It was a formula. It was a recipe for how to draw energy from water. Only this wasn't like drawing energy from oil or coal or nuclear reactors. The formula could help them create more power than all the power plants in the world did. From a single drop. That's right. A single *drop* of water. If Luna was the ultimate source of light, then this formula was the ultimate source of power.

"I have an idea," Sandra Sussman, a cosmologist on the rig, said. "With Luna getting brighter every day, I'm not sure we can deal with her anymore. Why not send her into space? Using a tank of water, we could fuel a spacecraft for millennia. She could report back what she observes. She might find other messages out there. Other things that will benefit the Earth immensely."

Even DeeDee, who loved Luna dearly, had to agree that this was a decent plan. It meant losing Luna, but keeping her wasn't a viable option. Life on Earth was no life for this particular wombat. They had samples of Luna's hair and blood, so they could always study those. Her actual presence, however, would only cause others pain. She was indeed destined to be alone.

So they built a spacecraft, equipped with state-of-the-art communications devices, and on a sunny October morning a year later, they prepared to launch Luna into space. Her vocabulary had grown to the point that she could converse and read at a high school level. (That's a good high school, not one of those crappy ones where kids come to class with switchblades.) She no longer needed a laser to communicate either. She could type on a keyboard with her little paws.

"I'll miss you," DeeDee told her through a speaker in the spacecraft.

"I am still so sorry for what happened to you," Luna wrote, using her keyboard.

"Don't be," DeeDee said. "It was not your fault."

"I love you," Luna said. "I will always love you all."

She did love them all. They had found a purpose for her. They had given her something noble to do that would benefit the entire world.

The spacecraft was about the size of a VW bug, and for Luna, it brought back memories of Rosie and how she used to drive them back and forth from the studio. Rosie was likely dead by now. Everyone Luna knew before the oil rig was likely dead. Which meant, besides DeeDee, who was she leaving behind? No one.

The spacecraft took off at 10:23 a.m., and it looked like a comet shooting into the sky, a glowing orb with a trail of smoke. At the speed it would travel, Luna would be passing the moon in a day. She would pass Mars in about four months. She would reach Jupiter in four years. And she would pass Pluto and the edge of the solar system in thirty years.

Communications traveled at the speed of light. So Luna could have conversations with the scientists and only have to wait seconds for a response. At first.

DeeDee was her main contact, and the two forged an even greater friendship through their correspondence. DeeDee talked into a microphone, which then broadcast on a speaker in Luna's spacecraft, and Luna typed her responses on her keyboard, which were translated into an electronic voice that DeeDee could hear.

When she passed Mars, Luna wrote, "It's more orange than red and reminds me of the cheese balls I used to eat with Hamish."

"Are you hungry, dear?" DeeDee asked.

"I'll be okay," Luna wrote. "I learned long ago that I don't need food to survive."

"I wish we could send you a million cheese balls to eat anyway," DeeDee said. "I wish everyone else in the world knew you were out there and how brave you are. But we have to keep it a secret. We don't need the Russians to know what we're up to."

"I have your voice," Luna said. "That's enough."

DeeDee told Luna about events on Earth, about how the formula was being harnessed into wonderful things—like energy grids that promised to build up third-world societies. Also into awful things—like weapons that threatened to wipe out first-world societies.

Luna told DeeDee about the beautiful sights of outer space, the asteroids and meteors, and DeeDee reported it all back to the other scientists, all the while knowing that Luna was doing it for her benefit, to give her the mental image of places and things she could never possibly see.

As a way to repay the favor, DeeDee talked to Luna about emotions. Luna was getting more intelligent by the second, but she was also *feeling* a heck of a lot more. She was still a wombat, but she was experiencing all the emotions that any intelligent being would experience. Most of all, fear. But she didn't fear death. She feared losing DeeDee's voice. It was inevitable, of course. The distance would become too far, or the spacecraft would get ripped apart, severing their connection. And even if those things didn't happen, DeeDee would eventually die. They spoke about these things sometimes until they realized that speaking about them wouldn't make them any less true.

Over the first few years, they spoke multiple times a day. But response times stretched from seconds to minutes to hours. The speed of light was fast, but not fast enough. And DeeDee could only dedicate so much time to talking to Luna. She had to sleep, and eat, and wait for Luna's responses.

To keep Luna company and feed her mind, DeeDee started broadcasting books on tape to her. Luna was becoming such a good absorber of information that she asked for multiple books to be broadcast at the same time, at high speeds. After a while, she didn't even need to hear the words.

"I learned Morse code once," Luna told DeeDee. "Can you send the books in Morse code?"

DeeDee spoke to some engineers, who designed a computer that could send the text of books in Morse code. It transmitted so fast that it would've sounded like static in the speaker of the spacecraft, but Luna could understand it perfectly. Her intelligence was reaching unprecedented levels. It was doubling by the day. She devoured thousands and thousands of books.

When she reached Jupiter, she described its brilliant swirling colors and its many strange moons, but she also made observations that furthered science. She understood astronomy and cosmology now, having absorbed countless books on the subject, and so the scientists barely needed to analyze the data she sent back. She did all the analysis for them.

Soon, all the scientists wanted to talk to Luna, and Dee-Dee was left with only a few minutes here or there to correspond with her dear friend.

"Things are getting dangerous in the world," DeeDee told Luna one day when Luna was passing Saturn. "More people are arriving on the rig every day. Powerful people. People who want to use you and the formula for purposes I certainly don't approve of."

Luna responded with Morse code. It sounded like static, so the other scientists who reviewed the tape wouldn't notice it, but DeeDee understood what it was. She made a tape of it, then brought it back to her cabin to slow it down and translate.

"You told me once that you have a pair of walkie-talkies," Luna's message said. "Turn one of them on tonight and tune it to 345 Khz."

DeeDee followed Luna's instruction, and that night when she tuned the walkie-talkie to that frequency, she heard an electronic voice.

"This is Luna," it said. "I have modified the spacecraft so that I can speak to you directly, without anyone else listening in. I too am concerned about what's going on. First things first: we need to get you off that rig. So someone will be coming to get you. They will relay false information about your father. Do not worry about what they tell you, but look worried. You'll be out of there before you know it. Pack the walkie-talkies and we'll chat again soon."

"Whatever you say, my dear," DeeDee responded, because at this point, Luna was not only her most intelligent friend, but also her most trusted one.

Minutes later, there was a knock on DeeDee's door. It was chief scientist Gladys Gershwin. "DeeDee, I'm so sorry," she said as she stepped into the room.

"What is it?" DeeDee asked.

"A message just arrived," Gladys said. "It's about your father. He's had a heart attack."

DeeDee's father was a former astronaut and national hero. Everyone on the rig adored him. Knowing his life was in jeopardy was a serious matter indeed.

"Oh dear," DeeDee said. "Is he okay?" She said it in a worried tone, which wasn't really faking, because she was worried. She had no idea what sort of plan Luna had cooked up.

"That's not clear," Gladys said. "A helicopter is arriving in thirty minutes and will take you to the hospital to be with him."

The helicopter arrived twenty-six minutes later, and DeeDee was shuffled aboard by two women whose voices sounded vaguely familiar. As soon as they were airborne, DeeDee heard the voice of the pilot, who sounded *very* familiar.

"Dad?" DeeDee said.

"We received some intel from your friend Luna," he said. "We're here to help."

"Do you know who Luna is?"

"Well, I know she needs computer assistance to speak, but I also know she understands the space program better than anyone I've ever met."

"That's true," DeeDee said.

"She thinks we need to get you somewhere safe. And I agree."

From an isolated cabin deep in the Adirondacks, DeeDee spoke to Luna. Luna sent her a message through the walkie-talkie that described how to build a complicated communications device out of materials she could find at the hardware store. No one else could intercept these communications either. They would be exclusively between Luna and DeeDee.

DeeDee's blindness made things difficult, but she managed. Her father had food and other items secretly delivered to the cabin every week, and DeeDee reported Luna's findings to her father, the only other soul she could trust.

"The scientists aren't in charge of the rig anymore," Luna told DeeDee one afternoon as she traveled toward Uranus. "Bad things are beginning to happen."

"How bad?" DeeDee asked.

"Bad enough that I'm going to send you plans to build your own spacecraft," Luna said.

Which she did. Immediately. But it was too late. By the time the message arrived, a few hours later, Earth had exploded. Everything and everyone on Earth was dead.

TO BE CONTINUED . . .

Friday, 12/29/1989

EARLY MORNING

WHEN YOUR BEST FRIEND AND YOUR BOYFRIEND HAVE BE-trayed you. When they've read your most private thoughts and . . .

When your parents are at their wits' end but don't have a clue what's going on with either of their children, with anything it seems, and . . .

When the snow is falling again and you know that it's beautiful but beauty can smother and you've had just about enough beauty, thank you very much, and you've had about enough of your brother, thank you very much, and you don't know what you can believe, besides the science and the science is promising you that you can't trust anyone, then you only have one option: all you can do is . . .

Explode.

I can't sleep. I'm angry in ways I didn't think were possible. In ways that hurt my insides. In ways that make my body shiver and my teeth throb. There are nerves in your teeth, Stella. In the core. Hot and throbby and Jesus, it gives me the heebie-jeebies just to think about them.

I've been pacing around my room, plotting my revenge. Okay, not my revenge, but my . . . my . . . my . . . soliloquy? No. My proclamation. The things I'm going to say, I mean *scream*, at Glen and Mandy. And at Alistair. Mostly at Alistair.

His life has become my life. Every one of his choices has guided me to this miserable point. It's like I'm using one of those origami fortune-tellers, but instead of telling me who I'll marry someday, it's telling me my future is based entirely on my little brother. Yes, the 1980s are almost over, and if the 1990s are going to be the decade of little turd brothers, then count me out. Because I don't think I can handle it anymore.

It's three a.m. and I'm about to leave my room. My fingers are twitching like they're tapping out Morse code. The message? *SOS, SOS,* of course.

I can't ever remember being so nervous about anything. If you'd told me a few months ago that talking to my little brother would make me so anxious, I'd have laughed in your face, made reference to Opposite Day, and then put Alistair in a headlock and started giving him noogies.

A lot can change in a few months and a lot did, and now I don't know what sort of person I'll be confronting. One thing is for sure: I'm not knocking. When you knock, you've already lost an argument. You've announced to the person that you're willing to let them set the terms, to invite you in or not. So, my first move in this confrontation is to bust down Alistair's door.

Okay, not bust down, exactly, even though kicking it in like a cop would be a cool thing to do. Totally unnecessary, however. You see, there are no locks on the bedrooms here in Casa de Cleary, a sad fact that I've protested for years.

"What if there were a fire?" Dad always says. "We couldn't get in and help you fast enough."

"I'll jump out the window," I always respond.

"We're not gambling our fates on windows that sometimes stick," he counters. "Don't worry. We'll respect your privacy."

For the most part, they have. Mom has slipped in a couple of times when I've overslept and was going to be late for school, but she's always apologized later. You see, there's a *Frantic* button that gets pushed on moms when you're late for school, and it causes them to do things like pour Cheerios into your lunch bag and apple juice in your cereal bowl. You can't really blame them for acting irrationally. I mean, God forbid your child misses homeroom or, gasp, ten minutes of first period Earth Science.

I guess the *Frantic* button has been pushed on me too. Only I'm not going to be apologizing for my intrusion. My fingers are still twitching as I rehearse the first few lines of my tirade, saying them into a pillow and getting louder with each word.

For two days, I've been trying to figure out why you lied and stole from me, but it seems that everyone lies and steals

from me now, so it means you're just like everyone else. A.
BIG. FAT. LOSER.

I've gone over it three times. I'm ready.

A LITTLE LATER IN THE MORNING

I don't have time to write, only to say that I plowed through
that door and started to holler, "For two days—" But then I
clamped my mouth shut. Because there she was, wrapped in
a blanket, sunken into the beanbag chair.

Fiona Loomis.

THE MEMORY OF FIONA LOOMIS

My head hurts. Behind my eyes, deep inside. I can hardly think. I can hardly breathe.

We were out in the road, you and I. Isn't that right? And I kissed you, didn't I? Or did you kiss me? And the air was spinning. Was there snow? Yes, there was. The snow was spinning, and I was drawing pictures in the snow on the road. You were telling me to get away from my uncle. I was telling you to get away from Charlie.

Now you're telling me it's almost eight weeks later?

This doesn't make any sense. This . . . It's like you're saying I'm in Thessaly, but this isn't really Thessaly. This is some weird other version of it. Some version where I don't belong. But you are here and Keri is here and this sure looks like your room.

Where's the poster with the bikini babe? Prudence, right? That's what we call her. Did you take it down? I hope you did. I'm glad, because it was a stupid poster. It didn't belong here.

I belong here, don't I? I'm supposed to be here, aren't I?

I need water. Do you have water?

God, it's like this isn't anything like a dream, but this isn't anything like the real world. What did . . . ? Someone did something to me. To my memories. To be . . . To be . . . To be . . .

I saw a flamingo. Or was it a heron? A big bird. A strange beak. I remember that. And a hammock. Ice cream. Lots of ice cream.

And eyes. Big eyes staring at me.

It's so cold here. Is it always this cold?

Keri, I feel like I haven't seen you in forever. But you look younger. Both of you. Is it that I got older? I know you showed me the newspaper with the date and all that, but how could the year almost be over? There hasn't been Thanksgiving. There hasn't been Christmas. There hasn't . . .

Why are you looking at me like that? Are you sad? Are you . . . I'm not sure I want to do this anymore. Turn off the tape.

Now. Now!

Saturday, 12/30/1989

AFTERNOON

Insanity. For almost two straight days.

I've hardly eaten, I've hardly slept, I've hardly had a chance to even pick you up, Stella, let alone comment on the aforementioned insanity.

To see Fiona's face was so horribly wonderful. Wonderful for obvious reasons. Where the horrible part comes in is when I began to imagine what she was going through. Her brain was obviously scrambled. Beyond scrambled. Pulverized.

I put her back together.

That's what Alistair said about Sunita Agrawal, the girl from Nepal, the Astronomer. And that's what it felt like with Fiona. She'd seemed . . . *put back together*. But not put back together particularly well. Watching her slumped in the bean-bag, I couldn't help but think of the Candy Cane Girl.

At some point, I lost track of the exact course of events, but I know that as soon as I opened that door, Alistair pulled out his old Fisher Price tape recorder and we made a tape of what Fiona said. And as soon as the tape stopped, I went upstairs and woke my parents. Then there were cops. Then there were Loomises. First Fiona's mom, red-eyed, bone-white, and shell-shocked. Then her dad, crying, which I never expected to see from that guy. He collapsed on a chair in our living room and buried his splotchy face in his arm. Everyone was basically a mess. You can't for a single second blame them for that.

Word spread fast, maybe through Mrs. Carmine, who I'm convinced has secret tunnels that lead from house to house and hides in every closet in the neighborhood to collect gossip. Helicopters were the roosters for the morning, hovering overhead and waking everyone at dawn. The news trucks that we knew so well were back too, parked at their favorite spots along the roadsides and in vacant lots.

Alistair had the tape for a full two hours, long enough for me to listen to it again and jot it down, but when the police questioned us, we were forced to hand it over.

"Where again did you find her?" they asked Alistair multiple times.

"Like I told you," he said. "She showed up at my window and I helped her climb in. She was cold, so I gave her a blanket. We knew that it was important to have evidence of what she said, so Keri and I started the tape recorder and let her talk."

"And she didn't say anything else?" they asked.

Alistair shook his head and said, "She was confused."

I nodded in agreement. The understatement of the decade.

The police didn't speak to us for all that long, though they said they'd probably want to speak to us again. They were too busy with Fiona and her parents, who they shuffled off to some undisclosed location.

The TV has been on in our house all day. I'm not sure who turned it on, but no one has bothered to turn it off. Whenever I glance over at it, I see either a news report about Fiona or some show counting down *The Best of the Eighties!* Music videos. Movies. TV shows. Et cetera. It'd be fun to watch that fluff if I didn't have so many other thoughts and images clogging my head. *The Worst of December 29 and 30!*

The image of Fiona in the beanbag chair, befuddled and terrified, miles away from the daring and confident little Heavy Metal Fifi who had my brother wrapped around her bony finger. It crushed me and is still crushing me to be lost in her vacant eyes.

The image of her parents hugging her while she shivered and wept and the cops loomed in the doorways of every room of our house in a way that only cops loom.

The image of the Dwyers, standing in the road, peering over the barrier of police cruisers, asking, "Anything? Anything on Charlie?"

Nothing. Nothing on Charlie.

EVENING

In the madness of the last two days I haven't had much time to revisit my accusations of Alistair. Did he read my diary?

Well, it seems that Mandy and Glen did, so it's certainly believable that he did too. Did he steal ideas and make up stories in some weird scheme to win me over? A bit farfetched, I know, but consider the alternative. Do I care anymore, now that Fiona is back? Not really. And yet when I saw the unopened phone bill on the kitchen table this evening, I knew I had to put the investigation to rest.

I snatched the bill and the cordless phone and headed for the bathroom. I locked the door and turned on the shower, but I didn't shower. I sat on the floor and tore open the envelope. I found a number on the bill that had a ton of digits. This had to be it. I dialed quickly, so I wouldn't chicken out, and I let it ring a few times. Fourteen and a half hours ahead, if I remembered correctly. It would have been Sunday at noon where I was calling, a perfectly reasonable time to answer a few questions about what the hell is going on.

The voice that answered was low and scratchy, a just-woken voice, or maybe an exhausted one, considering what time it was there.

"Hello."

"Hi," I said. "I'm calling to speak to Jenny Colvin, please."

A pause, and then, "Is this a joke?"

I knew at that moment who I was speaking to. The same woman who answered the phone before. Jenny's mother, I assumed. She had sounded so sprightly the last time, so happy, but now . . .

"I'm not joking," I assured her. "I have a quick question for Jenny, is all."

"So do I, dear," she said, though the *dear* was anything but sweet. "Why won't she come home?"

"Excuse me?"

"If you're having a go at me . . . then I . . . certainly don't appreciate it," she said, the words muddled by sobs.

"I'm confused," I said. "You're saying she's not home?"

"Hasn't been home since before Christmas."

I drew the phone away from my face. What I was doing felt absolutely filthy. My hand lingered over the button to hang up, and yet I didn't press it. I drew the phone back to my ear.

"I'm sorry," I whispered. "I didn't know."

"Not that it surprises us," the woman said. "Her sis had these sorts of problems too, spouting fantastical nonsense, threatening to run off and never come back. But she never went through with it. She grew up and got better. Jenny, on the other hand, always has to outdo her sis. I guess that includes going through with the running-off bit."

"Her sister?" I asked.

"Sigrid," the woman said.

I hung up immediately. I tore up the phone bill and tossed the paper in the toilet. Then I flushed away the evidence.

THE BEGINNING

You can survive without a soul. Princess Sigrid did, after all. The Dorgon had consumed Tom Rondrigal, who had taken Sigrid's soul into the afterlife with him. The Dorgon had then consumed Sigrid's trusty advisor, Po, leaving the princess entirely alone in the onyx tower. The cook still put a drop of that potion of forgetfulness in Sigrid's evening stew, and her short-term memory was wiped clean every day.

Even though she didn't have a soul, Sigrid still had feelings, but like her new memories, they were fleeting. They abandoned her within moments of her feeling them. They never imprinted themselves on her because there was nowhere to imprint.

So Sigrid indulged in nostalgia, in the old memories and feelings she hadn't lost. Those included her journey into other worlds, into other bodies—her time as a girl made of candy canes, as an alien, as a dark and disturbing joke, and as thousands of baby birds. There was no doubt that the journey had been a harrowing and horrible experience, but she began to miss it. That's the thing about the harrowing and the horrible: you tend to underestimate just how harrowing and horrible they are. You tend to tell yourself that feeling something is always better than feeling nothing.

And that's what Sigrid told herself. Her life was now as bad as it gets, as empty as it gets. Having feelings and memories that didn't last was torture. Confusion, anger, and even pain were better than numbness.

So one morning, she opened the hollowed-out book that concealed that old Dorgon potion, the one that allowed her to live other lives, and she put a drop of it on her tongue.

Poof!

She entered the body of a girl named Kerrigan Cleary. Keri for short.

Keri was a mess of a girl, a bubbling cauldron of emotion and confusion. As Sigrid entered her body, she was flooded, overwhelmed with feelings. Immediately, Sigrid regretted her decision to take the potion. Having no emotions was bad, but being torn apart by emotions was perhaps even worse. What had she gotten herself into?

Sigrid knew that the only escape from a body was death, and she certainly didn't wish such an awful fate on Keri. The girl was a wreck, but she was also sweet, and very very funny, thank you very much. So Sigrid decided to try to make the best of the situation. She'd do whatever she could to help young Keri.

Since Sigrid no longer had a soul, all she could offer Keri was her old memories. They didn't seem like much, but they energized Keri. They coursed through her mind and emerged at the end of her pen. They became stories, written down in a diary, and those stories accomplished two things.

They made Sigrid feel like she had a soul again.

They made Keri feel less anxious, more in control of her life. Kinder. More understanding.

And together, the two girls got stronger.

Now, when Keri sat on her bed, staring at that diary and asking herself, *What does it all mean?* she could tell herself a new mantra.

"Who cares, as long as it's working."

Sunday, 12/31/1989

---◦---

MORNING

WE'RE ALL OVERJOYED AND WE'RE ALL TERRIFIED. WE DON'T know what the hell is happening.

The phone rang all morning, like a scream in a haunted house. Mom and Dad fielded the calls because the calls were for them. Until there was a call for me. Mom handed me the phone without saying who it was.

"Hello," I said.

"Did you see the paper?" There was no need for formalities. I guess that's how far our relationship has gotten. I guess that's how far it's going to get.

"Why would you do that, Glen?" I asked. "Why would you read my diary?"

There was a pause. "So I could do something nice for you," he said, in a voice so clueless to his violation that I knew this was the end of things.

"There's nothing nice about violating someone's privacy," I said.

"But did you see the paper?" he asked, in that same voice.

What was he even talking about? Honestly, I didn't care. "All I see is that I don't know why I got into this relationship in the first place. I'm sorry, Glen, but it's over. It never should have started."

I hung up.

AFTERNOON

Did you see it? Did you see it? Did you see it?

Did I see what?

Did I look out the front window and see Dorian Loomis walking down the street with Fiona, his hand on her shoulder? Did I see the two of them alone, sharing some private words, a conversation I'd never be able to hear?

I did.

Did I see a team of police and dogs out in the swamp behind my house, poking around past Frog Rock, searching for clues and appearing to find zilch?

I did.

Did I see my brother, lying on the couch on his side, looking bewildered? Did I see his eyes go wide when I asked him if there was anything I could do to help? And did I see my reflection in his eyes, my face crinkled with worry, when he replied, "Absorbing them all was a terrible idea, wasn't it?"

I did.

EVENING

After lunch, Mom told me and Alistair that we were all going for a drive and we followed her to the minivan, where Dad was waiting with thermoses of hot chocolate.

Out of the neighborhood we drove, past the news vans and cop cars. Through town, past the Skylark and the memorial tree. To the countryside, where fields crusted with snow looked like big sheets of blank paper.

I figured we were going to an early dinner somewhere, because no one was in the mood to cook today, but then Dad said, "Have Mom and I ever showed you the place where we met?"

"You mean you two actually existed before we were born?" I said.

"Barely," Dad said.

And Mom said, "Aww. Still so sweet."

Then Dad pulled us over to the side of the road next to some farm that looked like any farm on any road out of town. He cut the engine, which cut the heat, which was okay because we were all bundled up anyway, and Mom started pouring the hot chocolate into short plastic mugs.

"Everything all right?" I asked.

"Fine," Dad said. "This is it."

I rolled down my window and stuck my head out into the frigid air. It was dead silent. It was almost dark, but there was a rind of color on the horizon. "This spot?" I asked. "This is where you met?"

"This very spot," Mom said as she handed us our hot chocolate.

Alistair leaned over me and peered out of my window too. "It's . . . stark," he said.

Dad looked back at us and smiled. "It was even starker then. I was twenty-four and still in grad school. Sometimes I'd go for long drives to clear my mind, and on one of those long drives, on a cold winter day like this one, I ran out of gas. At this very spot."

Mom picked up the tale from there. "I was twenty-three and I had my first job," she said, "which involved driving mail from the processing plant in Ontonkowa to the post office in Thessaly. Not a bad gig for a kid. And the reason you two exist."

"Really? What about the stork and the cabbage patch?" I asked as I rolled my window back up.

"That came later," Dad said with a chuckle. "Your saint of a mother—"

"Let me guess," I said. "She saw you on the side of the road, picked you up, and drove you to the gas station, and you fell in love and lived happily ever after."

"Hardly," Mom said. "You know me better than that."

"As I was saying," Dad went on, "your saint of a mother has always abided by the tenets of the United States Postal Service, and that day was no different. She slowed down, but didn't stop. The mail can't be late, after all."

"What?" I hooted. "Mom! You didn't stop?"

She shrugged out a good old-fashioned, *Eh, whattya gonna do?*

Dad passed his hot chocolate back to Mom and then he blew into his hands to warm them up. The breath snuck out of the cracks between his fingers and made extra, wispy little fingers in the air. "What exactly was it you shouted at me?" he asked Mom.

"'Plan ahead next time,'" she said with a smile.

"And you just left him there?" I asked. I'm not sure if my lip curled in disgust, but Mom certainly recognized the sour look on my face.

"Oh, he was fine," she assured me. "Someone helped him out a few minutes later."

"That's right," Dad said. "A kind old man who was on his way to do some ice fishing. He had a gas can and gave me a gallon to get me on my way. Poured me a cup of coffee from his thermos for good measure."

"Sounds like you should have married that guy instead," I said. "Jeez. This isn't a romantic story at all."

"The romance happened soon enough," Dad said. "I topped the car off in town and since I needed some stamps, I decided to stop by the post office. I figured if I saw your mom there, I could give her a piece of my mind."

This time my lip didn't curl. It probably quivered a bit, though. 'Tis a foolish endeavor to cross Mom. "You didn't," I said.

"I did," Dad replied. "I stormed in there and shook the room with my hollering."

"And what did she do?" Alistair asked. For most of the story, he'd been staring at his hot chocolate, but now that he looked up, he appeared as invested in the tale as I was.

"I did my job," Mom said. "I sat in the back, sorting mail, trying to ignore him."

"Except!" Dad said. "She's forgetting one thing. As I was on my way out, she jogged up and slipped me a note. It read—"

"'Forgive me,'" Mom whispered in a very sweet way. "'I get off in an hour. If you're still around, please let me buy you some pie.'"

"And you took her up on the offer?" Alistair said.

Dad shrugged. "I like pie."

"So first date was at the Skylark?" I asked.

"Hungry Paul's," Mom said with a little *tsk, tsk, tsk*. "Everyone in Thessaly knows Paul's has better pie."

Alistair nodded knowingly.

"Why have you never told us this story?" I asked. "You tell us every story."

"Oh, I've told you it before," Dad said. "Multiple times. Maybe you just weren't listening."

Maybe. It's possible.

"Or maybe you forgot," Mom said. "I don't think we've ever

brought you out here before, though. We wanted you to see this place."

My window was starting to fog up. The sunlight was gone. Everything was melting into the darkness. "Ain't exactly Paris, is it?" I said.

Dad chuckled and said, "No. It ain't. But it's where this family got its start. A barren field, a cold day, an empty tank, a snide comment, and a slice of pie. And now that we've shared something with you two, we want you to share something with us."

Mom cleared her throat and added, "There are no police. No doctors. There's no judgment. All Dad and I need is to know what's going on. We need something, because we're not dummies. We realize there's more to the story of Fiona and everything else that's been happening. Can you give us something? Honest. True."

I wasn't sure what *I* could give them. Maybe you, Stella? That scared me more than Glen or Mandy or even Alistair seeing you. What would Mom and Dad think of their weird little daughter after reading all of that?

Luckily—or unluckily, depending on how you look at it— Alistair saved me from saying anything.

"It's all my fault," he said.

I expected my parents to object, or at least Dad to object, but they didn't say a thing. They sipped hot chocolate and waited for Alistair to elaborate. So he did.

"You've given me a chance to tell you all something, and I'm going to take it," he went on. "Because this will probably be my last chance. Because things are going to change. Soon."

"Change how?" Dad asked.

"Me," Alistair said. "Soon I'm going to be different. Maybe I'll be the kid you once knew again. My old self. Maybe things will be like they once were. I don't know. What matters is that I'm going to finish things."

"Finish things?" Mom asked.

"I brought Fiona back," he said plainly. "Problem is, she's not Fiona anymore, is she? Not totally. I did my best with what I had to work with. But it took too long, and my best obviously isn't good enough. I want to bring Charlie back too. I want to bring them all back. There's only one other way I can see to do it now. But it's dangerous and it's cowardly, and it might mean we have to start things over."

"Fiona came back on her own," Dad said. "From wherever she was. Don't blame yourself for that. Don't blame yourself for whatever happened to her. You are not a coward, and there is nothing wrong with starting over. We can all start over. Together. As a family. Consider this the moment that we start over."

"You were kids once, right?" Alistair asked. "Before you met each other on the side of this road?"

"Of course," Mom and Dad said at the same time.

"And I'm sure you lost something when you were a kid," Alistair said. "A pet. A friend. A grandparent. Something that made you hurt more than you've ever hurt, or made you question everything you know about the world and how it works."

"We all experience loss," Dad said. "As kids. As adults. It's never easy. It's part of life."

"I know," Alistair said. "That's the point. But when you're a kid, it's different. You lose something and then there's this hole inside of you and you want to fill that hole, but you don't have the experience or wisdom to do it. So you ask for answers. From the air, from the clouds, from the stars, from anyone who might listen. And when voices finally respond and promise that there's a place where you can get what you want, where your wishes can come true, then you go. You go to that magical place and you stay and you create and you try to heal. You fill that hole. Which can be brave. Which is important. But while you're there, you realize that what you want and what you need are two different things. And that's when you're done with the place, and you leave for good. But leaving for good means you forget the place even existed at all."

"What are you telling us?" Mom asked.

Alistair took a deep breath and said, "The place does exist. It's as real as anything. Maybe even realer. Maybe you've even been there, all of you. Only you don't remember. And now . . . and now . . . I'm putting that all at risk. Taking a chance. Because I don't know what else to do."

His voice slipped away and Alistair put a hand on his brow.

Fog now covered every window, because of all the breath, and enclosed in the cold, dark shell of the minivan, we only had one another to look at.

"This has gone too far," Mom said. "This is why Dr. Hollister is so important, this is why . . . I don't want to upset you by saying this, but you're scaring us, honey."

He was. Yes, I was scared. But I also understood what he was talking about. Some of it, at least. He was talking about Aquavania. Still, there were so many questions, so many things I didn't understand. Like what exactly happened before he shot Kyle, before that first time he went to Aquavania? What led to all of that? And what exactly happened all those times he went back? What exactly did he do there?

Alistair ran his hand across his face, and then looked at me with something close to sympathy. Or maybe it was a confused look. Was it possible that he was even more confused than I was? I don't think he was signaling for me to help him, to save him, but I wanted to save him. I wanted to be more than the big sister who just stands by and listens and loves.

"Have you ever thought about telling your whole story?" I asked him. "Everything that's gone down in the last few months? So people can understand it a bit better? I can help with that. I can write it down, or put it on tape. If you tell us exactly what happened, maybe we can understand better and maybe we can help."

"It always helps to talk things out," Dad added. "Always."

Alistair lifted his head and whispered, "Maybe I've already talked it out. Maybe I've already told my story. Maybe now that it's told, I don't want to think about it anymore. I've absorbed everything I can. It's time to let it all go. I'm ready to forget."

No one responded. Maybe we were all ready for the same thing.

THE PHOSPHORESCENT WOMBAT, PART V

---◆---

LUNA FLOATED ALONE IN DARK NOTHINGNESS. THERE WERE NO broadcasts from Earth. There were no books on tape, no voices to keep her company. Nothing but the noise of outer space.

They say that outer space is quiet, and it is, to human ears. But Luna didn't have human ears. She hardly had wombat ears anymore. Her body had evolved to receive not only sound waves, but radio waves, light waves, all varieties of waves. With all those waves zipping about, outer space is noisy indeed, but when Luna floated past Pluto she didn't yet have the ability to interpret the meanings of all those waves. That would take time.

Time she had.

Decades went by. Centuries. Luna was the same shape she'd always been—squat, round, and wombatty—but she was brighter than ever. She was as bright as a comet. Brighter, in fact. She was a celestial object now, though the diameter of her glow was still significantly smaller than the diameter of a moon, planet, or star.

Her brain kept on being bombarded by waves, and the waves eventually made more and more sense. They told stories, in their own way. Chemical compositions of stars, the movements of galaxies in the distance, even communications from distant alien civilizations reached Luna's mind.

She was learning. She was feeling. She was glowing. More, more, more.

Within a few thousand years, she reached another solar system. Now her glow was the size of a small planet, and she noticed something intriguing. The star in this solar system started to dim as she passed it. Only slightly, but enough that she could tell.

The reason was obvious to Luna. She was stealing its light.

By this point, her spacecraft was mostly useless. Thanks to that amazing formula, it still was running off its original tank of water, but the electronics inside had started to degrade. Luna had the knowledge to fix them, but also knew that she didn't need them anymore.

So she abandoned ship about a hundred light-years away from Earth, letting the spacecraft follow its own momentum. Through her understanding of biology and quantum mechanics, Luna knew how to propel herself through space at ridiculously fast speeds using nothing but . . . excess gas. Let's leave it at that.

Luna could now explore the universe as she pleased, turning this way and that, moving forward and backward, gaining more knowledge, absorbing more light. The one thing she sought out more than anything, though, was feelings. She wanted to recapture the warmth she knew from her friendships with Rosie, Hamish, and DeeDee. But the more feelings she experienced, the further away she was from that original feeling. That original feeling got buried beneath it all.

A million years passed. She sped up and left the Milky Way galaxy. By this point, her glow was bigger than any star in the universe, and keen astronomers on other planets would be able to spot her once her light reached them.

Luna's speed was approaching the speed of light, however, which meant as soon as someone saw her, then she was probably long gone, streaking her way into another solar system, borrowing light from the stars in her path.

After a while, stars started to blink out as she passed them, because Luna sapped them of *all* of their light. After another while, it wasn't only light that she was stealing. It was every beam and wave—sounds, signals, thoughts, and even feelings. Not only could she understand the noise of outer space, she was absorbing the noise of outer space. She was becoming outer space.

Luna was now the most powerful thing in the universe, more powerful even than black holes. Scientists on Earth had believed that nothing could escape the pull of a black hole, but Luna proved to be the exception. Nothing could escape the pull of Luna. When she passed black holes, *she* absorbed *them*.

Deep down inside, she was still Luna, but the Lunaness was hidden beneath so much . . . stuff. So much . . . everything. It's hard to be a humble little wombat when you're essentially the most awesome thing in all of creation. It's hard to take a moral stance on anything when morality doesn't even exist anymore. Death. Birth. It's all the same when you're that powerful.

At three billion years, Luna's glow was as big as a quarter of the universe. Everything inside her glow was dead or incorporated into her mind and soul. The creatures that lived beyond her glow began to worship her, for they could sense her presence and her inevitable arrival. There were countless names for Luna, but they all meant the same thing.

The Ending.

When you've lived for three billion years, and when you move at nearly the speed of light, the passage of time doesn't feel the same as it does for a kid sitting through eighth period math on the day before vacation. Time for Luna was merely another part of the skyscape. Another wrinkle in the universe. Another fold in everything.

Ten billion years. There was almost no universe anymore. Luna's glow covered almost everywhere. She was almost everything. In those final moments, as her glow reached the edges of the universe and around the edges to meet itself on the other side, like caramel enveloping an apple, she revisited how it all began.

The road. Rosie and Hamish. The sign.

PERFECTLY FINE WOMBAT.

Using the English language, there were tens of thousands of anagrams that could be made from the letters in *perfectly fine wombat*. They featured words like *inept*, *farce*, *lefty*, and *womb*. Using all the other languages of Earth, hundreds of thousands of anagrams existed. Rearranging the sounds in the words, even more meanings emerged from even more languages collected from other planets. Using symbols that could be drawn from the lines in the letters, there were even more meanings. *Perfectly fine wombat* could be scrambled up and made to represent almost anything.

However, its first meaning was clear. There was nothing special about this wombat. And yet this wombat was everywhere, was everything, and at the very moment that Luna's light covered the entire universe, something astonishing happened.

The universe sprouted holes, like pockets of air in a loaf of bread. Then Luna opened her mouth to yawn—apocalypses are tiring, after all—and out of her mouth came a torrent of glowing animals. Nonillions of entirely suitable bush babies, exceedingly adequate tapirs, completely satisfactory coatimundis, and so on.

(FYI: a nonillion=1,000,000,000,000,000,000,000,000,000, 000.)

The nonillions of glowing animals plugged up nonillions of holes. The holes led to other universes. Some a lot like our universe, some a lot different. The animals were now the corks that separated the universes. Their glows were glows of knowledge, emotion, wisdom, and creativity.

When all the holes except for one were plugged, Luna had a choice of what she could do with her universe. What she chose to do was to start over. To give the planets life again, to give the stars light again. To turn back the clock, to start time over and let her universe, just one universe among countless universes, find its own path.

So Luna became nothing but a perfectly fine wombat. Her glow was faint, like the day she met Rosie and Hamish, and her feelings were straightforward. She had one desire: to feel water pitter-pattering on her head, like she did on that rainy afternoon along the road, like she did when Rosie gave her showers.

Her wish came true, and she ended up in a pool beneath a waterfall, along a creek that flowed through a forest similar to the forest where she'd met Rosie and Hamish. In that pool, beneath that waterfall, she plugged up one last hole. She became the cork that held back a universe that some people call Aquavania. It was a universe of possibility, of creation, a place where kids could go and create anything they could imagine.

Yes, she was a perfectly fine wombat, but she wasn't a perfectly fine cork. That was okay. She didn't need to be. As that waterfall cascaded over her, and as the water flowed from the pool down the creek into a river, then into the ocean and up into the clouds, which rained the water back over the land, it carried with it whispers from Aquavania.

The whispers said, "Come visit sometime."

And kids—the ones who were hurting, and scared, and

confused, the ones who saw death, the ones who felt death, the ones who needed to create, the ones who had holes in them—they heard the call. They came to visit. They lived in Aquavania. They constructed worlds there. They fixed themselves. Then they went home. Then there were more whispers and more kids and on, and on, and on, and on, always . . . to be continued.

Monday, 1/1/1990

MORNING

WHERE DID LUNA COME FROM ORIGINALLY? WHO PUT THE SIGN around her neck?

Hell if I know. Maybe someday I'll write that story, but could that ever satisfy anyone? They'll always ask, *Well, what came before that?* Knowing me, I'll probably say *I don't know, a whirling bandicoot, I guess. And before that, a burping ocelot.*

Forget that stuff. That's not what this story is about. This story is about . . . well, it's about how God is a wombat, because why can't God be a wombat? I'd prefer a wombat to some bearded dude who hands out commandments, asks us to kill our kids to prove that we love him, and floods us to the edge of extinction because he had a bad hair day or something.

When I first came up with the story, that was the first thing I thought about. A wombat who becomes God. A wombat who destroys and resurrects our universe, but who in the end only wants to feel the pitter-patter of rain on her head. A wombat who loves and makes mistakes like any of us. A wombat who glows, but doesn't know why. A perfectly fine wombat.

Of course, I added the Aquavania stuff later. After listening to Alistair's tales. Because it fit. And I was inspired. If I had told you from the very beginning that the story was about a wombat who becomes the greatest and most horrible being in all of creation, the reason for our existence and our destruction, and the ultimate source of inspiration in the world, well, you wouldn't have believed me, would you have, Stella?

Now, as I read it all over again, I wonder about Luna. Is she more than God? Is she supposed to represent Fiona Loomis? Is she supposed to be a version of my brother? Is Luna really me?

They call that literary analysis, Stella, and I'm not particularly good at it. My job is to write. Your job is to figure out the deep stuff.

And there is deep stuff going on here, isn't there? For the love of Luna, I hope so. Deep stuff beyond inspiration, I mean. Because whether inspiration comes from an actual place or not doesn't matter if you don't choose to do something with it. And if you do choose to do something with it, the stories you create don't matter unless they make ripples in the world.

Not to be all egotistical or anything, but my stories have made ripples. Things have changed. Small things at first. I've called them coincidences, but they've spread, become bigger, more significant. Ripples are turning into waves. It's time for them to crash onto shore.

AFTERNOON

It's a new year. A new decade.

Mom made an extra special breakfast today with eggs, bacon, pancakes, fruit salad, the whole nine. Dad even poured me a small cup of coffee, saying I was old enough and I looked like I needed it. I did need it. No, I wasn't up late watching the glowing New Year's ball. I was up late writing about the glowing wombat.

Alistair piled his plate high with all the grub, like he'd just come off a lifeboat. It pleased Mom. Hungry boys have pleased moms since the dawn of time, I bet.

"Family meeting in the living room at nine," Mom said. "Okay?"

As I poured maple syrup onto my pancakes, Dad topped off my coffee and then massaged my shoulders. It felt good, but I knew this was one of his methods of easing me into some bad news.

"Okay," I said with a sigh.

"Sure thing," Alistair replied.

It was around eight o'clock then, and the sun was barely up. We cleared our plates and went our separate ways to shower, dress, and prepare for the day. As I reached the door to my room, I felt a tap on my shoulder.

"Do you really want to help me tell my story?" Alistair asked. "Do you want to help me finish it?"

"Of course," I said.

"Grab your coat," Alistair said. "And don't say a word to Mom and Dad. We've gotta get out of here."

So that's what I did. I grabbed my coat. I didn't say a thing to Mom or Dad. Alistair brought Fiona back. If he could do that, maybe he could bring Charlie back too. We needed Charlie, and we needed to move on.

On the way out the door a few minutes later, I found a package sitting on the front step. A thin, rectangular gift, wrapped in the Sunday comics and addressed: *TO KERRIGAN*.

"Let's go," Alistair said as he motioned to the bikes that he had quietly wheeled from the garage. So I stuffed the package in my backpack—which I had also stashed you in, Stella, just in case I needed to write stuff down—and I hurried to meet him.

Twenty minutes later, we were fighting our way through the biting wind on the edge of town. Alistair wore his own backpack, one that bulged and strained at the zippers. It was hard to talk at the speed we were riding and with our scarves wrapped around our faces, so I couldn't ask exactly where we were going. All Alistair had said was "to the river."

Nearly an hour later, we were on a dirt road. I'd been down this road before, but that was long ago, back when they didn't even plow it. It was plowed now, though not well, and we had to ditch our bikes after a while and proceed on foot.

The cabin my uncle Dale used to own was buried in snow.

No one had been out to it in ages, it seemed. The roof sagged a bit. The whole thing appeared destined to cave in with the next significant blizzard.

Alistair led the way down to the Oriskanny River, to a bend where the water formed a deep pool. I had swum in that pool before. I began to wonder if it was somewhere around here that Alistair had seen Luke's body. Years had passed since then, but the thought still made my insides quiver.

There was a rock near the water, and Alistair brushed the snow off and set his backpack on it. He unzipped the backpack and pulled out that fishbowl, which he carried down to the water. He dipped it in and scooped up an icy bowlful, which he carried back to the rock. Sitting down, he held the bowl in his lap.

"I absorbed them all," he said. "Every last swimmer. All their knowledge. All their dreams and desires. I thought it would help me figure out the best way to bring back the ones who are trapped inside me. But it was a mistake. Like the old lady who swallowed the spider to catch the fly. Remember that song?"

"At the end, she swallows a horse," I said. "She's dead, of course."

It was a joke. A dark and disturbing joke. And I regretted saying it immediately.

A hint of a laugh snuck from Alistair's nose, and he said, "You may see something strange in a moment. Or you may see nothing at all. I'm going to Aquavania one last time. And I'm throwing myself off the tower and over the waterfall."

The water in the fishbowl swirled with dirt and sticks. It was a dark and earthy brew. "I don't like the sound of that one bit," I said.

"It's the only way to fix what I've done," he said. "What Charlie's done. All the mistakes. It's the only way to release everyone and start over . . . I hope."

"You hope? You don't know?"

"No one has done this before," he told me. His hands were running up and down the sides of the bowl. He was caressing it.

"But what happens to you?"

"I'll either come back without any memories of what happened," he said, "or I won't come back at all. And maybe there won't ever be another Riverman. The Riverman has always passed on the responsibility to another, but I can't put this burden on someone else. And yet if I don't . . . well, I'm not sure what happens then."

On the trees, there were no leaves left to rustle. The birds had all flown south. The only sound was the gentle flow of the current, the chimes of ice splintering along the riverbanks.

"I don't care what you do, as long as you stay. I need you to stay," I said, and I moved closer so that I could hug him, so that he could feel the words as well as hear them.

"And *I* need *you* to tell one more story," he said, and his fingers stopped moving over the fishbowl. "If I don't come back, I need you to tell Mom and Dad that I brought you here to show you where I saw Luke Drake. And then I fell in the river and was swept away."

Of all the things my brother has asked me to do, this was the worst. This was the cruelest. I couldn't possibly agree to it.

"No!" I screamed. "I will not! Because I've promised you enough. Now it's time for you to promise me."

"Okay," he said. "That's fair."

"Promise that you'll try again, that you'll keep trying to get them back," I said. "Jumping off a tower into a waterfall? That's idiotic. Disappearing? That is not an option, little brother. You need to keep doing what you've been doing. You've done it twice already. You can do it again."

"One sacrifice, one person," he said. "That's all it might take to bring back . . . thousands."

He pressed his hands against that fishbowl, gripping it like a crystal ball, like it was so much more than a piece of glass. And it was. It was his way into Aquavania. I saw that now. Una went there through a waterfall. Jenny Colvin was supposed to use a fountain. Alistair's portal was that fishbowl.

"I don't care about thousands," I said. "I care about you. All of us do. Promise me. No one needs to be sacrificed."

His grip on the fishbowl loosened for a moment, and I saw my chance. I've always been quicker than Alistair. So when I lunged forward and grabbed the bowl from him, he hardly reacted. His face looked confused more than anything. As I wrested it away from him, water splashed on my arms and hit me on the skin between my sleeves and my gloves. The cold was like a jolt of electricity, and I dropped the bowl. Its murky, watery guts emptied on the ground and it rolled away from us, down the riverbank and into the river.

It didn't sink. Its bottom rested on the surface and acted like the hull of a boat. The current pulled the bowl to the center and then downstream. In a matter of seconds, it was making its way around a bend, and for a moment, with shadows cast on it in a very particular and peculiar way, it reminded me of a head.

Alistair stood and watched it disappear. He didn't go after it. His mouth twisted up. He might have smiled. He might have even been glad to see it go. But I couldn't tell for sure, because he quickly wrapped his face in his scarf and turned away from me.

"Stay," I said. "Please."

He turned back. His eyes were completely lost, a little boy's eyes.

He nodded.

Then he sat back down on the rock, and I sat next to him. He didn't say anything else, not for a few minutes at least. So I didn't say anything either. Silently, together, we watched the water.

The wind was picking up and tearing its way through the fabric of my pants. My gloves were wet and my fingers were starting to get numb. So I lifted my backpack and prepared to leave. That's when I remembered the gift inside. I pulled it out. Alistair glanced at it, then back at the water.

As I tore away the wrapping, the first thing I saw was a note.

Dear Kerrigan,

I believe in us, but maybe you never will. I'm sorry I was so stupid, and I understand if you never forgive me. I'm just happy to have had the chance to get to know you. Thank you for giving me that chance, whatever your reasons.

Your Not-So-Secret Admirer and Your Number-One Fan,
Glen

P.S. Th-th-th-th-that's All Folks!

Beneath the note was a clipping from yesterday's *Sutton Bulletin*, enclosed in a glass and metal frame. It wasn't news, though. It was a story. My story.

"The Ending," by Kerrigan Cleary.

THE CHRONICLES OF
KERRIGAN CLEARY

———◦———

IT'S BEEN A WHILE, STELLA. AFTER EVERYTHING THAT happened, I wasn't sure I wanted to record the events of my life anymore. Too much trouble. Too much emotion. Too much everything.

I sympathize with Justine Barlow, the jogger from "The Ending." Sometimes it feels like my problems are multiplying exponentially, wherever I go, whatever I do. I'm not alone in those feelings.

I wasn't thrilled about Glen's publishing my story without my permission. I never intended to share it. I know it was "a gift," but whatever good intentions he had couldn't wash away the fact that he stole from me. That he invaded my privacy. Mandy too. Because she helped him.

However, from bad deeds come good things. People told me they liked the story, some even related to it. Among those people was Phaedra Moreau. Yes, *that* Phaedra Moreau. I wouldn't go so far as to call her my nemesis, and yet I never ever expected to call her a fan.

"I know it seems like I've got this awesome life, but even I get overwhelmed sometimes," Phaedra told me in the locker room a week after "The Ending" was published. "Sometimes I feel like that chick in your story. Like I can't run away from, well, everything. Like stuff keeps piling up in my way and it's awful and, well . . ."

Phaedra sighed. It was probably the best chance I've ever had to take her down a peg, to make fun of her or, I don't know, laugh at her. Instead, I channeled the power of Princess Sigrid. I found a well of kindness in myself. I sighed too and said, "Thank you for telling me that."

"It's a great story," Phaedra replied. "Except for the last part. Not a big fan of that. It was kinda stupid. I didn't get it."

I burst out laughing, because this was the Phaedra that I knew. Not that we were ever going to be friends, but there was something comforting about knowing that even when she was being nice, Phaedra was a bit of a jerk.

Mandy is a bit of a jerk. I guess I've always known that. We haven't talked much since that day in Hanlon Park. It's amazing how quickly your best friend can become an acquaintance, someone you say awkward hellos to in the hall and that's about it.

When she yelled at me that day, Mandy said I was selfish. She was probably right. She said I didn't deserve Glen, and she was probably right about that too. I dated him for all the wrong reasons. Still, it shouldn't have been up to her to put an end to things. Even if she would never admit it, I know the reason she helped Glen get my story published was to sabotage our relationship. She knew it was sneaky to look at my diary. She knew how I would react. She knew me.

But she doesn't know me anymore. I'm better. I'm kinder. I'm more complete.

Which reminds me, Stella, I should tell you what day it is today.

SATURDAY, 8/11/1990
EVENING

Today is Fiona Loomis's thirteenth birthday. I know that it's her birthday because best friends know these sorts of things about each other. In the last seven months, Fiona and I have grown as close as two girls can grow. Because of geography. Because of circumstance. Because we really like each other.

I won't sugarcoat things. It's been a tough stretch. Fiona's memory is spotty at best. She has talked to her fair share of police and doctors. No one, not even Fiona, has an explanation for what happened to her, why she disappeared, where she ended up, or how she came back.

Well, I suppose *I* have an explanation. But I haven't shared it with her yet. She's not ready for me to be telling her those things, though I do plan to tell her someday.

Right now, I'm there for her. To listen. To comfort. To make stupid jokes. To laugh. To watch movies. To bake cookies. To tell her it's okay that her dad moved out, that dads move out all the time.

Things have changed at her house. I don't press her for the gory details. I let her talk about what she wants to talk about, and she rarely mentions her family. I know her sister, Maria, moved back home and her mom has stopped drinking and is doing support groups and things like that. Life appears to be headed in the right direction, and while I realize things aren't always what they appear, sometimes they are. Often they are.

There have been others like Fiona. Kids who were missing and came home with faulty memories. Sunita, of course. But more since her. In other countries mostly, so we don't hear about them much, and I doubt anyone has connected the dots to what happened here in Thessaly.

Except for me. I spend a lot of time at the library now. Ms. Linqvist, the librarian, helps me do research. I tell her I'm going to write a book on missing children someday. She understands why the subject interests me and she queries other libraries, computer databases, and so on to find newspaper stories about disappearances. It helps that I have a few leads, names that Alistair once said.

Werner. Chua. Rodrigo. Boaz. Jenny Colvin.

According to the articles we've located, they're all home again. Confused. Slightly broken. But home.

"I only hope that someday we'll be reading a story about Charlie Dwyer," Ms. Linqvist said to me last week.

"Me too," I told her.

Still no Charlie. Kyle has done his time for illegal gun possession, returned home this June after a month in a minimum-security prison. I still see him and his parents going for walks. Well, they're walking. He's sitting, being pushed. I guess that's how it'll always be.

I could ask Alistair about Charlie, about what happened to him and if he'll ever be back. But I've already done that. So many people have done that, far too many times. The answer is always the same: a stone-faced "I don't know."

I'm not entirely sure what happened out there by the river on New Year's Day. That fishbowl floating away was the end of something. Or the start of something. Same thing, I guess.

Alistair doesn't talk about Aquavania anymore. Not to me, anyhow. His silence could mean at least a couple of things.

Option One: He still visits Aquavania and goes about his work as the Riverman, silently, diligently, putting back together the ones who were lost. Only he's not telling me because he's humble like that.

Option Two: He's forgotten all about it. Maybe in that split second before I grabbed the fishbowl from him, he went to Aquavania and did exactly what I'd begged him not to do. Maybe he threw himself into that waterfall and risked everything. And maybe the risk was worth it. Maybe in the blink of an eye he was back and all those kids were on their way home. Maybe Charlie's not far behind them.

Is there an Option Three? One where there is no Aquavania, where there never was an Aquavania? Anything is possible, I suppose, but it doesn't seem likely, does it, Stella?

Stuff isn't exactly back to how it used to be, of course.

Alistair seems happier, calmer, more satisfied. He acts goofy and sweet like a kid is supposed to. But Mom and Dad aren't about to forget that day along the side of the road and all the strangeness that led up to it. They refer to that time as Alistair's breakdown, even though it appeared, at least to me, to be the opposite. To me it was the moment that Alistair built up all of his courage.

My opinion didn't matter, though, because I didn't have much of a say in things. Not surprisingly, Mom and Dad did the Mom and Dad thing and decided not to send Alistair back to school in the new year. Instead they hired a tutor to keep him on top of his studies. Dr. Hollister agreed it was a wise move, and Alistair didn't object.

Recently, they took it a step further. Come fall, I'll be starting high school. But last week, Alistair already started boarding school. It was another mutually agreed upon decision. While I get a continuation of my life in an old place, he gets a fresh start in a new place.

The school isn't like most boarding schools. They have psychiatrists on staff. Group meetings to discuss emotions and so on. Apparently, my parents had proposed the option to Alistair as far back as December, and eventually he warmed to the idea. I guess Thessaly was getting to him, as it seems to get to a lot of people. So they waited until the time seemed right—or the financials went through, I don't know for sure. All I know is that we drove out to Vermont eight days ago and dropped Alistair off at a place that looked like a college, all brick, stone, and ivy.

I hugged my brother next to a willow tree and I told him, "I will always love you."

He said, "I will always love you too."

I think it's the first time he's ever said that. Actually, I'm sure of it.

My memory is good; stellar, in fact. Still, I like to write things down. I sometimes wonder if maybe that's all Princess Sigrid needed to do in the first place. To write things down. To have a look at her ideas and feelings. To experiment with characters and other worlds. To create. Maybe it would've helped her empathize with other people without actually having to live their lives. Maybe she never needed to sell her soul in the first place. At the very least, by writing things down, she would've always had a tool to remember.

As for me, stories help me feel complete. Even though I haven't written in you in months, Stella, I've never stopped writing stories. My latest story is longer, however. It's called *The Whisper*. It's basically a sketch right now, jotted into the diary my parents got me for Christmas. I'm not sure I have it in me to write an entire novel yet, but that's what it will become someday. Because it's epic.

It's the tale of Alistair's adventures in Aquavania, of Una and Banar, of the Riverman in his—or her!—various forms. Even if I finish it, I don't know if I'll ever let anyone read it. Maybe it will be something exclusively for me, to remind myself that believing in ridiculous things isn't always so bad.

Why isn't it so bad? Because my brother is getting better.

Because we have Fiona back. Because some of those lost children are home.

I don't know how they are home. I honestly don't care.

I went over to Fiona's house for lunch today. Her mom made a cake, and Maria and I sang at the tops of our lungs, which made Fiona plug her ears, but also smile. I asked her what she wanted for her birthday, and she said something a little strange.

"Meet me out by Frog Rock, tonight after sunset," she said.

"Why?" I asked.

"Years ago, your brother and I made promises to each other," she said, "that if one of us ever left Thessaly, then we'd bury something out by Frog Rock. I have to see if Alistair kept his promise."

So that's what we did. We dug a hole beneath the stars together, me and my best friend. Did we find anything? Does my brother keep promises?

Well, he kept this one. Because buried next to Frog Rock was an old ammo can—Dorian Loomis's ammo can, of all things. In that ammo can, there were cassette tapes. *PLAY ME* was written on them in Alistair's distinctive scrawl. I mean, come on, little brother, like someone needs to be told what to do with a mysterious cassette tape!

It was getting late and Fiona couldn't spend the night, so she took the tapes home with her. She's playing them now, I suppose, though I can't presume to know what's on them other than a message meant for her. If she wants to tell me what that message is, I'm here to listen.

I will speculate, obviously. And I will write more of my stories. Maybe not ones with happy endings, maybe not ones with endings at all. I'm simply going to see where inspiration takes me. Because inspiration is still out there somewhere, and it's assuring me that it's okay if everything doesn't work out perfectly and every question isn't answered. It's okay if the oceans are deeper than we suspect and the stars go farther than we could ever imagine. Because there's something absurdly comforting about the notion that we live in a universe of infinite possibilities.

ACKNOWLEDGMENTS

———◆———

THIS NOVEL IS DEDICATED TO MICHAEL BOURRET AND JOY Peskin for obvious reasons. At least the reasons are obvious to me. They have supported the story—the trilogy!—from the very beginning. Back in 2012, when I approached Michael with fifty strange pages, he believed that I could deliver another thousand or so even stranger ones. Or at least he pretended to believe. That's all I needed to keep writing. And I will always thank him for that.

Joy edited those thousand or so pages, helping me ditch a few hundred along the way. Good riddance to those ditched pages. The story didn't need them, but the story definitely needed Joy's guidance, her wisdom, and her encouragement. She was tireless in finding holes in the plot, in the characters, in the world. Then she patched those holes up and made it look like they were never even there.

There were others who have been with this trilogy since

the beginning. Beth Clark designed the books and they are lovely things indeed. Yelena Bryksenkova illustrated the covers and I couldn't have asked for more beautiful representations of Alistair, Fiona, Charlie, Keri, and their furry friends. Angie Chen saved the day many times throughout the process, keeping the books on schedule and looking their best. Kate Hurley and Karla Reganold copyedited and proofread all three volumes and humored my grammatical eccentricities. Mary Van Akin sang the trilogy's praises and people listened because she can really sing. The rest of the gang at Macmillan and the folks at Recorded Books, including Claudia Howard and Graham Halstead, have helped share my tales far and wide. Lauren Abramo and the other agents at Dystel & Goderich have been kind and supportive since the day I decided to join Michael's roster of authors.

My family has been there all along too, of course. Mom, Dad, Tim, Toril, Dave, Jake, Will, Jim, Gwenn, Pete, and all the other members of the Starmer, Van Scotter, Amundsen, Finney, Glitman, Evans, and Wells clans (as well as their respective dogs): I love you. Cate and Hannah: I love you the most (sorry, everyone else) and, really, all my books are basically dedicated to you, because you dedicate so much to me.

Finally, a storyteller doesn't exist without someone who's willing to listen. You, the reader, have been willing to listen and have stuck around to the end. That's quite incredible of you, and I am forever in your debt. Thank you, thank you, thank you . . .